BRANDED

BILL MACVEIGH

ISBN: 978-1-5356-0742-1

DEDICATION

To Nellie Ruth Jones
Lincoln County teacher for 40 years
True pioneer woman, mentor, and friend!

THE TALL, LEAN MAN SAT proudly in his Western saddle as he surveyed the hustle and bustle swirling around the busy plaza. His big Morgan stallion, seventeen hands high, stood quietly as his rider observed all the activity moving in every direction. It was evident that a line of heavy trade wagons were being unloaded. The man noticed every detail of the action from dark, intense eyes. His wide-brimmed, flat-crowned hat sat low over his eyes, making it hard to see his features. He wore a tan shirt, brown vest, and brown pants that rode over Western high-heeled boots. What some men lazing around the plaza noticed about the man was the fine string of eight mares and two more stallions on lead ropes behind him. Two of the horses were different than any breed the men sitting and watching had ever seen. One stallion and a mare were light cream in color with black spots on their hindquarters. All the animals were clearly the finest the men had ever seen in these parts. The tall man on the horse asked a man passing along the rough road and wearing a sombrero if there was a good place to stay. The man in accented English directed the tall man on the horse to the La Fonda Hotel around a corner of the plaza. The men lazing under a porch also noticed the big pistol in a leather holster on the man's left hip. The men sitting on a wooden bench under the porch watched the man pull his fine horses along the street. These men were always interested in watching newcomers to their land. In rapid-fire Spanish they speculated about the stranger and his horses and wondered from where this man might have traveled.

Redmon Drury found the Carlos Abreau stable located close to the La Fonda Hotel. He made arrangements with Carlos to have his stallion and packhorse rubbed down and all the horses given corn. Redmon Drury carried his clothes pack, a fine leather case containing some long objects, and a pack containing his money toward the hotel. He moved with an easy grace in spite of his height. He had developed his cat-like quickness and moves through hard experience.

Redmon Drury, at twenty-five years old, had been on his own in the world from the age of fifteen. It was not unusual for men to be on their own in the West at a young age. What set Redmon Drury apart was how he began this journey, and his background. Redmon was the third son of Lord Red Roland Drury. The name Drury remains well respected around Penrith on the River Eden in England. The Drurys received their title and land two hundred years earlier when an ancestor, Orrick Drury, saved the king's life in a battle with France. The group of four men sitting on the wooden bench watched as the man they saw earlier ambled around a corner back into view. They noticed the long leather-bound case the man was carrying and wondered what it might contain. They also noticed that the man was much taller than they originally thought. These men enjoyed speculating about what they observed around the teaming plaza.

Redmon eased through large double doors into the lobby of the La Fonda Hotel. When he looked across the lobby, Redmon's blood suddenly ran cold. Standing across the lobby talking to some men was a man he had not seen in ten years. Redmon had crossed an ocean as well as a continent only to discover that the man he hated above any other was here in Santa Fe in the New Mexico Territory. Redmon had never thought he would ever see his nemesis again when he took a ship away from England. He stood and studied his hated enemy for a few moments and immediately recognized the overbearing, arrogant, pompous demeanor that he remembered from ten years earlier on the fateful night that changed his life completely. Redmon decided that Wilfred Chatham of Chatham Manor would not recognize him. He was now much taller, at almost six feet three inches, with much broader shoulders. He also sported a well-trimmed beard and mustache. Redmon checked into the hotel and inquired about getting a hot bath and having his suit pressed. The desk clerk arranged for both of Redmon's requests.

Redmon Drury walked into the dining room some time later wearing his well-tailored suit and saw Wilfred Chatham sitting at a table among the men he'd been conversing with earlier in the lobby. Redmon chuckled and made his way to the table next to his hated former rival. He sat so he could hear what was being said at the next table. He quietly placed his meal order so his British accent wouldn't be heard at the adjoining table.

"Gentlemen, I want those people off that land and I want them off soon. I care naught whether they have clear title. They have the best springs in the area and I expect us to control them. I am bringing a large sum of money into this enterprise and will not be stopped. You told me that there is only the girl and her father left on the ranch. We have either run out or killed all their ranch hands so they cannot hold out much longer. They must be running low on supplies. They have rejected my offers to buy them out so we have little choice but to finish them completely. The existing authorities are so far away that no one will ever know what happened to them. I expect you men to accomplish what I require within the following week or two. Is that understood? We did much the same to some of the smaller landholders near our manor in England. I expect we will control all the land from the Gallinas Mountains north to the San Cristobal ranch, and east and west for a hundred miles. Gentlemen, I have Hereford cattle being shipped over from England to go with the five thousand head of longhorns we have coming from Texas. Have I made myself perfectly clear? I want those people off that land by whatever means necessary!" commanded Chatham.

"We understand, boss, but those Wilbankses are tougher than you think. That Allison Wilbanks can shoot as well as her old man," one of the men replied.

"If you gentlemen cannot handle the situation and procure that ranch land for me, I will find some men who can," Wilfred Chatham said.

Redmon Drury sat quietly, ate his meal, and contemplated what he just heard. It was obvious to Redmon that Wilfred Chatham was trying to build a huge cattle ranch by stepping on people that he considered beneath him. Redmon experienced the Chatham form of punishment and their so-called justice ten years earlier. Redmon decided that he would think over the plan he just heard being discussed by Wilfred Chatham and his cohorts. He would like nothing better than to even some accounts as he thought about it.

After walking around the plaza for a time, Redmon retired to his room in a thoughtful mood. He enjoyed hearing the Spanish language being spoken again as he walked. The late setting sun was reflecting on the adobe buildings and Redmon enjoyed the beauty. The buildings glowed with a golden hue. Redmon finally retired, and was asleep for some time when the regular nightmare came again as it always did the past ten years. The dream was made more intense this night after seeing Wilfred Chatham for the first time in ten years.

⬚ ⬚ ⬚

Redmon and Roselind Chatham were running across the heather between Drury Manor and Chatham Manor. They were close friends and played together from the time they discovered one another at age five. They snuck around together in both Drury Manor and Chatham Manor, avoiding the adults as well as their parents, brothers, and sisters. It always turned into a game for both Redmon and Roselind in each other's manor house. When they reached the age of thirteen the childish games changed. They shared their first real kiss. As time passed, Redmon and Roselind became freer with one another. Soon there were no secrets between them.

There was a secluded pool between Drury Manor and Chatham Manor where they swam together during warm weather from an early age. They swam there for years, always in the buff. When they were fourteen they made love for the first time in the pool. It was something that seemed to be natural and happened without any thought. Roselind's body developed early. In Roselind's and Redmon's minds they would marry when they were somewhat older. Then it all suddenly went wrong for them. Lord Reginald Chatham arranged a marriage contract for Roselind with Lord Charles Benford for his son Edward of Benford Hall near Ambleside. The two young lovers were devastated, for they surely loved one another. Redmon did not know that his father Red Roland met with Lord Reginald Chatham and attempted to arrange a marriage contract for Redmon and Roselind. Red Roland knew of the closeness of his son and the daughter of the adjoining manor. The young lovers did not have any idea that Red Roland knew of their relationship. Lord Roland was rebuffed by Reginald Chatham, saying that Roland Drury's request must be some kind of jest. He made the comment that the Drurys should be no more than stable hands for the Chathams. That comment caused a rift that would never be repaired between the two noblemen. Lord Reginald Chatham always displayed an inflated sense of his and his families' worth and station in British society. Roselind, after hearing of the unwanted marriage contract, asked Redmon to get her with child so she wouldn't have to go through with the marriage.

In Roselind's mind, if she were pregnant with Redmon's child, her father would be forced to let them be together and marry. The two young people went to work trying to complete her desire. For some inexplicable reason it did not happen no matter how hard they tried.

The young lovers continued trying until they were finally discovered and caught in the stable by Mortimer, the Chathams' eldest son, who would eventually inherit the Chatham manor and lands. Wilfred Chatham, Roselind's older brother, was also in the stable with Mortimer. Wilfred always hated Redmon because he could never match him in looks or physical prowess. Suddenly, Redmon was dragged away from Roselind by the two brothers and held by some stablemen of the Chathams.

With Roselind screaming and crying her protests, it was Wilfred Chatham who came up with the punishment given to Redmon for violating their sister as they called it. A branding iron was brought from the smithy. Redmon fought like a young madman, but it didn't do any good. When Redmon saw what was about to occur, he refused to scream out when the glowing iron was placed on his right breast by a sneering Wilfred Chatham. Redmon growled out his agony as a Chatham "C" was branded into his skin. The final and ultimate insult came when Wilfred Chatham urinated on the new brand in Redmon's skin. Then the Chatham stablemen were ordered to carry Redmon to the boundary of Drury land and dump him there.

A hate-filled Redmon Drury lay on the heather for a time and finally rose to make his way to his and Roselind's secluded pool. He slipped into the cool water.

The brand hurt unmercifully. When he was deep enough in the pond, he immediately dunked his head to wash off the urine and the spit, and hissed at the thought of the indignity of what just happened. He remembered the last words of Wilfred Chatham as he laughed and urinated on Redmon, "You Drurys are always attempting to overstep your bounds, but you are not fit to lick Chatham boots. You have defiled our sister and have received what you justly deserve. You are low scum and nothing more! Men, get him out of our sight!" As the stablemen picked him up and carried him out, Redmon heard Mortimer laughing. Roselind's cries continued with the final insult when Mortimer spit on Redmond as he was carried past.

Redmon stayed in the water until the burning hurt subsided somewhat. He hoped Mortimer and Wilfred would not hurt his Roselind. A deep, all-consuming hatred settled in Redmon's heart for Wilfred Chatham and his brother. That hatred saw no bounds. Redmon finally left the pool and walked home.

The Chathams did not see fit to leave him with his clothes. The cool evening air raised goose bumps on his skin as he walked toward home. His chest was hurting, but to Redmon that meant nothing now. It was done, but his hatred for Wilfred Chatham would simmer until one of them died.

He made it into the stable and found salve to put on the brand Wilfred Chatham gave him. The salve lessened the fire and sting of the brand somewhat. Finally, Redmon quietly crept into the manor house and made his way up the back stairs to his room. His chest hurt as he dressed, but he vowed that Wilfred Chatham would eventually pay for branding him and for what he and Mortimer did at the end to humiliate him further.

When he was dressed, Redmon made his way down the main staircase only to find Mortimer Chatham talking to his father. Redmond's brother Roddrick was standing close by. He could see that his father was angry and beginning to raise his voice.

Roddrick saw Redmon advancing on Mortimer Chatham and stopped him by putting his arms around Redmon and holding him back. Mortimer told his father that they caught Redmon using his sister, and punished Redmon for placing Roselind in such a compromising position.

"I will apologize somewhat for the severity of my brother's form of punishment, but your son deserved to be chastised for his actions. I will warn your son to stay away from Chatham Hall and away from Roselind. She will be married soon in spite of this. We will expect to have no further communication whatsoever between our properties."

Mortimer was turning to leave when Redmon stopped him cold "Mortimer Chatham, I will be glad to face your cowardly brother man to man. I will kill him for what he did to me. I think he only has the courage to face me when I am being held down by four stout yeomen!"

Mortimer wheeled around. "You used Roselind, but we can still get a proper match for her. If you have the audacity to attempt taking a Chatham's life, we will have you hanged, which you richly deserve for trying to ruin Roselind who is far above you in station. Our father will soon have the constable come here and arrest you for trespassing on Chatham lands and for what you did to Roselind. We will have our revenge for what you have done to a Chatham. You are exactly what Wilfred called you… low scum!"

Finally, Red Roland exploded and said, "Mortimer Chatham, you are a pompous ass! You are still young so I will excuse your ignorance. You have continually insulted our family, but expect us to accept your actions as well as your insults. Beware, for the high and mighty often fall to the depths of the common. Your family's arrogance may well be your undoing. Your father was the one who should have displayed the backbone to come and face me, but yet he sent you. Now remove yourself from our house and never darken our door again! If your father takes exception to what I have said to you, he may face me with a sword."

Everyone in the neighborhood knew that Red Roland Drury was an expert swordsman. Reginald Chatham would never take the challenge. When Mortimer Chatham was gone, Roland Drury turned to Redmon and said, "Let me see what they did to you."

Reluctantly, Redmon slowly opened his shirt to reveal the raw brand on his chest, a fresh burned capital C on his right breast. The brand looked red and terrible to Redmon's family. Suddenly, there was a strangled cry from his mother Joselyn and little sister Madeline, who both had been standing nearby and listening to the confrontation with Mortimer Chatham. The eldest son Rodney was not present as he was away attending Eton College.

Red Roland exploded. "Those arrogant bastards! Redmon, I cannot condone what you did with Roselind, but seeing that brand makes me want to kill Wilfred also. I believe what Mortimer said. Reginald Chatham is vindictive and will want to punish you further. I know that the Chathams will now make it as difficult for the Drurys as they possibly can. We must be prepared for them. If you try to kill Wilfred, which he richly deserves, they will surely see to it that you are dead. Knowing the Chathams as we do now, they may very well attempt to accomplish that anyway. The Chathams have a completely overblown sense of their worth in British society. I never thought I would be forced to say such a thing Redmon, but Drury Manor may not be safe for you now. You have thrown down a challenge to Wilfred

Chatham and he will probably come after you, hoping to have you killed. He will not come after you man to man. His father would never allow that. They will send men to do it for them, because they are able to do so. Redmon, first we will remove that cursed C from your chest. Then we will decide what must be done." Red Roland Drury had never been so angry in his life.

"No, Father, I am going to leave the brand. It will remind me of my hatred for Wilfred Chatham. It will remind me of how a man who is arrogant and unjust must be brought down to dwell with the rest of us mere mortals. I want to always remember what the all-powerful Wilfred Chatham did to me!" Redmon spit out in an anguished voice.

Joselyn and Madeline Drury were openly crying, and Red Roland, along with Roddrick, could only stare at Redmon. That night, Joselyn treated the fresh burn. After bandaging the brand, Joselyn Drury held her son and told him how much she loved him. There was worry as well as dread in the Drury manor house that night. Red Roland and Joselyn wondered just how quickly Reginald Chatham could alert and influence the local constables to arrest Redmon.

Two days later, Redmon Drury was on a ship leaving Gretna Green through Solway Firth. His family was there to see him off.

Joselyn Drury and Madeline, who would soon be thirteen and as beautiful as her mother, held Redmon before he boarded the North Star sailing to Canada. Red Roland and Roddrick took Redmon's hand and treated him like a man. The local constable had earlier come to Drury Manor to arrest Redmon for threatening to kill Wilfred Chatham, as well as trespassing on Chatham lands. However, when the constable learned what Wilfred did to Redmon, he left the manor shaking his head.

The Drurys realized that the constable's visit would only be the beginning if Redmon remained in England, so they booked passage on the North Star. Redmon wanted to stay to face Wilfred Chatham, but it was not to be. His parents convinced him that leaving would save not only Redmon, but also probably the family.

The morning the North Star sailed was dismal and overcast. The weather mirrored the mood felt by the Drurys as they watched Redmon walk up the gangplank carrying his two large bags. Red Roland was angry as he watched his son leave the country.

The Chathams it seemed possessed a long reach. Red Roland kept wondering how Reginald Chatham was able to influence their local authorities. Also Wilfred Chatham was developing a reputation for his harshness and cruelty toward the yeomen that inhabited Chatham lands.

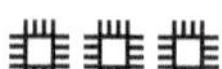

Redmon woke and stared at the ceiling. He had relived the night of the branding over and over for ten years. He always saw the sneering face of Wilfred Chatham, heard the words, and felt the sting of the urine on the fresh burn in each dream. He would never forget how he was treated and humiliated by Wilfred Chatham. He could still hear Roselind's screams as he was branded by Wilfred Chatham. He vowed vengeance that night, and now ten years later by some trick of fate he accidently found the only man he ever really hated. Apparently, Wilfred was planning to hurt the people named Wilbanks. He learned to live with the brand because it fueled his will to survive and fight against those who thought they were better than those around them. Redmon drifted back to sleep and the dream slowly returned as he relived the past again.

The North Star was loaded with people going to Canada to start a new life, some by their own choice and others by the will of the British government. There was also a hold filled with people from the debtor barges emptied from the River Thames in London and transported to the coast to be put on the North Star. There were probably some convicted felons mixed in. Redmon was lucky to have a small cabin, along with money his parents provided him for the trip.

Not many of his fellow landholders realized what a fine land manager Red Roland Drury was, certainly not the Chathams. He was even able to add land over time to the Drury holdings. The Drurys owned as much land as the Chathams, but the arrogant neighbors were unaware of that fact.

⊞ ⊞ ⊞

The North Star had only been a few days at sea when Redmon realized that a young earl named Winston Maybury thought he could buy the pleasures of the young female passengers even when they rebuffed his advances. One pretty young passenger, Constance Richards, was the young earl's early target. Redmon heard the girl refuse the man twice.

The young earl seemed not to understand the word no, so he sent his servant again when Constance was strolling the deck, except this time the servant attempted to force Constance down the ladder to the earl's cabin. Redmon stepped in and stopped him. Suddenly, a knife appeared in the man's hand. He lunged at Redman and that was his mistake. Redmon hacked down on the man's arm and shot his right fist out and connected with the man's chin. The servant hit the deck and did not move. Hearing the commotion, Captain Morris and the second mate were there. Redmon explained what had happened and Constance Richards confirmed his account. The man was put in irons and placed in the ship's brig. Constance

Richards was a paying passenger with a cabin on the North Star and would be protected by the captain.

Young Earl Winston Maybury was given a warning by Captain Morris to leave Constance Richards alone including the other young women on the ship. Earl Maybury tried to intimidate the captain by reminding him who his parents were and that they could have his ship confiscated and the captain himself put in irons for his actions. The captain, to his credit, showed character and told the young aristocrat to give that his best effort. Constance Richards thanked Redmon over and over for rescuing her from the man trying to take her below deck.

Redmon decided to make it his mission to thwart Winston Maybury for the remainder of the voyage. The young earl had one retainer left who attempted to entice a pretty young woman from the debtors' hold and take her to the earl's cabin. Redmon caught the man carrying the struggling girl down the ladder as he was coming out of his cabin. "Let me go, you goon!" Redmon heard the girl say.

Redmon stopped and blocked the passage. "I believe you should release the young lady. She clearly does not want to be taken anywhere."

"Get outta me way. Me master wants this lass and he always gets what he wants."

"Clearly your master needs to learn to control himself," Redmon replied.

The girl continued to struggle and managed to hit her abductor on the nose, causing him to grunt out in pain and drop her to the deck. Redmon quickly stepped in and hit the man on the chin, knocking him to the deck. Redmon immediately reached down, took the girl's hand, pulled her up, and pushed her toward the ladder. When he looked down, the man was beginning to stir, so Redmon followed the fleeing girl up the ladder. When they were on deck, she whirled and was in Redmon's arms. "Thank you, oh, thank you. That awful man hit my father who was trying to protect me. I must make sure he is well."

Redmon immediately realized that the girl he rescued was well spoken. He wondered about this girl being in the debtors' hold. He learned that the girl's name was Grace Walden just as an older man came striding up to them along the deck. Grace introduced her father Conner Walden. After introducing himself, Grace explained that Redmon had rescued her.

Connor Walden was profuse in his praise and appreciation for Redmon saving his daughter. They found a place along a rail and Redmon learned why these people were in the debtors' hold. Redmon could see that the Waldens' clothes were of quality but faded and dirty. Redmon learned that the Waldens owned a good estate, but Walden's son was found with the daughter of a nearby duke. Lionel Walden was put to death for ruining the duke's daughter, and the Lord Essex set about taking the Walden's land and putting them in the poor house as retribution. Grace's mother died when they were forced to leave their lands and move to London, so here they were. They found themselves in a debtors' barge because of the power of a nobleman.

Redmon alerted Captain Morris as to what happened, but the debtors' hold people were not treated the same as the paying passengers. They were on their own. During the process of saving the two young women, Redmon made a formidable enemy of the young Earl Maybury. His man pointed to Redmon as the one who kept him from bringing Grace Walden to the earl.

One morning, Redmon was standing with Connor and Grace Walden at the railing watching a pod of whales surfacing, blowing, and going back under the surface when Redmon felt a presence at his elbow.

"I know not who you believe you are, but do not intrude into my business again. I will have this girl," and he looked at Grace, "when I wish to have her. She is nothing but a girl to be used from the debtors' hold. If you interfere again, I will have you put in the gaol when we reach Quebec. My family could buy and sell you three times over."

If Winston Maybury expected Redmon to cower in fear from his threat, he would be disappointed, for Redmon laughed out loud. "Do not threaten me,"

Redmon said as he looked at the sallow-faced young man that could be a year or two older than himself. Winston Maybury was only five feet six at the most. "My father is Red Roland Drury, the Fifth Earl of Penrith. I know well the banes of nobility and how a large landholder may believe they can have and do anything they wish to those they feel to be inferior to themselves. I have dealt with such a family recently and will not do so again. Do not ever threaten me again. I suggest that you find anyone other than Miss Richards and Miss Walden, for they will now be under my protection." Redmon was bluffing but was not going to be intimidated by this small, arrogant aristocrat.

Redmon learned from Captain Morris that Winston Maybury's father was a high-ranking British official in Montreal. Captain Morris warned Redmon that the young earl's threat could be credible. The Captain advised Redmon, Constance Richards and the Waldens that they should disembark from the North Star before they reached Montreal where Earl Maybury's power could come into play. Constance told Redmon that her parents were to meet her at Tracy, north of Montreal. After talking to the captain, he suggested that Redmon and the Waldens slip off the North Star when it stopped at the dock in Repentigny above Montreal.

The North Star reached the mouth of the St. Lawrence Seaway six weeks after leaving England. Winston

Maybury must have heeded Redman's warning, for he left both Constance and Grace alone. Maybe he was only biding his time waiting for retribution. Redmon learned that the young earl found a comely young woman from the debtors' hold to use. The girl was a prostitute in London and was diseased. Winston Maybury's desire to prove he was manly would eventually cause his death from the disease he received from Maude Abney on the North Star.

⛭ ⛭ ⛭

Constance Richards found her parents waiting at Tracy and was safe. Four passengers off loaded in Quebec. Captain Morris told the remaining passengers that the North Star would need to dock for safety during the night. After midnight, Redmon and the Waldens slipped off the ship in Repentigny. Captain Morris told them where to find an inn that would take them in. He told Redmon to ask for Angus MacFadden, a Scot living in French country. Redmon carried his two bags and noticed that Connor Walden was only carrying a small bag that must have held very little as they made their way down the gangplank.

The term 'black as night' could easily describe their departure from the North Star. They could hardly see their hands before their faces as they moved along a rutted street. Grace was holding an arm of her father and one of Redmon as they moved slowly along. When they found the inn, Redmon was forced to pound on the thick door three time before he heard some movement inside. The door was thrown open and a huge man stood there. "Who ye be now? Fair or foul, laddie!"

Redmon spoke quietly. "Captain Morris sent us and said that we would be safe with you."

"Aye, the captain be a good mon. Come in then and be quick about it. Tis late ye be comin'."

Angus did indeed take them in and Redmon paid for the room for the Waldens. The next morning they were actually able to get hot baths at a bathhouse. Grace washed out her clothes.

Redmon confided to Angus why they left the North Star and Angus suggested they take a small river packet north above Montreal on the Ottawa River to go inland. It would be leaving the following morning. Redmon took the Waldens to a trading post Angus had suggested and bought them some essentials. The Waldens protested, but Redmon simply replied, "We are friends and you would do the same for me."

Grace Walden quickly realized that she could easily fall in love with Redmon Drury. She sensed that there was something in Redmon's past that she did not understand. Redmon had treated the burn on his chest with ointment that his mother had sent with him. The fire of the brand no longer burned on the outside, but the deep-seated fire of hatred still burned inside Redmon from that dreadful night.

Early the following morning, the Waldens and Redmon were on the packet boat. Grace was wearing a new dress that Redmon had bought for her. All of them were freshly scrubbed and feeling renewed after the long voyage. The packet boat bypassed Montreal and entered the Ottawa River. Two days after entering the river, the packet boat reached Ottawa. They found an inn called the White Swan close to the riverfront. Four days after arriving in Ottawa, Connor Walden found employment as a bookkeeper at a new mercantile. Grace was also hired to help the female customers that came to the store. The storeowner even provided the Waldens with a small house. The parting from the Waldens was a good one for Redmon. Grace Walden hugged Redmon hard. "Redmon Drury, you saved me and have been wonderful for us. You will always be in our thoughts. I wish we could have met under different circumstances in England."

"Grace, you will find a man who is worthy of who you are. You will be a wonderful catch for the man lucky enough to have you!"

❁ ❁ ❁

Redmon caught the packet boat and rode it as far up the river as it would travel. Two weeks after leaving the

Waldens, Redmon reached Pembroke and decided to leave the boat. He found an inn named the Wild Rose. Because there was only a bolt on the inside of the door to his room, Redmon carried his bags with him to a log trading post he noticed earlier. He realized that he needed weapons, and then he would look for horses.

In the trading post Redmon found a matching volcanic carbine and pistol. Both were brass engraved .38 calibers. The carbine was a 30-shot while the pistol was a ten-shot weapon. Redmon thought both were beautiful. He didn't know a great deal about weapons, but was sure that he could learn to use both the pistol and the carbine. Then he saw a left-handed leather holster that would strap around his waist to hold the pistol and bought it along with plenty of ammunition. While riding the packet boat up the Ottawa River, Redmon had read a couple of penny dreadfuls. The small pamphlets touted the quick draw artists of the western United States. He wondered if the volcanic pistol he bought could be drawn quickly. There was also a leather scabbard for the carbine.

Next, he walked to a stable across the muddy road from the trading post. He looked at the available horses. The sky was clear on this morning but there was the feel of moisture in the air. The stableman kept trying to point out horses that he wanted Redmon to buy, saying that they were the best in the country. Redmon kept looking at a chestnut-colored stallion. The tall horse was somewhat gaunt. Redmon also noticed some scars on the horses back.

"Monsieur, you do not want that horse. He was not well treated by a trapper who sold him to me. He has been used hard carrying heavy packs of furs."

Redmon looked at the horse's teeth and realized that the tall horse was only two years old, maybe slightly older. He bought the horse cheap and chuckled. The tall stallion was a Morgan, which they raised on Drury Manor. He thought that when the horse was treated well he would fill out. He believed the stallion would be a fine animal as he looked at its conformation. Then Redmon saw another horse in a stall. "Is that horse for sale?"

"Monsieur, that horse is for sale but it is crazy. She will try to bite and kick you all the time. That horse is a she-devil. You will be sorry if you buy that horse."

Again Redmon bought the Morgan mare to the protest of the hostler who kept saying that Redmon would regret buying her. He led the horses away while the stableman shook his head at Redmon's perceived stupidity, and then laughed at his good fortune for getting rid of two bad horses, even though he didn't make much money on them.

Back at the trading post Redmon bought a saddle, bridle, and saddle blanket for the stallion, along with a packsaddle and blanket for the mare. She tried to bite him as he tied her lead rope to the hitch rail. He popped her on the muzzle, causing her to snort and back up. When they returned to the Wild Rose stable he got corn for the stallion and hay for the mare. The stallion attacked the corn as if the tall horse had never tasted such fine fodder before this moment. Redmon took the time to run his hands over the stallion and rub down his coat. He could tell that the big horse had been ill-treated. He could remedy that problem. He then rubbed a sack he found over the mare; and, even though she attempted to kick him once when he was near her hindquarters, it caused him to laugh and slap her on the rump.

When he came into the common room and sat down, the men sitting there eyed Redmon and his packs, especially his volcanic pistol and carbine. After eating a good meal, Redmon carried all his possessions to his room and bolted the door. In his room, Redmon handled the pistol then strapped on the holster. With the big pistol resting in the holster, Redmon began pulling it slowly. Finally, getting the feel of the weapon in his hand, he began to draw more quickly. Redmon realized that he might have the natural dexterity, with practice, to draw quickly. He decided that when he left Pembroke he would practice shooting both the pistol and the carbine.

Redmon slept well that night, but was anxious to get started on his new adventure. After going to sleep, he experienced the dream that came almost every night. He thought the dream might lessen in intensity when he crossed the Atlantic on the North Star, but it did not. If anything it became more intense. He began to see little details of that night that he did not notice at the time. The smell of the hay in the loft. The feel of Roselind's skin as he touched and loved her. The sudden grasping of his hair and arms. The curse from Mortimer when they were discovered. Being dragged from the loft by the yeomen with Roselind screaming her protests. It was always reliving what happened the night he was branded.

Redmon spent a great deal of time during his voyage from Gretna Green to Canada thinking about his years with Roselind and what she meant to him. He decided that he was being completely unrealistic about ever having Roselind as his wife. He had seen the actions of Reginald, Mortimer, and Wilfred Chatham over the years when he and Roselind were playing their hiding game. He saw their youthful arrogance when they thought no one was watching them.

When Redmon came down the stairs the next morning with his gear and the big volcanic .38 strapped on his hip, there were chuckles from the men in the common room. Redmon, now almost sixteen years of age, had not yet reached his full height and weight. The pistol looked huge hanging on his left hip. The men sitting in the common room thought this young man would have a great deal to learn in a land that was settled by hard men. French trappers were the first into Canada and they were tough men. Two old grizzled former mountain men were amongst those in the common room. During their formidable years they fought Indians as well as British trappers who now controlled the country.

Jacque Cousard and Louis Broulet both noticed that the young man looked capable and surprisingly seemed to display a somewhat hard look as they observed him. They thought the men in the room who were laughing just might be wrong about the young man. Redmon saw them and moved to a place across from them. He placed his gear at his feet, sat, and nodded to the old trappers. A young pretty maid was quickly at his elbow and took his breakfast order. Redmon heard Jacque ask Louis if he thought the young man could hold his own and survive in Canada.

Redmon chuckled and spoke in perfect French. "Messieurs, I will do my best to hold my own in your fair land. You men must know this land well. Could you tell me what to expect out in the West, where I wish to go? I must find a place for the winter."

Redmon had given his order in English, but spoke to them with respect in French because they had spoken to each other in that language. Jacque chuckled. "Monsieur, you speak our language well but you are surely Anglais, as the natives say. How is it that you speak French so well? Then we will help you on your way."

"My father insisted that I, along with my brothers and sister, learn languages as part of our education. I also speak Spanish but French is the language I like. My name is Redmon Drury, and I hope to learn how to survive in your land. I am young, but I wish to learn from men who know the land. My father taught me to listen to those who have walked the land and faced the dangers ahead of me."

"Monsieur, your father is a wise man indeed," Jacque replied.

Jacque and Louis told Redmon to follow the Ottawa River west and find a man named Emile Bouchard who owned a trading post at North Bay on Lake Nipissing. "Emile has many skills and will help you when you tell him that we sent you."

While eating his breakfast, Redmon listened to Jacque and Louis tell stories of how it was in Canada when they were young voyagers trapping fur for the French Fur Company. Redmon related the story of making an enemy of the son of Lord Maybury during the voyage from England. Both men knew of Lord Edward Maybury and told Redmon that he had better head west right away because, as they said it, "You have made a terrible enemy."

Redmon saddled the tall Morgan and strapped on the new carbine. As he approached the mare, he saw the devil in the animal's eyes. He reached to untie the lead rope and the mare tried to bite him. He popped her on the muzzle and untied the rope. He tied the mare's head close to a post, put a blanket on her, cinched up the packsaddle, and loaded his gear. When he had gone to the trading post the day before, Redmon bought trail supplies, blankets, a ground sheet, and a slicker. When he walked near the mare's hindquarters, she tried to kick him. He laughed and slapped her on the rump. With the rebellious mare in tow, Redmon headed away from the Wild Rose.

The two former French trappers watched Redmon, whom they liked very much, ride away. They also saw a hard-looking character watching the young man as he rode west. The two Frenchmen wondered if the young Englishman would even come close to reaching North Bay. Redmon was clearly in possession of a good outfit and probably some money. Redmon had also spotted the character in the common room that was constantly watching him intently. He saw the man watching as he rode away from the inn. Redmon realized that he was going to face his first test and would have to be ready. Because of Wilfred Chatham and the branding, Redmon now trusted no one.

He found a good trail along the river and increased his pace. There was traffic in both directions along the trail. Redmon realized the movement of people along the river trail might give him an advantage. Late in the afternoon, Redmon found a secluded spot in a slight bend in the river to camp for the night. He thought that if the man he saw was indeed following him, he would be forced to discover Redmon's camp among the many others along the river trail. Redmon could actually hear some noise from the other camps near him.

Jacque and Louis had warned him to keep his fires low and put them out early. They also warned him that he'd better learn how to use his new pistol and carbine quickly. Redmon put together a quick meal and put out the fire. He rubbed down both horses but spent some time handling the stallion. He had bought some corn and a feedbag in Pembroke and eventually put it on the stallion.

Next Redmon practiced drawing his new pistol. Redmon liked the feel of the pistol in his hand. He realized that drawing and firing the weapon quickly could insure his survival in this land. After drawing from the new holster, he used his knife and cut a small piece of leather away to make the draw easier. Redmon knew he would need to find a spot so he could practice shooting at targets.

He hoped that he could evade his pursuer, if there was one, until he became proficient at shooting. Finally, Redmon brought the horses in close to the camp and tied them up. The mare, true to her nature, tried to nip him. He popped her on the nose and she snorted and shook her head. He settled in the shadows facing away from the river and waited.

Night was descending as Redmon's thoughts went to his family and to Roselind again. He hoped his family was coping with the Chathams. As for Roselind, he thought of holding her and making love. He knew every inch of her firm but supple body, and they had learned much together from age five on. There were never any secrets between them, and Redmon honestly thought they would always be together. Then reality set in for the both of them.

❖ ❖ ❖

Drury Manor was doing well financially because of the stewardship of Red Roland, but it was a sad and angry house. The Drurys were not happy about sending Redmon away. Some two weeks after the North Star had sailed, they realized the mistake they made sending him away. Much had already changed for them as a family.

The Chathams were in some trouble of their own and found little time to harass the Drurys. Red Roland learned from a friend and local government official that the Chathams were heavily in debt. It seemed that Lord Reginald Chatham was not a good steward or manager of his land.

Lord Reginald and Lady Lydia Chatham were not prepared for the reaction from Roselind immediately after the branding of Redmon Drury. When Wilfred walked into the manor house, Roselind attacked her brother with a vengeance. She hit, slapped, and clawed him as she screamed out his cruelty. Finally, Wilfred threw her away from him. Hitting her head on the stone floor she was knocked unconscious for a short time. The rift between sister and brothers was now complete.

Lady Lydia ran to her daughter. When Roselind regained consciousness, she uttered the words that would split the family forever. "I'm not going to call you brother any longer for you are surely the devil incarnate. I will never speak to you or Mortimer again and I believe your souls will reside in hell. I truly believe that Redmon will put both of you there in hell where you belong. We have been lying together for over a year. He is my man in every way possible. He is more man than either of you will ever be!"

Wilfred moved toward his sister as if to strike her, but Reginald stopped him. "Enough of this! Roselind, you will become the wife of Edward Benford and that is final. I will not have the name Redmon Drury mentioned in this house again. Your brother did what was necessary to someone who is far below us in station. I have sent Mortimer to warn those Drurys and inform them that we will no longer tolerate them acting as though they are noblemen. I am going to have that low son of a Drury who defiled you arrested for his attack on you."

Roselind stared at her father. He was startled by the hate-filled look she gave him. "Father, our arrogance does not serve us well. As to marrying Edward Benford, I am sure he will appreciate learning that I have lain with the man I love and only want to marry him." Then she turned and ran up the stairs to her room leaving her parents and brother staring after her. That night Roselind Chatham disappeared from Chatham Manor. Her family did not have any idea when she left or where she went. They would not see her again for more than twelve years.

✦ ✦ ✦

The stallion nuzzled Redmon and he came awake suddenly. The sky was graying in the east. No attack came and Redmon was thankful. He rekindled his fire and put water on for tea. The air was heavy that morning along the Ottawa and Redmon realized that rain might be in the offing. He was on the trail early. For the first time the mare didn't try to bite him when he loaded the packsaddle. She did, however, reach and grab the packsaddle blanket with her teeth twice and throw it on the ground which caused Redmon to laugh out loud. He decided to call the stallion Lancer. Redmon noticed how the stallion was already filling out and looking much better.

He passed several camps that were just beginning to stir. An hour after beginning his ride, Redmon was forced to get into his slicker. The rain was heavy along the river. It became a thoroughly miserable day of riding. Late in the afternoon, the horses were plodding so Redmon stopped at an inn he found in Point Alexander with a stable. He was fortunate to get the last room by stopping early. Anyone who came late would be forced to sleep on the floor near the fireplace or on a bench in the common room.

Redmon was sitting over his evening meal when the grizzled character from Pembroke walked into the common room. Redmon tried to look as though he didn't notice but he certainly did. He knew that he very well could have to face the man soon.

Redmon was in his room early, bolting the door but keeping his pistol close. Before he lay down for the night, Redmon practiced drawing his .38 and worked the cocking lever. Surprisingly, he slept well that night and was up early.

After a breakfast in the low-ceilinged common room, Redmon headed out to the horses. From the corner of his eye he saw the man watching him saddle and load his horses. He hit the trail in a light drizzle. He pushed his horses because they were in better shape than only a few days earlier when he left Pembroke. He figured the man would try to attack him that night. He rode hard, but was wary in case the man tried to overtake him. Finally, the rain stopped and the sun came out, but there was almost a heavy feeling to the air along the river trail. He found a good place to camp just before sundown. Quickly, he put a fire together, rubbed down the horses, and put on feedbags. Redmon cooked a quick stew and then decided to build up his fire, hoping to bring the attacker to him. He wanted the grizzled man to believe that he was a complete tenderfoot as Jacque had called him, which he knew he actually was. Maybe he could use that to his advantage.

He would liked to have the chance to get in the river for a bath but could not take that chance. With the horses tied in what he hoped was a safe spot, Redmon put more wood on the fire and moved into the shadows with his pistol and carbine at the ready. As it happened, Rosie, as he decided to name the mare, alerted Redmon to the approach of the grizzled man as Redmon thought of him. Rosie gave him the direction that the man came from towards the camp. Suddenly, a shadow appeared from downstream. Rosie snorted and the shadow went still. Several minutes passed before the man moved and made for Redmon's packs. The thief was carrying a pistol in his hand and seemed ready to shoot.

Abruptly, the man realized his mistake because the weapons he wanted were not with the packs. He wheeled with the pistol out in front of him looking into the dark. Redmon moved slightly and the man fired. The shot passed close by and Redmon fired back. His shot did not miss and the man crumpled near the fire. The attacker's pant leg even caught fire.

Redmon waited some time before moving. He put out the man's burning pants, and was able to add some sticks to the fire. When it flared up, Redmon rolled the man over and saw that his shot had hit the robber in the heart. Redmon felt fortunate for this man was probably a seasoned camp-robber. He was sick at heart for having killed the man, but he realized also that this man had planned to rob and kill him and take his horses, weapons, and money.

Redmon rolled into his blankets but did not sleep well. Killing a man was never in his plan unless it was Wilfred Chatham. When dawn finally came, Redmon found the robber's horse and knew at first sight that it was a good one.

He was able to take a dip in the river and have a quick breakfast before getting on the trail pulling two horses behind him. Each night he found good camping spots, and again each night the recurring dream came. It never lessened in intensity.

Two weeks later he rode into North Bay. He found the trading post easily as well as Emile Boushard. Redmon told the trader that Jacque Cousard and Louis Broulet had sent him.

Emile immediately put a huge smile on his face and welcomed Redmon. After taking care of the horses, Emile gave Redmon a small cabin close to the trading post. That first night Emile asked Redmon to have dinner with him and Redmon related for Emile his entire background, holding nothing back. He told Emile about the grizzled man who tried to attack his camp. As they talked, Redmon saw the crossed dueling swords and foils hanging on a wall and inquired about them.

"Redmon, in my former life I was a master of sword in France. My father sent me to the finest schools and to the finest academy to learn the art of arms. Then I ran afoul of a nobleman much as you experienced with your Lord Chatham. I was forced to leave France because the daughter of a count loved me."

"Would you consider teaching me the sword?" Redmon asked. I've had some lessons but never finished. My father, Red Roland, is considered a master of the sword. I would wish to follow in his footsteps. I truly believe I will go home someday and face Wilfred Chatham, and I want to be prepared. I know he and his brother were also taking lessons from a master of the sword. I will work for you in any capacity you might have for me."

"Can you shoot that rifle you have with you? I have never seen such a fine weapon as that one. If you can shoot, Redmon Drury, I will need you to hunt for the post. I have a native guide who will teach you wilderness craft, but you will do the shooting."

❖ ❖ ❖

Roselind gathered some clothes, sturdy shoes, and the money she had carefully saved and left Chatham Manor well after midnight. The big house was quiet, for the family and servants were all abed. She felt completely hurt and betrayed by her own family. She always knew that Wilfred was cruel, but she never dreamed that he would do something like brand Redmon. The most terrible part of the entire episode was that her own brothers, and especially Wilfred, made her stand and watch as they tortured the love of her life. She was finished with them as brothers! Roselind was carrying bread, cheese, and some roasted meat she had taken from the kitchen as she quietly left the place she once called home. There was bile in her throat as she looked up at the large manor house that had suddenly caused so much pain in her life.

She planned now to seek refuge with the only people she knew who would treat her well. Roselind's hope was to get to Redmon so they could be together.

Roselind made her way to the abandoned cotter's cottage where she and Redmon had made love often. She only wished they had made their way there that fateful night rather than to the Chatham stable loft. Tonight she was sure her family would go first to Drury Manor to look for her.

Roselind knew that she had loved Redmon Drury from the time she was five years old. They had expressed their love for one another for the last three years, but they knew it deep in their hearts far longer than that. She and Redmon had taken the time to make the small cottage clean and comfortable for themselves.

The night was dark and dreary, as was her mood as she made her way to the isolated cottage after escaping Chatham Manor. Every night sound was enhanced as Roselind made her way across the heath. She seemed to hear the leaves as they rustled in the breeze. She saw bats swooping and diving in the moonlight that was just beginning to show in the east. Finally, she saw the outline of the cotter's cottage appear out of the gloom.

Roselind lay on the pallet where she and Redmon shared their love and cried for her man as she thought of Redmon. Her heart ached for Redmon for she knew they were a perfect match. Why they decided to choose the Chatham stable loft for their last lovemaking she could not explain. It was so spontaneous and led to their downfall. She relived those anguished moments when they were discovered and Redmon was dragged from her.

Roselind was proud of Redmon as he never screamed out in pain when her brother placed the red-hot iron on his chest. Her hatred for her brothers, Wilfred and Mortimer, was now complete.

She knew that Red Roland Drury set a time and met with her father to arrange a marriage contract for her and Redmon, but was rebuffed and made to look foolish by her father for even making such an attempt. Roselind realized at that moment that her own father was a man of very little character. She listened to her father as he attempted to belittle the fellow nobleman when Lord Drury came for the meeting. Her mother said not a word in support of Roselind and that hurt her deeply. Eventually, she met young Edward Benford with whom her father arranged the marriage contract. Roselind thought him to be an arrogant sniveling young man who would be just like her father and brothers.

For two days after leaving Chatham Manor she saw men searching the area, and even saw Wilfred riding toward Drury Manor with Mortimer and her father. Once, she was forced to hide in the tiny loft as she fortunately saw a Chatham yeoman approaching. He glanced briefly into the cottage, but went away. Apparently, the man who came searching did not notice how clean the abandoned cottage appeared.

Each night in the cottage she relived that terrible night of the branding and the pain did not lessen for her. On the fourth night she made her way to Drury Manor. As it happened, it was seventeen-year-old

Roddrick Drury that found Roselind behind the manor house and took her in. In a comfortable sitting room, Roselind poured out her tale and begged the Drurys to give her refuge.

"I love Redmon and he loves me! Redmon always told me that if I needed a safe place I should come here and you would protect me. My family betrayed me when they hurt Redmon. I will never forgive them for that injustice. Redmon and I can go away and not put you in danger from my family. Where is he? Is he not well because of what my brother did to him?"

Roselind learned that indeed her father and brothers came to Drury Manor looking for her. The constable was with them and was allowed to search the manor house, but Red Roland refused entry to the Chathams. Roselind was devastated to learn that Redmon took a ship to Canada only two days past. She chastised herself for remaining in the cottage too long. She broke down and cried afraid that Redmon was gone from her life, probably for good.

Joselyn and Madeline took charge of Roselind and got her bathed and fed. Red Roland was somewhat hesitant and worried about taking Roselind Chatham in, but Redmon vowed to protect her and he would keep his son's promise.

That night, wearing one of Joselyn's clean nightgowns, Roselind finally slipped between clean sheets in a fine bedroom next to Madeline's room. Roselind cried for her lost love for she truly believed that she would never see Redmon again. She thought of Canada as being a complete world away. If she only came sooner, she could have taken a ship to Canada with Redmon.

The Chathams rode for Gretna Green and learned that Redmon did indeed leave alone on the North Star two days earlier. So they knew Roselind was still in the neighborhood somewhere. Reginald Chatham knew that Chatham Manor was in deep financial trouble so he hoped to forge a family alliance with the powerful Benfords to save Chatham. Now they must find Roselind to complete his plans. They searched the neighborhood but found no word of Roselind or any trace of her. When the constable was allowed to search Drury Manor house, Roselind was not found anywhere in the house, and he assured the Chathams that he looked in every cabinet and under every bed.

✿ ✿ ✿

Two years passed quickly for Redmon at North Bay. He successfully hunted for the trading post and made a fast friend in Long Bow, the Huron brave who taught him forest craft. Redmon became a crack shot with both pistol and carbine. He could move through the forest like a ghost and track like a native. He wore buckskins and moccasins when off with Long Bow. The afternoons were spent learning fencing and swordsmanship from Emile Boushard.

Redmon quickly realized that he had learned very little from his instructor in England. Barnabus Gainsby was considered to be a master of the sword in England, but Redmon now knew the man's reputation was overblown after being taught by Emile Boushard. Red Roland insisted that Redmon and Roddrick learn from someone other than himself. Redmon now wished that his father had been the one who gave the lessons, for he saw his father in action once when Red Roland did not know Redmon had followed him to the dueling field. A nearby nobleman had made advances toward Joselyn and a duel ensued. Red Roland dispatched Sir Gilbert Gladstone easily, who was purported to be a master of the sword himself. Redmon never said a word but was proud of his father.

At the end of the second year with Emile, his mentor declared Redmon as being a near master in proficiency, which was quite a compliment. Redmon grew in height to over six feet two and bulked up in the shoulders and chest. Now at eighteen, Redmon sported a beard and mustache that he kept well groomed. He was also growing restless of late with each passing day.

He and Emile practiced every day with the sword or foil come rain or come shine. Emile set aside a room for practice during bad weather or they sparred outside when possible. Their sparring sessions at the trading post never failed to draw a crowd of watchers when they were outside. All the men who frequented the trading post knew that Emile Boushard was a master of the sword. They quickly realized that Redmon Drury was achieving that level after watching the sessions for two years. Redmon was now cat quick in reflexes and strong as a young bull. Because of the branding he never gave in to any trial.

Emile realized early in their relationship that there was some kind of demon inside Redmon driving him to be the best at everything he attempted, and the sword was no exception. They fought to a standstill during each session, and Emile was amazed how quickly Redmon became an expert with the blade.

Emile Boushard had killed men with his blade but realized that Redmon Drury would be his most difficult opponent if he were forced to face him. Emile knew that this Wilfred Chatham would have no chance if Redmon ever challenged him. Emile was the one who realized that it was time for Redmon to move on. He felt as though he actually helped raise Redmon Drury and turn him into a man. The two became more than mentor and student. A very close bond was formed during their two years together during which time they always spoke French with each other. Redmond had learned many things from Emile as they became fast friends.

A few months after Redmon sailed for Canada, two important things happened for the Drurys and Roselind. First, Wilfred Chatham married Melissa, the only child of the wealthy Lord Thomas Dudley.

Then, the lenders called their loans on Reginald Chatham, but Thomas Dudley refused to cover the loans of his new in-law. Sir Dudley's reply when Wilfred asked him to bail out his father Lord Reginald was, "Your father made the debt so he can very well find a way to extricate himself from his financial problems. I did not incur the debt. Your father did that for himself, and will deal with the lenders on his own. He should have managed the Chatham lands in a more judicious manner."

Behind the scenes, Red Roland Drury quietly bought the loans owed by the Chathams. Red Roland was able to buy up the loans at a reduced rate so the lenders could see some money from the Chatham property and retrieve most of their money. Constable Diggins informed Lord Reginald Chatham that he, Lady Lydia, and Mortimer would have two weeks to vacate the manor because they no longer held its title. Wilfred had already left to reside with his new wife on the large Dudley Manor near Leeds. Little did Sir Dudley and Melissa know that Wilfred Chatham was already putting a plot of revenge into motion because Sir Dudley had adamantly refused to cover the Chathams' debt. Melissa Dudley would have no idea what a devious and ruthless man she had recently married.

On Drury Manor, Roselind became part of the family until she and Roddrick discovered one another. It began innocently enough as Roddrick and his sister Madeline spent more and more time with Roselind. Red Roland had been honest with Roselind and told her that he had bought the loans on Chatham and was having her parents and Mortimer evicted. Roselind agreed that after what her family did to Redmon that little consideration should be given to them.

Drury Manor doubled in size with the purchase of the Chatham lands. Roselind quickly settled in with the family and became a Drury rather than a Chatham. She and Roddrick continued to grow closer with each passing day. Roselind never realized that a family could talk, laugh, and be as close until she resided with the Drurys.

Rodney Drury finally came from Sheffield and learned the complete details about the branding of Redmon. Rodney had become a practicing barrister in a firm. He was not interested in living on Drury Manor or farming. He soon realized that Roselind was a good addition to the Drury family. Roselind, for her part, liked Rodney and thought he was much like Redmon in personality. For her safety, Roselind was kept hidden away for a period of time. She now looked forward to every day so that she could live with and be a part of the Drury family.

Roselind discovered that the Drurys possessed a wonderful library and were all well-read. Her family's perception of the Drurys was completely incorrect. She was learning to speak French along with Madeline. She was getting an education at Drury Manor that she never received at Chatham Manor. Both Red Roland and Joselyn were constantly telling Roselind how smart she was. Which was something that never happened at Chatham Manor. Joselyn also held Roselind in her arms as a mother would hold a daughter and Roselind responded in kind.

After Roselind's parents and her brother Mortimer were gone from Chatham Hall, she and Roddrick rode freely across the land. Six months into her tenure at Drury Manor, Roddrick asked Roselind to marry him and she accepted.

They were married quietly by the local Anglican minister, who came to Drury Manor for the ceremony. They would take up residence at the former Chatham Manor after repairs were made and renamed it Eden Hall. Their first night as husband and wife in the refurbished master suite in the new Eden Hall was a revelation for the newlyweds. Roselind came to realize that she could love two men in her lifetime, and Roddrick discovered why Redmon loved Roselind. She was honest and straightforward with him from the very beginning of their relationship. She gave herself completely, and they discovered that they were a perfect fit, as Roddrick described their wedding night.

On Sundays, all the family, with the exception of Redmond, was together for dinner at Drury Manor or Eden Hall. Joselyn announced that a letter had finally arrived from Redmon! It had been almost a year since he left his home and sailed to Canada.

During dinner Joselyn read the letter from Redmon. They marveled when he described his travels, along with his adventures and his descriptions of Canada. He related stories of Emile Boushard and Long Bow. He told of the fencing lessons with Emile and learning forest craft from Long Bow. He described the Morgan horses that he was breeding and how he had found them. He reported that Rosie had produced two fine foals from Lancer, one colt and one filly, both being fine animals. When he told of fighting off an attack on the Ottawa River, his family gasped. He told them that when the time was right, he would move on west. In the letter Redmon expressed his hope that his family did not suffer on his account at the hands of the Chathams. Then he spoke of his hope that Roselind was not mistreated by Wilfred and Mortimer. He also wrote that he hoped that one day he might find a woman as good as Roselind to love. Tears were rolling down her cheeks as Roddrick took her hand under the table.

Joselyn wrote a long letter back to Redmon. She communicated everything that happened after he left. She informed her son that the Drurys now owned the former Chatham lands and that Roddrick and Roselind were married. She wrote that they were living in the former Chatham Manor house but renamed it Eden Hall. Joselyn wrote that Redmon could come home if he wished, for everything was now changed because of the Chathams' leaving. Roselind's parents and brother Mortimer were now residing in London in a house owned by Sir Thomas Dudley. There was news that Sir Thomas had died suddenly giving ownership of the vast Dudley Estates to Wilfred Chatham.

In both Leeds and London, the Chathams learned that the Drurys now owned Chatham Manor, and wondered how on earth they would have the money to make the purchase of the loans. Then the real shock and ultimate insult for the Chathams came. Roselind was now married to Roddrick Drury and they had taken up residence in Chatham Manor house, already renaming it Eden Hall.

Reginald and Mortimer wanted revenge against the Drurys. They would rather blame the Drurys for their financial troubles rather than themselves for losing Chatham Manor and its lands. Lady Lydia fired off a letter addressed to Eden Hall. When the letter came, Roselind recognized her mother's handwriting. When she read the scathing words, Roselind cried. Her mother called her many unkind things, including being no more than a depraved prostitute for marrying into the lowly Drury family. When Roddrick read the letter, he held his young wife while she cried again. That night Roselind gave herself completely to Roddrick, for she realized that she was now part of a family that truely cared for one another.

✠ ✠ ✠

The doctor who had attended Sir Thomas Dudley thought there was something odd about the color of his patient's skin. He harbored his suspicions but there was no proof of foul play. Dr. Seth Jenson certainly did not care for the overbearing Wilfred Chatham. The man watched every move Dr. Jenson made while around Sir Dudley and couldn't seem to get rid of the doctor quickly enough at each visit. However, Melissa insisted that Dr. Jenson attend her father. Two days after his last visit, Sir Thomas Dudley was dead. Dr. Jenson could not explain how a perfectly healthy man at age fifty died so quickly after becoming ill. His skin seemed to have an odd, yellowish tint that he suspected to be caused by some kind of poison. Unfortunately, the doctor could prove nothing. In his heart, Dr. Seth Jenson knew that

Sir Thomas Dudley was murdered by his new son-in-law Wilfred Chatham.

✿ ✿ ✿

Redmon was excited when he received the reply from his mother. That night after his sparing session and dinner, Redmon read the letter through twice. He was shocked to learn of the developments at home. He even thought about going home but then came to his senses. His brother was married to the woman he loved. He was happy for Roddrick and thankful that Roselind was safe. Redmon knew that his brother would take care of her and protect Roselind, and that was what he ultimately wanted for her. He had dreamed of her often and remembered every curve of her beautiful body. Now he knew that she was safe and that was enough for him.

Two days later Redmon said his goodbyes to Emile Boushard and Long Bow and rode west. Redmon decided that he had spent two of the best years of his life in North Bay. The winters had been harsh, but they were also good when he was inside by a warm fire, and the conversations with Emile and Long Bow were extraordinary. He was able to trap for fur and make some extra money, and then there were always the sparing sessions with Emile. The spring and summer months were spent with Long Bow in the forest, and they were the best. Before mounting

Lancer, Emile presented Redmon with a fine dueling blade along with a foil.

"Monsieur Redmon, continue to practice when you can. You were a fine pupil, the best I was ever fortunate to teach. I will miss your comradeship and our bouts every day."

The parting from Long Bow was also difficult. The tall Huron in his slow speech kept it simple. "Red Mon," he said, for he always called Redmon in two syllables, "may your trail be clear and your skies blue."

Redmon drifted west, working when he felt like doing so and then moving on. When he was twenty years old, he reached his full height of six feet three inches. He sported the Drury dark blonde hair and penetrating blue-gray eyes. He was ruggedly handsome.

In Winnipeg, he took a job driving a freight wagon between Winnipeg and Lake Winnipeg and Lake Manitoba. In Winnipeg, he found another fine Morgan stallion and mare and bought them. He was now quite an imposing character and most men left him alone. The men who did challenge Redmon received a beating for their troubles.

After a time he moved on west again. In Virden, Manitoba, he took a sheriff's job for a year. The years were passing quickly it seemed. While in Virden, Redmon learned in a letter from his mother that Roddrick and Roselind were now the parents of two children, a boy named Clendon and girl Clarissa. The letter made Redmon somewhat homesick, but he stayed busy with his job as Sheriff. After solving the murder of a prominent business man, Redmon decided to move west again.

When Redmon reached Regina and then Moose Jaw he heard about the Rocky Mountains. While buying supplies in Medicine Hat, Alberta, Redmon noticed two men eyeing his horses and his outfit. He chuckled when he saw them mount and follow him out of town. The two characters must have decided that two to one odds were good for them.

That night he camped on the Oldman Creek. Redmon had survived eminate attacks before and knew what was coming. The two men struck his camp just as the sun was going down. The men made a grave mistake thinking that Redmon would be easy because he was alone. He fought them and they died in the attempt. Redmon added their two horses and outfits to his string. In Lethbridge, he sold the robbers' horses and their outfits and rode south into Montana.

✻ ✻ ✻

When he reached Helena, Montana, he took a riding job on a cattle ranch. This was his first experience on a ranch. The Diamond A was owned by Tom and Irene Arnold. They were transplanted southerners from Virginia who came to Montana after the South lost the Civil War only three years earlier. Redmon heard stories of the war, but Canada and North Bay were so far removed from the South that it had little effect. As it happened, Tom Arnold attended the Virginia Military Institute where he learned the sword. He noticed the two leather-wrapped blades on Redmon's packhorse and asked about them.

"Well, Mr. Arnold, I studied under a French master of the sword in North Bay, Canada for two years. We practiced every afternoon after I hunted for the trading post. My teacher's name was Emile Boushard. And, I have been able to practice with some military men in Canada as I came west." Tom Arnold asked Redmon if he would consider practicing the sword with him.

After seeing his string of Morgans, Arnold decided to have Redmon work with the horses on the Diamond A rather than ride the ranch with the other cowboys. This assignment, for some unknown reason, would rub one particular cowboy the wrong way.

⊞ ⊞ ⊞

The Arnolds had a very pretty daughter named Melanie. She couldn't keep her eyes off Redmon as he was talking to her father about a job.

When Redmon moved into the bunkhouse, there was one ranch hand that took exception to his being on the ranch. Chad Brown was a Texas cowboy who immediately began calling Redmon a Yankee because of his accent. Redmon tried to ignore Chad Brown's taunts because he had just signed onto the ranch crew. He didn't want to have trouble so soon after taking the job. Redmon quickly realized that the other ranch hands were beginning to view Redmon as a coward because he would not brace Chad as they called it. One afternoon Redmon finally decided that enough was enough. He would tolerate no more of Chad Brown's goading or taunts. Chad walked into the barn one afternoon and began giving Redmon a hard time, calling him a stupid Yankee coward.

Redmon grabbed the cowboy and threw him out the big barn doors and into the ranch yard. One of the men working at the corrals alerted the other hands to the fight. Redmon followed Chad out the door and met him. Chad tried a right cross, which Redmon countered, and knocked Chad down with a hard left to the chin. In quick succession Redmon knocked Chad Brown to the ground four times. Chad attempted to get Redmon in a clinch. As Redmon threw the Texas cowboy away from him, Chad grabbed his shirt and tore it open, exposing the brand on his right breast. All the ranch hands saw it as did Tom, Irene, and Melanie Arnold, who came from the main house to watch when they heard the commotion. Melanie was the Arnolds' very pretty daughter who had an attraction to Redmon. She had a hard time keeping her eyes off him whenever Redmon was around.

There was a gasp from both Irene and Melanie when they saw the brand. It was ugly, puckered skin but the capital C was clearly visible on Redmon's chest. Redmon was now angry for having the brand exposed.

When Chad came at him again, Redmon proceeded to whip him completely until Tom Arnold called, "Enough!" Chad Brown was lying on the hard-packed ground in front of the big barn with Redmon standing over him. Chad was a bloody mess, and his eyes were swollen shut from the beating. Without saying a word, Redmon turned and walked to the bunkhouse to get a clean shirt.

The Arnolds and ranch hands stared after him as he walked away. Redmon never said one word during the fight. He had just whipped a notorious bully and a supposedly tough Texas cowboy to a pulp, and Redmon was not even hit once. All on the Diamond A now wanted to know the story behind the C brand on Redmon's chest, but no one dared to ask him about it after what they just witnessed Redmon do to Chad Brown.

※ ※ ※

Redmon and Tom Arnold fenced every afternoon and that always drew the ranch hands to watch. Redmon's ability with the sword, along with the brand on his chest, really got the men speculating about this stranger that signed on as a hand while they rode the range. Redmon owned an outstanding string of Morgan horses and his weapons were the most unusual, but also the best any of the ranch hands had ever seen before. Most men now carried a Colt or a Smith and Wesson pistol and Winchester rifle, or even an old beat up carbine from the Civil War. Redmon's were also well used but well cared for. All the men on the Diamond A watched him break down and clean both the volcanic pistol and carbine in the bunkhouse. He was quick and efficient. A couple of the wiser men on the ranch crew noticed that Redmon demonstrated quick, cat-like movements in every motion he made. He never wasted any energy when he moved.

Chad Brown was constantly shooting off his mouth, betting that the big pistol Redmon carried was just for show. Colly James, an established ranch hand, told Chad that he'd better not think about trying the big Englishman with a pistol. After Redmon had previously beaten Chad's head into a fine fare-thee-well, he should have known to leave well-enough alone.

During the next two fencing sessions, Tom Arnold wanted to ask Redmon about the C brand on his chest, but also realized that a man's past and his secrets were his alone. Tom also recognized cultured speech when he heard it. The men from the bunkhouse told him that Redmon carried several fine leather-bound books into the bunkhouse and read constantly. Redmon Drury was but a young man of twenty-three, or four, yet seemed to have quite an interesting past. Tom noticed that Melanie was quite smitten with the young Englishman and that troubled him somewhat.

During the fencing sessions, Tom recognized that Redmon was holding back. His skill and abilities were far superior to those of Tom, but Redmon never tried to show up the ranch owner. Tom knew that Redmon Drury could defeat him easily, eventhough Tom was the best swordsman in his class at the institute. He had lost some of his skills during the Civil War as he had little time to practice, but found some time to hone his skills again after the war when he met a cavalry man that could fence. Tom owned his own blade, but he had never seen one as fine as the blade that Redmon wielded.

With Chad's face still battered a week after the big fight, Tom decided to send Redmon and Colly James into Helena with Irene and Melanie to buy supplies. Tom would follow along later with two men. Tom Arnold said nothing to Redmon, but Colly knew that a new man recently moved into the area and was attempting to cut a wide swath for himself around Helena.

Charlie Connerly came into the area with more cattle than the land he owned on the Connerly Box C could support. Any good cattleman realized quickly that Charlie Connerly would need to push his cattle onto other ranchers' grazing land to keep the number of cattle he brought in. The land was still open range. The ranchers owned their land but there were no fences to set boundaries. Each year there would be a large roundup in the area and each ranch would separate their brands and get a count. There were a couple of confrontations between Diamond A hands and the Connerly Box C hands out on the range. So far no shots were fired between the two ranches, but it was a tense situation just the same. There was a rumor floating around that Charlie Connerly just hired on what was now being called a gun slick by the hands from the ranches in the valley.

Colly was driving the wagon with Irene and Melanie sitting on the seat with him. Redmon was riding Lancer next to the wagon. When they rolled into town there were some hard-looking men in front of the saloon, and then again when they drew up at the mercantile. One character in particular was eyeing Melanie. Then he noticed Redmon when he saw the big pistol on his hip for a left-handed draw.

Redmon was always observant when he saw men wearing guns. One man in particular seemed to be peering at them as they drew to a stop. The man sported a tied-down holster that caught Redmon's eye as he climbed out of the saddle and helped Melanie down from the wagon.

Redmon put out his arm and a surprised Melanie placed her hand on his forearm as he escorted her up the steps into the store. Everyone close heard the man with the tied-down pistol utter, "Now ain't he the fancy one. This Diamond A bunch must be real ladies' men," which drew a laugh from the men standing around listening and watching Redmon and Melanie go into the store.

Colly quietly warned Redmon that the man must be the gun slick they were hearing about on the Diamond A. Redmon nodded and took Melanie to the counter with her mother. Ben Mathews, the store owner, greeted Irene and Melanie warmly and took their list of needed supplies. He quickly warned the Diamond A ranch people to beware of the hard-looking bunch that was in town. Redmon noticed that the man with the tied-down pistol had followed them into the store and was watching them intently. Irene felt that she and Melanie would be safe in the store especially with Redmon and Colly there.

Redmon walked around the store and found a Western saddle and matching bridle that he wanted. Melanie moved around to a counter and was looking at some yard goods as Redmon was carrying his new saddle and bridle to the counter so he could pay for them. Then he heard a protest from Melanie in another part of the store. He dropped the saddle and bridle and walked quickly toward her. Irene was trying to protect her daughter, but the man pushed her away and she fell into the counter. Redmon moved quickly, grabbed the man, and shook him loose from Melanie. He dragged him to the front door of the store, flung him down the steps onto the dirt, and then waited for the man to get up. A leering Abe Giddings stood and looked up at Redmon. "You're a dead man," he said and his hand flashed to his Colt for the draw. His pistol was half way up when Redmon's bullet took him in the chest. There was a complete look of surprise and shock on Giddings face for only a moment. Then the would-be gunfighter collapsed on his back staring up at nothing, his Colt .44 still clutched in his hand at his side. Redmon saw another man drawing on him and he wheeled, levered the volcanic and fired again. Another man dropped.

Suddenly, another shot rang out and Colly downed a man that was going to shoot Redmon from his blind side. Redmon quickly moved to Colly's side and they faced the remaining Box C hands, but they were all staring at the body of Abe Giddings and then at Redmon. All the Box C hands thought Abe Giddings was the fastest man with a pistol they ever saw, but the big Diamond A man outdrew and beat him easily. Abe Giddings was constantly demonstrating his fast draw for the other men at the Box C headquarters and embellishing stories of his fighting in Texas cattle wars.

Two men with stars on their chests came running up to the scene of the shooting. Another man came from the opposite direction. "Sheriff, I want those two men arrested for murdering my ranch hands!" Connerly shouted.

Sheriff Drew Benson was looking at Redmon and Colly who were still holding their pistols in their hands facing the Box C men arrayed in front of them. "You men put those guns away. There won't be no more shooting here!" the sheriff bellowed.

Ben Mathews, the store owner, stepped out on the porch, along with Irene and Melanie Arnold.

"Sheriff Benson, there was no murder here. That man," and he pointed at Abe Giddings, "was attempting to molest Melanie Arnold in my store. This man, nodding at Redmon, was defending her. That Giddings fellow drew first and got what he deserved. The man on the ground over there tried to shoot Redmon from his blind side but Colly got him first. Sheriff, it appeared to me that this whole thing was a planned shooting by the Box C men."

"Shut up, Mathews!" grunted Connerly. "You'll pay for talkin' like that."

"Don't threaten me, Connerly. I've lived in Helena my whole life and I'm telling the truth. Your men tried to drygulch these men and I saw it." Mathews answered back.

Wallace Gillett, another Helena rancher, stepped forward.

"It's like Ben said. The Diamond A men were defending themselves. It looked like a setup deal all the way. This man handled that Abe Giddings so their plan didn't work."

"Gillett, are you on the Diamond A payroll? There's no way this tinhorn could'a took Abe Giddings in a fair gunfight." Connerly almost yelled.

"You came in here thinkin' to take over our range, Connerly." said Gillett. "You brought in a gun slick to handle us valley ranchers, but he wasn't slick enough."

Sheriff Benson had heard his fill. "I'm declarin' this a fair shooting. Connerly, if your men go after any of these men here, I'll be arresting you for attempted murder."

Charlie Connerly signaled to his men and they all walked to their horses and rode out of town. They didn't even pick up their own downed men, which spoke to Charlie Connerly's lack of character. The dead men were left for someone else to deal with. The Connerly men did take their horses with them. One man stood over Abe Giddings for a long moment, shook his head, climbed into his saddle, and rode away after the others.

Tom Arnold rode up to the store just in time to see Redmon put his arm around Melanie protectively. He saw three bodies on the ground in front of the store. His main concern now was for the safety of Irene and Melanie, but they seemed to be well. Tom wanted to know the story of what happened here. Tom stepped on the porch and Irene and Melanie ran into his arms. Redmon quietly turned and walked back into the store. He retrieved the new saddle and bridle, paying for them at the counter.

Some men were watching every move that Redmon made for they saw the draw he made against Abe Giddings when Abe was said to be a fast man with his pistol. So now they knew the Diamond A had one of their own.

Redmon sat on a bench outside the store with the new saddle at his feet. He was staring off into space. It appeared now that he stumbled into a difficult situation when all he wanted to do was find a place for the winter and do something new. He heard one man term this as a range war. He had no desire to be involved in such a thing as a so-called range war. All he wanted to do was help with the horses on the Diamond A and then move on when the time was right. Now, he would have the label 'gun slick' attached to him and he certainly did not want that. He was thinking so hard that he didn't notice who sat next to him. He was startled back to reality.

"Redmon, thank you for protecting Melanie. I hate to say it but this place is going to get hard for you now. There will be men gunning for you so they can build a reputation. I know winter is coming but you may need to move on," Tom Arnold told Redmon.

"Mr. Arnold, I ran away from England when I was fifteen," Redmon replied. "That is when I got this brand on my chest. The son of another nobleman gave it to me. I vowed to never run away again. If I run now, I may never stop. Besides, one of my mares will foal soon and cannot travel. Sir, if you want me to leave, I certainly will. But it seems to me that you still have some trouble here with this Charlie Connerly. I would like to see this through."

"Will you tell me about that brand some time?" Tom asked.

"I will tell you my tale when we are back at the ranch. I have carried the burden of the branding inside and outside now for eight years. I am ready to explain the whole of it as it is finally time to put it behind me."

That night in the main house Redmon explained to the Arnolds that his father was an English nobleman named Lord Roland Drury. Then he told them everything about himself and Roselind and the Chathams, and what Wilfred Chatham did to him when he and Roselind were found together.

"Mr. and Mrs. Arnold, what Roselind and I did together was wrong by English standards, but we fully planned to marry," Redmon admitted. "My family now owns the former Chatham lands because the Chathams lost them to debt lenders and my father bought those loans."

He finished his story by describing all his travels from the time he landed in Canada and what he experienced at each stop along the way. The Arnolds were amazed by all that Redmon was able to do in such a short time.

In the bunkhouse, while Redmon was talking to the Arnolds, Colly James described for the men everything that happened in the store and then outside. The men realized that Redmon Drury would ride for the brand as it was called in the West. When Redmon walked into the bunkhouse it was quiet.

Redmon walked straight to Colly. "Thank you for watching my back as you call it. If you ever need my help, I will be there. You saved us today."

The men of the Diamond A saw that Redmon was trying to give Colly, the established Diamond A hand, all the credit for defending them during the shooting in Helena.

The men of the Diamond A crew now had a confidence that their crew could handle anything that the Box C threw at them.

❖ ❖ ❖

Redmon began pairing horses for a breeding program. The Morgan mare produced a fine filly. He used Lancer's first colt stallion as the stud. Redmon's string of Morgans was the finest that anyone could remember seeing.

The Diamond A hands were continually pushing Box C cattle off the Arnold range as were the other ranchers in the area. Some shots were fired between Gillett, G bar hands, and Box C riders. Another Box C rider was killed and some of Charlie Connerly's men quit and rode south. Connerly was forced to sell many of the cattle he brought in. His range could not graze them all. Charlie Connerly finally realized that if he wanted to remain in the area, he would have to become a good citizen.

Conditions settled in the Broadwater, and the winter seemed to pass quickly. Chad Brown finally came to Redmon and they made peace. They even hunted together during the winter and brought in elk, deer, and even a buffalo to add to the menu.

Redmon related stories about England and Drury Manor for Melanie. The cowboys in the bunkhouse liked hearing about Canada and the Great Lakes country. They saw his buckskins so he told them of learning forest craft and hunting with the Huron brave Long Bow. The men liked hearing about being a freighter around the big lakes, and then as the marshal of Virden, Alberta. These Western men liked watching Redmon and Tom Arnold fence and were fascinated by their finesse. They recognized the cat-like grace the sparing required. These Western men realized that Redmon Drury would be a dangerous opponent with gun or knife, in this case a very long knife. Redmon told them that even though it was illegal to do so in England, duels were sometimes fought to the death in secret with swords and dueling pistols between men of the noble class. Redmon, wearing his buckskins, also did some trapping during the winter and the men liked watching him prepare the fine skins that he brought back from his outings. He presented Melanie Arnold a fine jacket made from ermine. Plus, he was able to sell his other skins in Helena for a good profit.

⁂

When the second thaw came, Redmon left the Diamond A and headed south. Two weeks later, he rode into Wyoming. He was amazed by the Yellowstone country. He camped on the Yellowstone River. Seeing the hot springs and the geysers was something he would never forget. Wearing his buckskins, Redmon steadily rode south pulling his horses along behind him.

He met a mountain man named Julius Fry who advised him to angle toward the Green River so he could follow it all the way to Colorado. Redmon found the Green River and headed south from there. A couple of days passed along the Green when he realized that he was being followed.

In a protected spot he looked back as Long Bow had taught him. Two Indian braves were coming along his trail. He knew he couldn't disguise the trail of seven horses so he looked for a place he could defend. Late in the afternoon he found it. He figured the braves wanted his horses and weapons. At a sharp bend in the river he found good grass for the horses and some downed wood that he could use to make a small corral. Quickly, he rubbed down Lancer and the packhorse and put them on the grass in the makeshift enclosure. After arranging his packs, starting a fire, and putting on a coffee pot, he waited. Redmon found that he liked coffee and thus began the habit of drinking it on the Diamond A. Cowboy coffee they called it. Black and strong.

Redmon learned from Long Bow that Indians could wait out the sun and moon if they wanted to catch their intended victims by surprise. He hoped that the two braves following him might be as impatient as most white men tended to be or that they would underestimate him. Redmon placed his pistol close to his leg, drank coffee, and waited. He watched Rosie because he trusted her to warn him if the braves approached.

The night descended almost suddenly and it was pitch black out away from his camp. Redmon realized that his fire would light his camp, giving the braves the advantage in the extremely dark conditions. He quickly spread the fire so it would go out, and then he retreated back into the shadows. Much too slowly it seemed, the sticks burned, and they slowly went out one by one.

Redmon eased down behind his packs until the last ember died out. Now he would have to depend on the horses to warn him. Ever so slowly his eyes began to adjust to the dark around him. The time seemed to pass so slowly. He thought it might be about midnight when a half moon peeked over a mountain ridge to the east. Ever so slowly the landscape began to take on a pale hue. He could distinguish trees and rocks. He carefully relaxed his muscles and found a more comfortable position for his back and legs. Redmon had learned to be a very light sleeper while on the trail across Canada. Finally, he dozed off but kept the volcanic pistol next to his leg.

The attack came at dawn when the sun was almost in his eyes. Redmon had drifted into an uneasy slumber when Rosie suddenly stamped and snorted. It all happened so quickly that Redmon couldn't believe it afterwards. A brave came running out of the early morning mist with a knife raised high as he leaped at Redmon. Redmon raised his .38 volcanic and fired. The bullet caught the brave in mid-leap and he dropped immediately, laying still on the ground. Redmon heard a dull thunk behind him in the horse enclosure, and then the horses began milling and snorting. Redmon kept his pistol ready waiting for the next brave to attack. The horses kept snorting, stamping, and snorting in the small enclosure. Finally it was light enough to see. The first attacker was clearly not moving so Redmon slowly surveyed the small clearing.

When he looked into the horse enclosure, Redmon couldn't believe his eyes. The second brave was being trampled by his horses! He quickly checked the brave that he had shot and discovered that he hit him in the heart. Next, he pulled the horses out of the enclosure and tied them. When he looked at the brave who had tried to take his horses by coming across the river, Redmon saw what happened. There was a clear rear hoof print in the middle of the brave's forehead. Rosie kicked the brave when he came near her and her colt.

Redmon walked out of the enclosure and patted Rose and rubbed her muzzle. She no longer tried to bite Redmon, and even nuzzled him occasionally. The mare probably saved him from a rear attack. He believed the once crazy mare was even more valuable.

Redmon restarted his fire and put on a fresh pot of coffee. He took a quick dip in the river and then cooked breakfast. It took some time but Redmon found the braves' horses and was astounded by what he found. He had never seen any prettier or finer animals, and their conformation was outstanding. They were a color between white and silver gray with dark splotches of hair on their hindquarters. He had never seen horses like them before. Immediately, he began thinking of the possibilities. There was a young stallion in addition to a young mare that was of a light cream color.

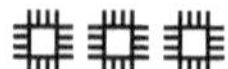

Redmon continued south for a short time along a well-used trail when he came across a mountain man pulling two horses loaded with packs of furs. Barnabus Caine noticed the knives Redmon was carrying along with the bow and quiver of arrows that were hanging on the stallion. The items were obviously from the Sioux tribe and he inquired of Redmon how he had come to have them. Redmon gave a description of the attack feeling fortunate to have survived it all. The mountain man confirmed that the Indians had to be Sioux because of the marking on the arrows. Barnabus gave Redmon simple directions to keep riding along the Green River all the way into Colorado. The mountain man also told Redmon that the Sioux warriors were riding stolen Nez Percé horses from the tribe in Idaho. Redmon learned that the breed of horse was called Appaloosa. Adding the fine horses to his string, Redmon picked up the trail south along the Green River, riding into Colorado three weeks later.

✦✦✦

Word was received on Drury Manor that Wilfred Chatham's wife, Lady Melissa Dudley Chatham, had died suddenly. Wilfred moved Reginald, Lydia, and Mortimer to the fine manor house in Leeds shortly after Lady Melissa died.

The word circulating among the nobility was that Lady Melissa Chatham died under mysterious circumstances. Some were saying that a quack doctor retained by Wilfred bled her too much and she became so weak that she died. The local constable investigated but could not prove anything. Roselind knew in her heart that her brother probably murdered his own wife. Her brother did some terrible things and she wondered if he would ever be called to task for his actions. Roselind told Roddrick that her brother's soul would surely reside in hell when his time on earth was finished.

Roselind and Roddrick Drury became good partners in every way. Under Red Roland and Roddrick's direction, Drury lands became productive and very successful. Roddrick and Roselind completely transformed the former Chatham Manor house into a comfortable home. The people who lived and worked Drury lands were happy. The former Chatham yeomen were amazed by the change. Eden Hall was now a vibrant and cheery place to live and work. Clendon and Clarissa were even learning to swim in the pond where Redmon and Roselind swam when they were young. The yeomen on both manors always protected the Drury children.

❖ ❖ ❖

Redmon found the Manning Circle M ranch and stayed for a short time. He enjoyed eating at the long table with the Mannings and their cowboys. Dan Manning and his men wanted to know about Redmon's horse string. He told them how he had built his Morgan string and related the story of the spotted horses. He downplayed shooting the one brave. His mare, Rosie, was credited for kicking the other brave in the head when he came close to her foal, thus stopping the attack. The men laughed when Redmon said there was a perfect Rosie hoof mark in the middle of the brave's forehead.

"I learned from a mountain man along the Green River that the braves were Sioux warriors riding stolen Nez Percé horses. He told me that the Nez Percé call their horses Appaloosas," Redmon told the cowboys.

The Manning crew was fascinated by Redmon's tale of coming from England, crossing Canada, and then heading south into Montana, Wyoming, and now Colorado. They were astounded when he described the Great Lakes. They liked hearing how he learned fencing and sword fighting from Emile Boushard. They hung on every word when he told of the Yellowstone country and its wonders. The ranch crew was intrigued to see his volcanic .38 caliber pistol and carbine. In turn, Redmon learned from them which rivers to follow in order to reach Denver to the southeast.

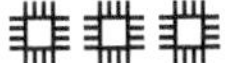

Three weeks of travel found Redmon riding into Central City. He found a stable for the horses and walked to the Central City Hotel. Dressed in his buckskins, the desk clerk didn't want give him a room until Redmon asked about having his suit pressed, a hot bath, haircut, and beard trim. After getting cleaned up, Redmon was sitting in the fine dining room eating from China with real silverware. He was listening to the conversations around him, when three men talking at a nearby table caught his attention.

"You know, men, it isn't right that Wilfred Donaldson is trying to take over Ol' Red Brandais's mining claims. That Donaldson is some kind of crook. Red has some good mines if he can stay alive long enough to develop them. These damn claim jumpers we have coming into the mountains are a scourge, and that Wilfred Donaldson is one of the worst of the lot."

One of the other men spoke up. "Well, it's gonna be tough for Red since Donaldson's men have him surrounded up there in the canyon like they do."

Redmon contemplated what he just heard the men saying. Someone else with the name Wilfred, and he was trying to hurt someone, too. After dinner Redmon learned where the Red Brandais mines were. He paid his room for the week, and slept well that night in a real bed. Following an early breakfast, Redmon saddled

Lancer and rode for the Brandais mine. He was again in his buckskins and wearing his pistol.

As he rode up a canyon, Redmon heard shooting. He saw some wooden buildings on a high mountain bench. Four men were below but obviously working their way toward the buildings above. Redmon could tell that only one man was firing from above. Redmon put Lancer in a protected spot and then pulled his carbine. He decided to shoot the attackers only if he was forced to do so, but would try to warn them away first by shooting around them.

He found a good spot and began shooting around the Donaldson thugs. He could see the men furiously trying to learn who was shooting at them. One man tried to rush the buildings and was shot down for his effort. Red Brandais was a good shot. Redmon continued to shoot close to the three remaining men who were attempting to duck under cover but there wasn't much of that to be found.

The time was beginning to drag so Redmon decided to finish the confrontation. He shot one man in the leg and one in an arm, and waited. Finally, the last man slithered down the hill to their horses and rode off through the canyon with Redmon chasing him with shots.

Redmon yelled out, "You two wounded men can get down to your horses and ride out, but you'd better ask Mr. Brandais if he will let you go without shooting you."

"I'll let 'um go, but they better not come back," Red Brandais yelled out and the men made their way to their horses. The one he shot in the leg was really hobbling as he worked his way down the hill.

Redmon yelled up the hill, "Mr. Brandais, my name is Redmon Drury and I heard about your trouble and decided to help. Can I come up so we can talk?"

"Come on up but keep your hands where I can see 'um."

Redmon retrieved Lancer and walked slowly up a game trail toward the buildings. He wondered why the attackers hadn't used the game trail. He decided that crooks were not the brightest coins in the box. A man with bright red hair blowing in the breeze and holding a rifle was waiting for him. When Redmon reached the buildings he saw a man of maybe fifty who stood some five feet nine or ten.

"Thanks, young feller. Them durned Donaldson men almost had me this time. I'm startin' to run low on food and ammunition. They probably would ah had me tonight. Who are yah and why did yah help me?" Red Brandais asked.

So sitting in the shade of one of the buildings Redmon told Red Brandais his entire tale as he called it.

"Mr. Brandais, when I was fifteen, a man named Wilfred ordered to have me held by four men and they branded me. When I heard that another Wilfred was trying to take something that didn't belong to him, I decided to step in and help. I will go to town and get food and ammunition for you. Is there anything else that you need?"

Red Brandais sat for a time looking into the distance. "Mr. Redmon Drury, I have a proposition for ya. I need a partner to help me work these three claims I've got here. I'm tired of bein' alone. I've found some color and somehow that Donaldson found out about it. He's some character that come into Denver. I've heard that he's been takin' over mines around the mountains by hook or by crook. Some call him a claim jumper. I've heard he's some kind of rough character that gets what he wants. I just don't want him to get my claims."

Redmon stuck out his hand. "Mr. Brandais, I will accept your offer but I have a proposition of my own. I have some money so I propose we hire a mine engineer and miners. You and I can act as guards against this Wilfred Donaldson character and keep him from trying to interfere with the operation."

A deal was struck and Redmon even wrote it all out on some paper that Red Brandais kept in one of his shacks. They both signed the agreement. Red signed with his real first name, Arthur. They would call the mines Brandais-Drury Mining Enterprises.

☷ ☷ ☷

Redmon immediately went back to town and bought supplies and ammunition. He asked around town for a mining engineer and after talking to him extensively, hired a young man that had just come to town. Adam Collins recently graduated from what they were calling the Colorado School of Mines. Redmon found five miners willing to work a new mine, and they all headed back to the canyon. Adam inspected the three claims where Red Brandais was doing some exploratory digging into the mountain and recommended sinking better shafts at two of them, so the hired miners went to work.

Timber was cut on the mountain to shore up the tunnels going into the side of the mountain. A month into the digging the engineer found the main vein of gold. The vein was rich, and word spread quickly to Denver about the Brandais-Drury mines and their strike.

Wilfred Donaldson became angry when he learned that the men he sent to take the Brandais mine were shot up and forced out by some stranger. It was the stranger who suddenly became Red Brandais's partner.

Word was being circulated that the new strike was a rich one. Wilfred Donaldson sent one of his toughest enforcers to get rid of this so-called new partner that Red Brandais took on. By doing that, he thought he could then eliminate Red Brandais and take over his mine.

Wilfred Donaldson was also going after the mines of some people named Brownley. He hired assassins and men to set explosions in the Brownley mines in several locations in Colorado. Donaldson was a former shoulder striker for the New York gangs. He came west following the railroad to make his own fortune on the backs of others who did the work.

Clem Nedney was the man Wilfred Donaldson sent to Central City to eliminate Redmon Drury. The man was a hired killer for the cattle wars in Texas. He left Texas just ahead of the Texas Rangers, and then drifted north looking to hire out his gun.

Clem watched Redmon and could have shot him from cover as he was ordered to do, but then learned that the tall stranger was an Englishman. The tinhorn was actually wearing a pistol on his hip.

"What could some English dude know about handling a pistol that only real Western men knew how to use?" Clem wondered. Nedney's ego was such that he wanted to face this Englishman head up and then kill him. He didn't like the fact that the man was pretending to be a Western man by wearing the clothes and carrying a pistol on his hip. He watched and waited, and caught the Englishman coming out of the hotel.

Clem stepped out to face him. "Hey you, tinhorn! I've been sent to get you outta the way. I could 'a shot you from cover, but I decided that I don't like some Englishman pretendin' ta be a Western man."

Redmon had noticed the man lurking the last couple of days. He asked around and learned that the gunman worked for Wilfred Donaldson. Clem Nedney didn't realize that Redmon never placed himself in an open position to be shot from cover. So here it was again. Donaldson wanted him out of the way hoping to still get the mine from Red. Redmon faced the man from under his wide hat brim, but never said a word. He concentrated on the man's right hand as it hovered over the butt of the pistol. Redmon could see that the man sent to kill him was growing impatient and expected Redmon to be afraid or beg not to be killed. Redmon let his left hand hang loose at his side. He hoped that he was ready.

Clem thought that this damn tinhorn should be beggin' for his life, but instead the dumb Englishman just stood and stared at him. Clem decided to finish this quickly so he flashed his hand to his Colt .44 knowing the tinhorn would have no chance against him, for no man ever had. The next thing he saw was a pistol spitting flame but his own Colt had not even come level. Clem's Colt went off into the ground. His cheek was now resting on the dirt of the street. Just before he died, Clem realized that the damn tinhorn got him. He had never figured on that!

A group along the rough street noticed the confrontation between the new mine owner Redmon Drury and a character they knew as an enforcer for Wilfred Donaldson. Most thought the Englishman would be shot down. The men were amazed when Redmon out drew Clem Nedney, a known gunfighter working for Wilfred Donaldson.

The sheriff came to Redmon and asked what happened. Redmon explained that the dead man told him he had been sent by Wilfred Donalson to kill him. A mine owner standing nearby, James Redding, who had listened and watched the action, confirmed Redmon's account. The Sheriff then ruled it a fair shooting.

✿ ✿ ✿

Red Brandais and Redmon Drury promptly became wealthy. Redmon opened an account at the Denver Miners Bank. Red decided to build a large quarried rock house in Central City. He would be able to manage the mines from there. Redmon began spending time in Denver, staying at the Brown Palace Hotel. He was fitted for good suits and dated some of the prettiest daughters of the wealthier families in Denver. He escorted the young ladies to restaurants and the theater, always sitting in a prime balcony box. He saw Wilfred Donaldson frequently at the theater and the man always glared at him. Redmon would simply nod and smile. Donaldson received a complete report of the shooting of Clem Nedney and realized that there was far more to this Redmon Drury than he first thought.

Redmon met and became friends with Reese and Victoria Brownley, a couple who owned mines that Wilfred Donaldson wanted. Victoria Brownley was also British, and she was absolutely beautiful. Redmon told Victoria that he was originally from Eden along the Eden River in northern England. Along with the Brownleys, Redmon became friends with their son Chad. A week after Redmon's last trip to Denver, he learned that Chad had been shot at one of the Brownley mines located near Durango and to the southwest of Denver, but had escaped the assassins and disappeared on his horse.

In the Brandais-Drury mines, the miners followed the vein and it became richer the deeper it went into the mountain. Redmon insisted that he and Red pay Adam Collins well, along with the miners. Red Brandais and Redmon bought some other claims and began developing them. Soon, other miners wanted to work for them because of the good pay.

Redmon helped Red build his house, but Red could see that Redmon was becoming restless. Redmon helped make Red rich beyond his wildest dreams and did so quickly with his plan for the mines. Redmon was never anything but honest with Red and that was important to him. Red Brandais could be called a confirmed bachelor, but Redmon helped Red meet a pretty widow, Audrey Mendlow, on a trip to Denver. Six months after they met, Red gave Audrey a ring and she accepted his proposal of marriage.

The next piece of news was that Chad Brownley came home after healing up from being shot. He brought a wife with him from the New Mexico Territory. The best part of the story was that Chad's new wife, Barbara, had shot and wounded Wilfred Donaldson one night while the couple was attending the theater. Her shot came from the Brownley's balcony seats across the theater from Donaldson. Wilfred Donaldson was then arrested by the Denver police for the attempted murder of both Chad and Reese Brownley, in addition to being the culprit behind the Brownley mine bombings. Donaldson's threat was over for the Brandais-Drury mines.

Redmon stood up with Red Arthur Brandais as his best man when Red and Audrey Mendlow were married. Redmon continued to ride as guard on their shipments of gold to Denver and the bank, but he was becoming ever more restless with each passing day. None of the young women he squired around Denver or Central City caught his fancy. Some were quite pretty, but Redmon thought most of them were silly and immature. In Redmon's estimation, there had never been a woman that he met who could compare to Roselind. Maybe he was being unrealistic about what a woman should be. He just felt as though something was incomplete in his life.

It was Red who finally told Redmon that he should finish his journey and find what he was looking for.

In the days after Redmon rode out of Central City heading south, Red would continue putting his share into Redmon's bank account. Redmon corresponded with his parents while still in Central City and let them know of his good fortune in meeting and becoming partners with Red Brandais. He told his family that if they ever needed money, it was there in the Denver Miners Bank.

The string of horses were frisky and seemed glad to be moving again. Redmon made some fine friends along the way. As he rode south, Redmon passed through deep canyons and valleys. He camped in high meadows where he felt close to the stars. There was snow in some of the high crevices on the peaks. Following the creeks and streams, he eventually dropped into the New Mexico Territory. He found himself in Las Vegas and learned of a military fort sitting on the high plains. Redmon stopped at this place called Fort Union. He enjoyed his stay at Fort Union and even met several officers stationed there who were willing to practice fencing skills with Redmon.

卅 卅 卅

So finally, here he sat at breakfast watching the man who placed the red-hot branding iron on his chest some ten years earlier. He knew now, after letters from his family, that the man probably murdered his father-in-law and even his own wife to gain the Dudley Estates. He had spent a long, almost sleepless night, remembering his journey, which began that fateful night ten years earlier when Wilfred Chatham had ordered him held by four stout yeomen and the glowing branding iron being placed on his chest. Redmon's long-hated rival was here in Santa Fe in the New Mexico Territory, so far from England, and was plotting and planning to hurt someone again.

He heard one of the men mention that work was progressing on the huge manor house Wilfred was having built that would be the center piece of his western cattle empire. Then he heard Wilfred order the men to ride south that morning and finish off the Wilbankses. Wilfred told the men he wanted to come down and move into the new house and take over the cattle range, and wanted to do it soon.

One of the men chuckled, "No offense to your Lordship, but I plan to use that Allison Wilbanks before we're through with them. She's the best lookin' gal in this whole territory."

"You can have her, Nate, but I want that land cleared of the Wilbankses soon. There are no authorities within one hundred miles of that land, so no one will know what happened to those people. You men have chased away or killed all their ranch hands. How hard should it be for you to finish one old man and one girl?" Wilfred exclaimed.

Redmon finished his breakfast, gathered his gear, and bought trail supplies. He chuckled when he realized that he sat so close listening to the conversation and Wilfred Chatham never recognized him.

The Chatham men's horses were stabled where Redmon kept his horse string, so following them would be no problem. He let the four men ride out pulling a packhorse and then followed along. Redmon realized that his horse string was putting a large cloud of dust in the air so he dropped farther behind the men. He did not want to alert the men ahead of him as to his presence. The men didn't seem to be concerned that someone might be following along behind them. They camped that night on a small creek below Santa Fe.

Redmon was still amazed by the immensity of the western night sky. The millions of stars seemed to give the landscape a partial light. He built a small sheltered fire and put on his coffee pot then he cooked a quick meal. He checked the direction of the breeze before building his fire to ensure that the men ahead could not smell his smoke.

As he rolled into his blankets, an almost full moon came up in the east and gave a surreal glow to the land around. The coyotes began yapping with the rising of the moon. He thought about seeing Wilfred Chatham for the first time in ten years. A younger Redmon Drury would have confronted the man who branded him right there in the dining room. His years of experience taught Redmon patience. He immediately decided to help the people named Wilbanks so he could eventually get to Wilfred Chatham. He had waited a long time for this chance. As amazing as it was turning out, he would not have to travel all the way to England to accomplish what he had wished for so long. He would be as ruthless as the men who were ordered to take over the Wilbanks land and do away with the real owners of that land. Redmon slept well that night knowing that Rosie would alert him if someone attempted to approach his camp. He had learned to sleep lightly, but well, when he was on the trail.

Redmon was up the next morning early and saddled his horse along with the packhorse. All the horses were watered and had grazed during the night. He moved along the creek slowly until he spotted the camp in the distance. He could see the twinkle of a campfire in the early dawn light. He watched the men ride out as the sun was peeking over the eastern horizon. He followed them through the day. He liked the wide open country and rolling swales he was riding through. There were rock-strewn mesas along with wide open vistas. White puffy clouds cast some shadows over the land at times.

Redmon realized that he was probably riding into a dangerous situation, but this was country that he liked in spite of the danger.It could not be called anything but a big country.

Late in the afternoon, one man split away from the group and rode south while the other three turned west. Redmon decided to follow the single rider. Less than an hour later, the man was sitting on his horse and seemed to be looking down. The man pulled a rifle and began shooting down at something below him. Redmon heard the unmistakable sound of shots being returned from below.

Redmon dropped Rosie's lead rope, pulled his own carbine, and rode forward. When he drew close enough, he rose up in the saddle and quickly began putting bullets around the lone man's horse. The horse jumped straight up in the air after Redmon's first two shots. The man surprised Redmon by getting control of his horse, and once he spotted who was shooting at him, he started riding directly at Redmon. Redmon dropped out of the saddle, slid the volcanic back into the scabbard, and waited with his left hand loose at his side. Two bullets kicked up dirt next to where Redmon stood. The man must have watched Redmon put away his carbine for he rose up in his stirrups and sighted on Redmon. One shot went past Redmon's side. Redmon drew and fired, knocking his target out of the saddle with his arms flying to the side and his rifle dropping in the prairie grass.

The man hit the turf, rolled twice, and lay still. His horse ran past but finally stopped near Redmon's horse string. Redmon holstered his pistol, walked to the man, and rolled him over. His shot had found the man's heart. This would be the first blow struck at Wilfred Chatham.

Redmon gathered the man's horse, loaded his body over the saddle and tied it down. He then retrieved the dead man's rifle. With all horses in tow, Redmon headed for the place where the man had sat on his horse shooting earlier.

Below him, Redmon saw a good-looking ranch layout tucked into a curve in the escarpment. He could see that the Wilbanks selected the site for their headquarters well because it was protected from winds blowing from the north, east, and west. The headquarters faced the south so it would get the winter sun. Redmon noticed that the headquarters would be easy to defend because there was no easy way down from the escarpment. Any attack would have to come from the south unless men jumped from the escarpment to a scree pile below. He rode east until he finally found a way down. In the distance to the east he saw what appeared to be a lake with low hills all around it. He would learn later that the water was brackish and salty, and the lake was called a playa.

He needed to ride around a ridge to reach the south entrance to the ranch headquarters. When he was close enough, Redmon hailed the house. He held up his hands for the Wilbanks to see. "The man who was shooting at you is no longer a threat. He tried to shoot me also so I was forced to kill him. I mean you no harm, and I know who is trying to take your ranch," Redmon yelled out. He knew the Wilbanks were studying him from the house. He thought they should be able to see the body draped over the saddle behind him.

"What do ya think, daughter? Could be just another trick by that bunch that has been hittin' us!" the older Wilbanks asked his daughter.

"Pop, we have to trust someone sometime. Let's find out who this man is. He said he knows who is behind the attacks. I think I recognize that horse carrying the dead man. I've seen it before in two of the attacks. Pop, let's give him a chance."

"Who are you and where did you come from?" Franklin Wilbanks yelled out.

Redmon called back, "When I stopped in Santa Fe, I heard the man who is behind all this order this man and three others to kill you. I want to help you if you will allow me to do so. I will explain why if you will give me a chance."

"Come on in, but keep your hands where we can see 'em." Franklin replied.

Redmon chuckled because Red Brandais had yelled the same words when Redmon helped him. Redmon rode forward until he saw a man and a woman standing on a porch with rifles at the ready. When Redmon saw the young woman, he was stunned. She was absolutely beautiful.

Franklin Wilbanks was concentrating on the horse string behind this stranger. Allison Wilbanks was looking at the new man sitting on his big horse. His face was in shadow below his hat brim.

"Mister, you can climb down. We'll have to decide what needs to be done with that man." Franklin told Redmon.

Redmon climbed out of the saddle, took off his hat, and faced Allison Wilbanks. They stared at one another. The spell was broken when Franklin Wilbanks spoke. "What are you two starin' at? Let's get these horses put up. We'll dump that hombre in the shed for now. Mister we'll bring your outfit in the house. I sure hate to bury that hombre close to our house."

They all moved at once pulling the horses toward the barn and corrals. Franklin commented on the fine quality of Redmon's horses and asked about the spotted stallion and mare. Redmon told of the Indian attack on the Green River in Wyoming and getting the Nez Percé horses there. After putting the body in a shed, they put the horses in the barn with corn. The attacker's horse went in a corral. Franklin said he thought the man's name was Nate Burleson and that he worked for some stranger who was trying to take their land.

Redmon and Allison couldn't seem to keep their eyes away from each other. He always thought Roselind was the most beautiful girl that he had ever seen, but Allison Wilbanks' beauty could not be compared to anyone he could ever remember seeing. She stood some five feet seven with long auburn hair and flashing hazel eyes, and her face was a vision of beauty. Redmon had seen and experienced some pretty girls and women over the years, but he thought Allison Wilbanks had a beauty all her own. She was trim but Redmon could see that she was quite shapely. She smiled shyly when she noticed that he was studying her. She and Franklin helped Redmon carry his packs to the house.

Franklin noticed the two leather-wrapped swords and wanted to know about them. He saw the Indian bow and quiver of arrows tied to the packhorse and would ask about them also. Both Franklin and Allison had recognized Redmon's British accent when he first called out to the house and talked to them.

"Mr. Wilbanks, I will explain everything when we arrive at the house," said Redmon.

Redmon was given a room down the hallway from Allison and shown where to wash up for dinner. He and Allison accidentally touched hands once and then stared into each other eyes. Redmon could not explain how or why, but he immediately knew he was home. Allison scurried away to prepare dinner but not before turning back and staring at Redmon without saying a word. How does one know that they have found their mate so quickly? Maybe it was part of the human condition, but somehow both Redmon Drury and Allison Wilbanks knew.

✠ ✠ ✠

During the meal, Redmon related his entire story for the Wilbankses. For some unexplained reason he felt that he could trust them, especially Allison. He learned that she was twenty-two years old, an old maid by most standards of the time. He told them that some ten years had passed, but his hated rival Wilfred Chatham was the man he saw in Santa Fe at the La Fonda Hotel. Redmon said he had listened to Wilfred give orders to four men to kill the Wilbankses and get them off their land so he could take it over. "It has taken ten years, an ocean, and a continent, but I finally found the man that branded me. I can tell you that Wilfred Chatham is evil. According to my parents in England, the belief is that he murdered his father-in-law, Lord Thomas Dudley, and then his own wife to get their lands and wealth. Now, according to what I heard him say in Santa Fe, he plans to set up a cattle empire here but you are in his way. I wish to stay and help you stop him. I have money from the mines in Colorado so I will require no wages. I am tired of running from something that happened ten years ago. I will do all I can to keep Wilfred Chatham or his men from harming you!"

Franklin and Allison could only stare at Redmon after he finished relating his story. Redmon noticed that Allison's eyes were misty after hearing his tale. Franklin finally spoke.

"Young man, I fought through the Civil War on the Southern side. My wife Corrine and I came to this land when we lost our place in Georgia. We were in the line of Sherman's march and our place was burned out. We hold clear deed to this land and Allison knows where that deed is hidden. I'm not afraid for myself, because I have seen war and death, but I don't want Allison hurt by those men. You said that you heard that Nate Burleson character say he wanted to use Allison, and that hurts me to hear such a thing. That bunch of scalawags has run off or killed our ranch hands. We managed to shoot some of them when they attacked us. I guess we did not kill enough of them to make them stop, so we can use your help. We haven't been able to ride the ranch and check our cattle because we've been bottled up here. That bunch has probably stolen or run off most of our cattle. They probably ate some of them at their camp. We're short on supplies because we can't leave the ranch. Too much longer and they would have been able to take us. Yes, we can use your help. Redmon Drury, I hope I can trust you because I am going to ask you to protect Allison and get her out of here if it comes to that."

"Pop, I'll not leave you or the ranch. Momma is buried here. This is our land and we won't leave it to this Wilfred Chatham man. Redmon, you don't really have to stay, but I hope you will." Allison looked at Redmon with a hopeful expression on her beautiful face.

Late that night Redmon put on his buckskins and moccasins and strapped on his pistol. Allison must have been awake and heard him stirring for she met him in the hallway outside his room with a questioning look. "Allison, I'm going to get some supplies and get rid of that Nate Burleson fellow. I will return as soon as possible. It is time to take the fight to Chatham. You told me where their camp is located so I will give them a little surprise with their morning coffee."

Suddenly, she was in his arms and he held her. "Please come back, Redmon. I would like to know who you are."

Redmon saddled Lancer and put a packsaddle on Nate Burleson's horse. Then he loaded the dead man and tied him down. He noticed some empty feed sacks in the barn and tied them on the packhorse. When he was clear of the canyon, Redmon rode west. It took an hour before he saw the building site where Wilfred Chatham planned to lord over his cattle empire. An almost full moon was up now lighting the landscape and made the white tents easy to see across the plain. It was now somewhere close to one o'clock in the morning.

Redmon rode around the building site until he determined where the cook shack for the workers was located. He climbed out of the saddle and led the horses forward. It was obvious that no one here expected an attack from the Wilbankses or anyone else for there were no sentries posted. The cook shack was empty and Redmon found the pantry. First he loaded the sacks he brought with flour, side meat, coffee, and canned goods. He took several of everything he saw in the pantry. He carried the full sacks out to the horses. Then he carried the body of Nate Burleson into the cook shack and sat him in a chair at the long table where the workers sat for meals, and put the dead man's arms on the table in front of him. He made the dead Nate Burleson look as though he were staring off into space. As an afterthought, before leaving the cook shack Redmon took off Nate's hat, tilted his head, and using his hunting knife, carved a capital D on Nate's forehead, then put the hat back on Nate's head.

Redmon stood back to see the effect he was making and it was eerie. Because Nate Burleson was stiff it looked as though he was staring off into space. Finally, he put the man's body back into the sitting position.

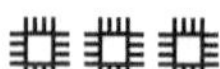

Slowly and carefully Redmon left the cook shack, loaded the supplies, and led the horses away into the night before he mounted and rode back east. Redmon was now throwing down the gauntlet to Wilfred Chatham and his men, warning them that their plans might not go as they wished. An hour later Redmon rode back into the Circle W and Allison was waiting for him. She helped put up the horses. When they were in the house, Allison turned to Redmon and he opened his arms and she went into them. "Redmon, I know we don't know one another yet. I have very little experience around men, except Poppa and the ranch hands when we used to have them here. We are so far from a town that I know little of the outside world. We have been to Santa Fe a few times before this trouble started, but I have never been anywhere else. I love Poppa and this ranch, but I would love to know about the world. Will you tell me all that you have seen and lived? I hope you will tell me all that you have done and what you have learned living around people."

Redmon put his finger under her chin, raised her face to his, and lightly kissed her lips.

"Allison, I believe finding Wilfred Chatham and then finding you was meant to be. I hope we can learn more of one another. I cannot explain the feeling I had when I first saw you, but it is as if I am home. What is coming will be dangerous but we can face it together. I will tell you of England, of Canada, and my travels." They kissed one more time and then went to their rooms to sleep at least for a short time.

※ ※ ※

The cookie, Amos Sudder, was in the cook shack early and saw the man sitting at the table. "Nate, I'll have some coffee on the fire real quick so hold on. You're in here early. You and the rest goin' after them Wilbankses today? Them house builders will be in here any minute."

When Nate Burleson didn't respond, Amos stepped out of the kitchen and walked down the long table. He put his hand on Nate Burleson's shoulder and the body fell forward onto the table. He ran from the cook shack yelling for Harley Edwards, the foreman of the Chatham C Bar. Amos alerted Harley Edwards, Ray Toms, and Ned James and they all ran back to the cook shack.

When they lay Nate Burleson on the floor, they all saw that he was shot through the heart. Nate was considered a tough man and good with a gun. The men's first thought was that Nate attacked the Wilbankses and either the old man or the girl made a lucky shot. Then they saw something on Nate's forehead that they did not notice before. There was a capital D carved into Nate's forehead. It was clearly done after he was dead, for there was no blood around the carving.

Then Amos yelled, "We 'been robbed. Somebody come in here and took a bunch of our food. We're gonna run short unless someone takes a wagon ta Santa Fe ta get some more, and they need to go real soon!"

Harley Edwards suddenly knew that this situation was completely different. Whoever shot Nate through the heart had brought him back, and had the gall to set him in a chair. Amos told them that he found Nate staring off into space. The pantry was raided. Harley just couldn't believe that either Franklin or Allison Wilbanks could have done something like this. Someone came right into their camp, took the food, and placed Nate in the chair, and none of them even knew the man was here. There must be a new card player in the game. Now they would have to figure out who it might be. They would have to eliminate this new threat and then finish the Wilbankses.

Wilfred Chatham hired Harley and his men to do the job. Harley would be the foreman of one of the biggest cattle spreads in the West once the Wilbankses were removed from their land. Harley Edwards knew one thing for sure. The idea of hurting a woman like Allison Wilbanks did not set well with him. He secretly planned to take her to a place of her choice once her father was dead. He personally never saw her, but some of the men said that she was beautiful. The idea of killing a beautiful girl made him sick.

They took Nate's body out and Harley got two of the builders to dig a grave and bury him. There was some grumbling from the building crew when they heard the story that someone had come into the cook shack and taken food. They were angry that someone brought Nate Burleson back and sat him up the way it was done. Amos Sudder described how he found Nate sitting at the table and staring off into space.

After breakfast Harley, Ray Toms, and Ned James saddled their horses and rode for the Circle W headquarters. Before they rode away to finish the Wilbankses, Harley ordered one of the men to take a wagon to Santa Fe for supplies. Amos Sudder gave the man a list of needed supplies for the cook shack.

❖ ❖ ❖

Redmon awoke groggy, but made his way to the spring behind the house and washed up. He kept thinking how good Allison felt in his arms. It felt so natural to hold her. When he kissed her the feeling was special, a feeling that he had not experienced in over ten years. He developed the habit of brushing his teeth with some soda using a stiff bristle brush he found in Canada and had bought several. He didn't know that Allison was watching from a back window. When she saw the brand on his chest she sucked in her breath. Immediately, Allison was angry with this Wilfred Chatham. She wanted to make the man pay for what he did to Redmon.

Allison heated water on the stove and had a bath in her room. Then she cooked breakfast. During the meal, Redmon told Franklin what he did during the night, causing Franklin to laugh, but he did not tell him that he had carved a capital D in the middle of Nate Burleson's forehead as a calling card for Wilfred Chatham. Franklin laughed again as he thought about the tale.

"I think they will come at us this morning because of what I did last night. We will need to be ready. I will be outside in the canyon waiting. If they try to send a man from above, I will be ready. I would like to force Wilfred Chatham to come down here from Santa Fe to take charge. I believe he has stayed away so no one could connect him to your deaths," Redmon explained.

⬚ ⬚ ⬚

In preparation for an attack, the front porch of the house was set up like a fortress with stacks of burlap feed sacks filled with sand from a dry wash. They even made shooting slits to cover the canyon opening below. Both Allison and Franklin told Redmon that they were tired of having their house set up like a fort. Much of the window glass was shot out in the front and back of the house.

After breakfast Redmon filled a canteen and gathered his volcanic carbine. But before he left, he took Allison's hand. "Please do not expose yourself. Keep your head down." Then they looked into each other's eyes and just knew how the other felt.

Redmon was sitting behind a rock below the escarpment when he saw the three riders come up to the edge of the rocks above and look down at the Circle W headquarters. One of the men pointed and Redmon knew the man was pointing out Nate Burleson's horse in the corral. He saw one man dismount while the other two rode east. He knew they were going to attack the Wilbankses from the front while the other man jumped off the ledge and then slid down from above to attack from the rear hoping to catch the Wilbankses by surprise. Redmon wondered why this tactic was not used before, but he was thankful it was not.

When Ray Toms, sitting above on the escarpment, heard shooting from the front of the house, he jumped the ten feet to the scree pile below the ledge and began to slide down the hill.

Redmon set his carbine against the rock, made sure his pistol was loose in the holster, and stepped around the bottom of the boulder he was crouching behind.

"I don't think they need or want you down there," Redmon addressed Toms.

Ray Toms pulled up suddenly with a startled look on his face, causing Redmon to chuckle.

"Who the hell are ya?" Ray asked and clawed for his pistol.

Redmon's draw was quick and smooth, and the surprised look on Ray Toms' face was complete. He was considered a fast draw, but his pistol was just clearing his holster when he felt the bullet hit him. He died instantly, rolling down the hill with dust and debris thrown up as he tumbled, finally settling at the bottom amid a cloud of dust.

Redmon retrieved the man's pistol and his own carbine, and moved around the curve of the hill until he could see the men attacking the front of the house. He sat, using a rock to lay the carbine barrel over. He sighted carefully. Letting out a breath, he squeezed the trigger. He saw a man throw up his arms, drop his rifle, and fall to the ground.

Then Redmon switched targets and levered his volcanic in smooth rhythm, putting bullets all around the other man. He didn't want to kill the man. He wanted this man to ride to Santa Fe and tell Wilfred Chatham what was happening here, hoping that his hated enemy would be forced to come and take charge at the site of his proposed cattle empire.

Finally, he saw the man crawling to his horse, so he let him go. He watched the man ride south and then back west toward the Chatham headquarters. Redmon found a slight game trail leading up to the escarpment where he retrieved the riderless horse. He then rode around to the other man's horse where he loaded the body and headed up to the house.

Allison was off the porch and in Redmon's arms as soon as he dismounted. Franklin came from the porch and watched his daughter and Redmon. For the first time in a while he thought they might actually survive this battle. He never wanted to alarm Allison, but he truthfully wasn't sure they would survive before Redmon came. Now he hoped they could finish this and that Redmon might stay. He knew that Allison missed her mother and was lonely living so far from other young people. He believed he was gauging Redmon's character correctly as being as good as his word.

Redmon and Franklin went around the house to load the second man over a saddle.

"Mr. Wilbanks, I don't believe they would think we would hit them two nights in succession so I will go again tonight and leave these two men and see if I can stir them up a bit."

Then Redmon looked at Mr. Wilbanks, "I know this is sudden, but will you allow me to court Allison once this situation is all straightened out? She is a wonderful girl. I promise to protect and treat her well."

"Redmon, your coming has saved us. Please don't get yourself killed tonight. That would hurt Allison a great deal, I believe," her father told Redmon.

The rest of the day, Redmon and Allison stayed together and talked. He told her of his parents, and his brother Rodney, who had left to attend the college at Eton. His eldest brother, who had told his father Red Roland that he had no interest in the land, was practicing as a barrister; or, as they called them in America, a lawyer, now resided just south of Eden, in Sheffield.

He told Allison of Roddrick and his sister Madeline. He was honest and told Allison that Roddrick married his own former love. He talked about Drury Manor and the former Chatham Manor. He described the countryside and also London. Redmon held nothing back and told Allison about the night he was branded by Wilfred Chatham. They held hands as they talked and the time passed too quickly for Allison.

At the Wilbanks ranch, they were all relatively quiet during dinner. They knew that the men at Chatham headquarters might be ready for a second visit by Redmon.

Redmon put on his buckskins again for the night's work. Allison hoped for his safe reurn.

⌗ ⌗ ⌗

Harley Edwards was stunned as he rode away from the Circle W. He knew Ned James was dead and figured that Ray Toms was dead also because he didn't show up after all the shooting. Harley now realized that there was a trained fighter on the Circle W. His last three fighting men were dead and the Wilbankses were still on their ranch. Whoever the new man was, he was a crack shot. His shot from the side of the hill killing Ned James must have been at least three hundred yards, and it took only one try. Harley decided he would have to ride to Santa Fe and bring Wilfred Chatham into this whether he wanted it or not. The man clearly stayed in Santa Fe to keep his hands clean of the murders of the Wilbankses. He wanted to be called Lord Chatham or Sir Wilfred, which Harley thought was a bunch of bunk. There was no royalty in America. Harley was beginning to lose interest in this whole land grab deal.

Wilfred Chatham learned at the state land office in Santa Fe that the Wilbankses possessed a clear deed to their land issued in 1866. So the only way to get them off the land was to buy them out or kill them and get rid of their bodies. The Wilbankses turned down all the offers to buy their land, so Wilfred Chatham wanted them dead.

Any law was over a hundred miles away in Santa Fe. Lincoln, the county seat, was even farther to the southeast. Chatham had no fear of the consequences he might face for murder of the Wilbanks.

Redmon was ready to go at about eleven o'clock. He was tired but this night might just bring the finish he wanted. He needed to flush out Wilfred Chatham. He knew that he wanted Allison Wilbanks as his wife and this would be a first step in making that happen.

Redmon realized that he and Allison would have a great deal to learn about one another, and he hoped she would be willing for that to happen. She was easily as regal as any of the noble women he remembered from London and England. She displayed a spirit that few could match. As he prepared to leave the house, she was in his arms and they shared their first real passionate kiss.

He mounted his horse and rode out of the canyon, pulling two horses behind him with her watching after him in the starlight. He liked the idea that she would be there for him when he returned. The moon was just about to peek over the eastern horizon when he reached the Chatham's building site. He would have two purposes this night—to leave the dead men, and to deliver a message to both Wilfred Chatham and the man Wilfred had sent to murder the Wilbankses. Franklin and Allison did not know it but Redmon had already put a D on the forehead of each dead man.

He dismounted and carefully surveyed the building site when he got there. He saw one guard and carefully worked his way to him. He stopped periodically to listen to the night sounds. He wanted to make sure that there was no other man lurking nearby. Redmon learned stealth tactics from Long Bow in Canada. He was standing behind the guard before the man even knew he was there and rendered him unconscious. He laid the man at the door of the cook shack and tied him up.

Then Redmon unloaded the dead men and laid them on each side of the guard in front of the cook shack door. Redmon had found some coal oil in the Wilbanks' barn so he brought it along and doused the large pile of wood beams and logs that were to be used in the huge house Wilfred Chatham was having built. When he was ready, he struck a lucifer and set the woodpile on fire.

He led Lancer and the other horses into the dark, pulled his carbine, and began shooting at the tents. He aimed high only to send a warning. He didn't want to kill any of the builders for they were only men trying to earn a wage. Immediately, there were shouts, and Redmon could see men scurrying from the tents in the glow of the fire that was quickly becoming an inferno and consuming the woodpile. The logs were pine, and because of the pitch in them, the logs caught and burned easily.

He put shots at the feet of several of the men causing them to jump in the air and yell. Finally, when the scene was total chaos, Redmon mounted and rode away into the night.

Allison ran to Redmon when he reached the barn and he scooped her up into his arms as soon as he climbed out of the saddle. "Oh, Redmon, I was so worried when I heard the shots. You can see the glow of the fire you set from here!"

"I am all right, Allison. Now we will have to wait to learn if this has the desired effect I am hoping for," Redmon replied.

Redmon quickly stripped the horses and put them in the corral. The attackers stole most of the Wilbanks' horses during the many months of siege so the three dead men's animals would somewhat make up for that.

❖ ❖ ❖

When dawn came to the Chatham camp, it was in shock. They found Ray Toms and Ned James at the door of the cook shack, along with a trussed up Ben Nesbit. With most of the building crew standing and listening, Ben told Harley Edwards that whoever took him was like a ghost. He wanted his time and was leaving. Half the builders also asked for their time. Some had already packed their kits and tools and were ready to go. Some said this was a place of death now with three more of Harley's men dead. The building crew looked down at the dead men whose hands were crossed on their chests with their hats covering them. The whole crew saw the capital D carved into the foreheads of the two dead hard cases.

After getting some men to bury Ray and Ned, Harley saddled his horse, loaded a packhorse with what supplies he could manage from the cook shack, and headed for Santa Fe. The day before he had one of the men shoot one of the Wilbankes steers and drag it to camp for meat for the building crew. What he saw on Nate's forehead and then on the foreheads of Ray and Ned disturbed him. It was clearly a message of some sort, but what kind of message and from whom? Harley had been a hard man from the age of fourteen, riding with Quantrill's Raiders in Missouri and then fighting in some Texas cattle wars. Something here was different. The new man, whoever he was, only killed the men who threatened the Wilbankses. He could have easily killed Ben Nesbit, but didn't. The D carved in the foreheads of his men…what could that mean?

❖ ❖ ❖

Redmon slept past sunrise, which he never did. After a breakfast Allison had kept warm for him, they noticed some men coming toward the house. The Wilbankses and Redmon were ready with their weapons.

One man came forward as the spokesman. "Could you folks spare some water? Ours at the camp was fouled from the fire last night. Half the crew has quit. Some headed back to the Rio Grande and Soccoro. We're goin' east to Roswell. We hear that they're building. By the by, Harley Edwards rode for Santa Fe to talk to that Chatham feller who wanted to take your land. We don't want any part of this no more."

The man looked at Redmon. "Are you the ghost who got them hired killers and hit our camp? Man, you shoulda heard Harley this morning when he found Ray Toms and Ned James. He was fit to be tied. Never heard such language."

Franklin let the men fill their canteens at the spring, and then watched the men ride away to the east. The men told Franklin that they were going to ride for the Pecos River and then follow it to Roswell. Now he knew that Redmon's attacks were having the immediate impact he wished for. Redmon and Allison decided to saddle horses and ride to the building site and have a look. They rode close enough to observe any activity and clearly no building was being done. When Redmon saw the rock walls of the house that was being built, he laughed. "Allison, I can't believe it. That would have been a copy of Chatham Manor where my brother and Roselind now live, and own. They renamed the property Eden Hall after the Chathams lost it. I find it interesting that Wilfred was trying to build the same thing here."

Allison stared at the size of the house. "Redmon, is Drury Manor where you grew up that big?" she asked in amazement.

"Well, Drury Manor is slightly smaller, but not much. Drury was always more homey, as you call your house. My mother saw to that," he explained, and winked at her. They rode close and he leaned down and kissed her, and she held onto him.

They rode back to the Circle W slowly, just enjoying being together. Redmon wanted to let the horses out of the barn so they could graze before Wilfred came from Santa Fe, if he actually did. As they rode back, he described the sea voyage from Gretna Green. He told her of the confrontation he had with the young earl Winston Maybury because he was going after any single female on the ship. He told her of the fine people Conner and Grace Walden who he helped. He described the St. Lawrence Seaway and how he and the Waldens escaped the young earl's wrath by leaving the ship in the middle of the night. He described the inns and common rooms where he stayed being much like those in England. Allison hung on every word. She thought it was fun to learn about places she could only imagine seeing.

When he let them out of the corral, Redmon's horses took to the grass as if they hadn't grazed in months. Allison was amazed by the beauty of the Nez Percé horses. Redmon told Allison about Rosie and how the mare saved him twice on the trail, and how she tried to bite and kick him when he first bought her. She laughed when he told her of Rosie's habit of reaching behind and pulling the saddle blanket off with her teeth and throwing it on the ground when he prepared to leave camp. He pointed out the fine animals she produced from his stallion Lancer.

Late in the day they put the horses in a corral, but he separated the Appaloosas, not wanting one of the Morgan stallions to cover the Appaloosa mare.

Dinner was enjoyable even though the threat of Wilfred Chatham and Harley Edwards was still hanging over them. Redmon helped Allison wash the dishes. He put soap on her nose, causing her to giggle. She felt so comfortable with Redmon. She did not want this Wilfred Chatham to take Redmon away from her. To be close to a man near her age was new for Allison. She was always so sheltered by her mother and father. Her mother Corrine was her teacher, and Redmon realized that Allison's mother did an excellent job. Allison was a lady in every sense of the word. Redmon thought, if she were dressed in a nice gown, with her hair done and some makeup, that Allison would be the most beautiful woman in any room full of beautiful women. He wanted Allison to be a part of his life.

⊞ ⊞ ⊞

Harley Edwards found Wilfred Chatham in the La Fonda dining room. Chatham saw him approaching his table and suddenly put a frown on his face. "Well,

Harley, what happened? I can tell from your visage that something has clearly gone wrong." Harley had been on the trail for two days and was dirty and tired. He hadn't slept much because of the attacks by the ghost, as the men at the camp were calling him.

Harley sat down without being asked and addressed Mr. Chatham, "The Wilbankses have a man with them who has killed Nate, Ray, and Ned. The man is clearly a trained fighter. I was lucky to get away alive." Then Harley explained about finding Nate sitting at the cook shack table with a bullet through his heart. The pantry had been raided and most of their food taken. Harley said he had passed Bud Wilkes heading back south driving the wagon loaded with supplies for the camp and told him to get there as soon as he could. Next, Harley told of their attack on the Circle W and about Ray and Ned being killed by the mystery man. "The man must have shot from three hundred yards to kill Ned. Then he came again that night. He overpowered the guard, tied him up, and put the guard, Ray, and Ned together in front of the cook shack door. Then he burned the pile of timbers for the house and started shooting at the workers' tents. Half the workers asked for their time the next morning and quit. Our water supply was fouled by the fire and no work is being done on the house. Now you need to hear the strangest part. The letter D was carved in the forehead of both Ray and Ned, and Nate had a D carved on his forehead the night before. Do you know what that means?"

Wilfred Chatham looked as though he was going to explode. "All right, we have attempted to kill them and you were incompetent in your task to get that accomplished. So I will go down there and buy them out to get them off the land. Everyone has their price. I want this finished now. I will not take no for an answer from these people. Hire some more men if you can get them to go with us tomorrow. I will handle this mystery man. Have you seen him? What does he look like?"

Harley replied that no one ever got a look at the man. In fact, the men at the building camp were calling him the ghost.

Wilfred bit out his words in an angry tone of voice, "The ghost, is it? Well, I'm going to kill this so-called ghost if those people refuse my offer for their ranch. I always get what I want, and always have. No one has ever stood in my way and survived."

Harley Edwards decided to take care of himself first. He got a hot bath, shave, and a meal. So far, all he ever saw or heard from this Lord Wilfred Chatham was talk. He was obviously flush with money, but Harley and the dead men were the ones doing all the fighting.

There had been nine men in his crew at the beginning. All were tough, hard men. The Wilbankses and their hands were responsible for the first five dead. As far as

Harley was concerned, Frank Wilbanks and his daughter were the real fighters in this deal. Harley decided that he could have had twenty men and would probably be in the same shape. Now this new man suddenly comes to the ranch and helps Franklin and his daughter. The man dealt with his three men so quickly that Harley was stunned. This stranger was brazen enough to come right into their camp undetected.

The Wilbankses were forced to barricade the front of their house and were holed up in their ranch house for quite a while. Harley knew that they must have been low on supplies. It would have been only a matter of time until the Wilbankses were forced to give up. Then this new man came and raided the pantry and killed his men. Together the Wilbankses and this ghost made a tough situation worse.

Wilfred Chatham was seething with anger after Harley Edwards gave his account of the disasters at his building site. These western types were all fools as well as cowards. He kept thinking about Harley's words. The letter D was carved into the foreheads of Nate Burleson, Ray Toms, and Ned James. What could that mean?

Wilfred Chatham never gave any thought to the deeds he wrought over the years. If someone was in his way, he dealt with them in what ever manner he felt necessary. Chatham Manor was lost to his family, so he got them a new one. Thomas Dudley was in his way, so he dealt with him. His harpy wife Melissa accused him of murder, so he did away with her in the same way he did her father. His own so-called sister betrayed him and the family. He made an attempt to hurt her and that group of ingrates she chose, but nothing came of his efforts. He was young then, but he was sure he could now easily deal with those lowly Drurys using the experience he had gained. He was still angry that the whelp got away from him before they could deal with him.

Suddenly, a memory dawned. "Could it be?" Then he dismissed the thought. The whelp was lost somewhere in the wilds of Canada, probably dead by now anyway. It would be completely improbable and Wilfred was sure impossible. This must be someone else deviling him.

🁢 🁢 🁢

Redmon and Allison grew closer each day. When they were alone, they held each other and kissed. Their attraction was strong and they took full advantage of that attraction. They talked and realized that they would have at least six or seven days before Wilfred Chatham and any men he could recruit came to attack them again.

Redmon and Allison hunted and brought in one antelope and a mule deer for fresh meat. One night, Redmon raided the pantry at the Chatham building site one more time. The supply wagon must have come back from Santa Fe, so there was plenty to choose from.

The next morning, the cookie Amos Sudder realized that they were raided again and threw up his hands. He worked as the cookie on longhorn cattle drives from Texas to Kansas, and even to Montana. He suddenly realized that he was caught in a tough, no-win situation. He only met this Wilfred Chatham once and thought him to be an arrogant, overbearing, aristocratic ass. Amos was familiar with this type of man.

Amos Sudder was not his real name. As did many men in the west, Amos possessed a past and changed his name to get away from that past. He was a well-educated man who ran afoul of a powerful English nobleman as a very young man. He worked hard over the years to lose his accent, even using slang in his vocabulary to sound more uneducated. He was never really happy about working for Lord Chatham.

Some of the men working at the building site rode to the Wilbanks' Circle W ranch. They told the men in the cook shack that the Wilbanks girl was beautiful, and that she and her father were good people and probably didn't deserve what Harley and his bunch of hard cases were doing to them. Suddenly, Amos made a decision and left the cook shack. He went to the tent where his gear was stored, and packed his kit. Two other men in the tent asked what he was doing.

"I'm headin' out. I think this deal is done. I'm going over to the Circle W and ask if they could use a cook. I don't think this ranch is going to pan out," Amos said, and carried his belongings to the corral, saddled his horse, and loaded his packhorse.

The men in the tent looked at one another. One said, "Well, hell, if there ain't no cook, I'm outta here. I'm gonna grab some supplies and hit the road." Word spread quickly that the cookie Amos Sudder was gone. An hour later the building site was deserted. The pantry was now completely cleaned out before they left.

Amos rode carefully up the canyon to the Wilbanks house. He could see that, along with the house, there was a good barn, what must be a bunkhouse, corrals, and various sheds. He helloed the house and heard someone yell, "What do you want?"

Amos replied, "I was the cook at the building site to the west. I was wondering if you could use a good cook. I think you've got most of my supplies here at your ranch as it is."

Amos heard a laugh from the porch. "How do we know you can actually cook something decent?"

Amos heard a woman's voice call out, causing him to laugh also. "Give me the opportunity to cook one meal for you. If you don't like it, I'll move on tomorrow."

"Well, come on up. You can put your gear in the bunkhouse," the voice answered.

When Amos reached the house he saw three people facing him, and all were prepared for trouble with their guns out and ready. "Well, this is quite a greeting for a cook," he remarked, and grinned at them. When Amos studied the tall man standing beside the beautiful young woman, he was shocked. Amos was sure he recognized the man, or at least the family resemblance. He would wait to decide if he was correct when he heard the man's name.

Franklin took charge. "I'm Franklin Wilbanks. This is my daughter, Allison, and the man who has been helping us, Redmon Drury."

So there it was, the name Amos knew. He could not credit this happening all the way out here in New Mexico. Amos decided that only honesty would work with these people. He took a deep breath and said, "I am honored to meet all of you. For many years I have gone by the name Amos Sudder. Redmon, I believe you are the man we have been calling the ghost at the camp. I will also tell you that I know your father Red Roland. You look just like him when he was your age."

Redmon stared at the man dumbfounded, but finally found his voice. "Mr. Sudder, to hear that you know my father is a shock. I will look forward to hearing the story."

Amos noticed that Allison placed her hand on Redmon's arm protectively. "I will be glad to tell you all of it tonight after I cook a fine dinner for you."

Franklin took Amos to the bunkhouse. Amos found a building that was immaculate. Franklin watched the cook's reaction. "My daughter likes to keep things real neat as you can see. There's a room at the end where you can wash up. Pick a bunk. There are plenty. Come to the house and Allison will show you the kitchen and the pantry that is fully stocked," Franklin chuckled and left.

This would be the best bunkhouse Amos ever stayed in. He put his gear on a bunk and found the wash room. There was actually a pump for water and a copper tub for a bath. He could heat water on the stove.

Redmon and Allison took care of Amos' horses. "Allison, I believe fate is working here. That man was working for Wilfred Chatham and now I learn that he knew my father in England. That has to be fate of some sort." He pulled her to him and kissed her soundly. "I know this may be too soon, but I love you. You are the woman I would like to hold for the rest of my life."

"Oh, Redmon, I have been hoping that you could love me. I have been so afraid that you might leave. I love you and never want to leave your side," said Allison.

Redmon added, "When this business with Wilfred Chatham is settled Allison, we will go to Santa Fe and marry. I have already asked your father and he agreed to let me court you."

That evening, Amos Sudder cooked a meal for Franklin, Allison, and Redmon. After dinner was finished, Franklin took one look at Allison and said, "Daughter, what are you going to do with all your free time? Amos you're hired. Now tell us how it is that you know Redmon's father. I'm sure he wants to hear the tale."

Amos began his story, "I will first tell you that revealing my past is difficult because I have put it behind me for some twelve years. My real name is Henry Sudderth. I am the third son of Lord Edward Sudderth of Hexham."

Redmon blurted out, "I know your family!"

"Well," continued Amos, "I decided to pursue a military career because my oldest brother William would inherit the Sudderth lands. Our middle brother, Jonathan, decided on a naval career. The last time I heard, he was the captain of a British frigate. I was made a lieutenant in a northern garrison because of my family's standing.

I was close to becoming a master of sword in our regiment when I began seeing the daughter of a prominent nobleman. Another man wanted her and an altercation between us ensued. The man insulted me as well as the woman I loved, so a duel was fought. I was sixteen years of age. I killed the man who was a year older. He was the eldest son of Lord Edward Maybury."

Again Redmon blurted out his reaction, "Oh, my God, this is surely fate! I will explain when you are finished with your story, Amos."

Amos continued, "Sir Edward Maybury, who it seems carried a great deal of influence with the Crown, was able to have me declared an outlaw for killing his son. I was immediately dismissed from the regiment and was forced to go into hiding. My family, who were also prominent, could not even help me because I was not near to home. Redmon, your father Red Roland took me in and hid me, and then arranged for my ship passage to America. Your father and mother were young at the time, but never hesitated to help me. Your father even provided money so I could make a start here. I will tell you that your mother was the most beautiful young woman I ever saw. She treated me well, and helped your father get me to the coast so I could ship to America.

I took the name Amos Sudder and moved on west. Several Texas cattle drives hired me on as trail cook. Some twelve years have passed and here I am. With a promise to be the chef in the big house when it was completed, I took the job as cook for the Chathams. Well, I have learned that Lord Wilfred Chatham set a plan in motion to steal your land by any means necessary. I finally realized that I was on the wrong side of this situation. So there you have my story in its entirety."

Quickly, Redmon outlined for Amos his history with Wilfred Chatham, and then the confrontation with Winston Maybury, the son of Sir Edward Maybury on the North Star during the voyage to Canada. A bond was forged that night between Redmon, Allison, and Henry Sudderth that would last some forty years. Henry told them that he would like nothing better than to have his real name back.

The next morning two of the men that were working on the building crew came and asked for riding jobs. Henry vouched for them, so they were hired.

Franklin, Redmon, Ralph Maynard, and Joe Walsh rode out to look for Circle W cattle. Henry and Allison would stay and protect the headquarters. Pockets of cattle were found and they herded them back toward the headquarters. It was Joe Walsh that noticed the two riders in the distance heading for the Chatham building site.

⌗ ⌗ ⌗

Harley Edwards took care of having the horses saddled and the packhorse ready to load when Wilfred Chatham came into the stable with a clothes bag and a long leather sheath.

When Harley asked him about it, Wilfred replied, "It's my sword. I am a master of the blade. I have killed men with it and always carry it with me when I travel. It is a gentleman's weapon. I fought three duels in England and obviously won for I am alive. No man has ever touched me with their blade."

Two days later, Harley and Wilfred Chatham rode to the building site and found it deserted. Harley had noticed earlier the four riders in the distance moving cattle on Circle W land and wondered where the Wilbankses found ranch hands so quickly. He was unable to find a single man in Santa Fe willing to ride for Wilfred Chatham. It seemed that word was being passed in Santa Fe by some of the former building crew who came back after they quit the building site. A story was being circulated that any man who rode for Wilfred Chatham would be killed by the ghost. Even some gringos refused to sign on with the Chatham outfit.

Wilfred was angry beyond words when Harley told him what was being said in Santa Fe about working for Wilfred Chatham. Then he wanted to kill someone when he saw his building site abandoned. It seemed that since some stranger had appeared on the scene, all his plans were going awry. He vowed to get them back on track tomorrow when he rode to this Circle W and bought them out. He would not allow two lowly commoners to ruin his plans.

✸ ✸ ✸

Harley discovered that the cook shack was completely stripped of food. He knew that the supply wagon had just returned from Santa Fe completely loaded and now all of it was already gone. Harley decided when he looked at the empty pantry and realized that Amos Sudder was gone that this land deal was probably over. Luckily, he had brought enough supplies to get by for a few days.

That night the mood was subdued in the cook shack as Harley put together a meal for himself and Wilfred Chatham. There were few words exchanged between the two men. Harley could tell that the so-called nobleman was brooding and angry.

The next morning when they were riding for the Circle W, Harley noticed that Wilfred had the sword hanging at the side of his saddle. Harley wondered if Sir Wilfred Chatham actually thought he could scare the Wilbankses into selling their land with a sword when bullets hadn't worked. The man's arrogance still amazed Harley. He wondered if this was how rich people treated poor people in England. If it was, he was glad that he was a cowboy in the west. He could always move on at his pleasure if the mood struck him. He had heard somewhere that poor people were tied to the land on these nobelmen's estates.

❁ ❁ ❁

Allison was feeding her chickens when she saw the men riding toward the house and she gave the warning. Immediately, guns were readied and waiting. It was Redmon who recognized Wilfred Chatham riding to the house. He took a deep breath and then let it out.

His hope to get the man to come here worked. Now he needed to hold up his end of the bargain. Chatham rode up to the house without asking permission, regardless of the attacks made by his men on the Circle W over a several-month period.

Wilfred Chatham sat in his saddle and surveyed the people watching him as if he were looking at lesser beings. Redmon immediately recognized the look. Wilfred looked at the oldest man he saw and cleared his throat as if something was caught there. "I am here to buy this land. I will expect you to be off the place in two weeks. If you refuse my offer, be warned that I will have an army of men here and level what you consider a house to the ground. No one will be given quarter, including the woman I see there."

Redmon studied the man who branded him so many years before and noticed the sword hanging from Chatham's saddle. So, the man fancied himself a swordsman? Evidently, so much so that he would actually carry one on his saddle out here in the west. It was obvious that the man did not recognize Redmon. Wilfred Chatham was even more arrogant as an adult than he was as a seventeen year old. Redmon surmised that getting away with murder made Chatham even more confident in his ability to do anything he wished with no consequences to face for his actions.

Finally, Redmon laughed and Wilfred changed his focus to Redmon. "You are an arrogant rogue to believe that you can come here and threaten the Wilbankses. It seems also that you fancy yourself a swordsman. I have a suggestion for you. We could settle this easily as one man to another. You have a sword, I have one in the house. If you are agreeable?"

Wilfred Chatham looked at the tall, bearded man as if he were observing a lowly serf in England. Redmon stared at Wilfred and then laughed again, hoping to prick Wilfred's ego.

"Do I know you?" Wilfred asked.

"Only in a past life," Redmon replied.

Redmon's statement about the past did not register, but Wilfred realized that this must be the man who so quickly turned his fortunes around. This was the man the men at the camp were calling the ghost. The man seemed to have a slight British accent when he spoke. Thinking that when he killed this man, Wilfred would easily be able to take over this land. Wilfred still did not realize that this man challenging him was Redmon Drury even after his statement about the past.

Wilfred Chatham sneered, "Gather your sword then, man, and we will have done with this farce." Allison immediately took Redmon's arm in fear, looking up at his face. "So! She is your woman. That will make this so much more enjoyable. I will sell her in Santa Fe when this episode is concluded."

Redmon touched Allison on the cheek. "Do not fret, Allison, all will be well. Mr. Wilbanks and Henry, please make sure the other man does not interfere," Redmon quietly told the people staring at him.

"Redmon, are you truly equipped to handle this challenge?" Henry Sudderth asked, and Redmon nodded.

Redmon went to his room and changed into his moccasins and a light loose shirt that he wore when sparing with Emile Boushard. He took up his sword and walked toward the front of the house. He needed to believe in his training with Emile Boushard. He believed that the arrogant Wilfred Chatham would try to finish him off quickly. Redmon was thinking of his strategy as he walked to the front of the house where everyone was waiting.

Ten years of waiting to settle with Wilfred Chatham was finally upon Redmon. The night of the branding would finally catch up with him, and in a place far from that stable. Redmon felt that his years and the miles he had ridden had prepared him for this moment. Wilfred was whipping his blade through the air as if to intimidate Redmon, causing him to laugh out loud.

Wilfred sneered out, "I should know the name of the man I am about to dispatch. Do you have a name or do you go by The Ghost." Wilfred chortled.

"Does it really matter?" Redmon said, presenting an awkward stance as if he were a novice. He wanted to determine Wilfred's training and style before revealing his own true ability. Only Henry recognized what Redmon was doing because Redmon told him that he learned the sword from a French master. At least Henry hoped that that was what Redmon was actually doing.

Wilfred immediately noticed that this so-called Ghost held his sword in his left hand. He had never faced a left-handed swordsman before but decided that this might actually be enjoyable. Wilfred attacked, thinking this contest would end quickly when he saw the inadequate stance taken by the obvious novice. He backed this tall, bearded man across the yard and attacked constantly, thinking this duel would be over quickly, but somehow this character managed to counter every move he made.

Finally, the thought crept into Wilfred's mind that his challenger might be more than he originally thought. He was always able to kill his opponents more quickly than this. Suddenly, the man being called the ghost touched him with his blade. Redmon had promptly gone on the offensive, displaying a completely different stance and fighting style. Henry Sudderth chuckled. "Miss Wilbanks, you need not worry. Redmon has this situation well in hand. He is far superior to this Wilfred Chatham in skill. He used the awkward stance at the beginning to bait Wilfred Chatham into thinking that he was a novice."

When Redmon scored the first time, there was shock on Wilfred's face. Redmon scored twice more and Wilfred realized that this man had carefully disguised his skill. Obviously, the man possessed the skill to act as if he knew nothing at the start, and was able to get away with that tactic.

For the first time in his life Wilfred Chatham was afraid. This man was backing him into awkward positions with each of his moves and Wilfred found that he couldn't do anything about it. Suddenly, Redmon's sword tip moved so swiftly that Wilfred couldn't react. Blood began running into his eyes.

For those watching, other than Henry Sudderth, they found themselves mesmerized by the action. The constant clanging of the sword blades and the swift movements were something to see. Allison was scared to death at first when she thought Redmon was overmatched, but she heard Henry quietly chuckle and say it would be all right because Redmon was gauging his opponent. All of a sudden, she could tell when Redmon changed tactics and began to be the aggressor. She was completely amazed by how fluid, smooth, and quick Redmon moved on his feet. Every movement Redmon made seemed to be measured and perfect as he began to take charge of the duel. She could see that his complete concentration was on the blade being wielded by Wilfred Chatham. It was clear that Redmon was much stronger and in better physical condition than the land grabber. Redmon moved Wilfred into positions that his adversary clearly did not expect to face. It was evident that Wilfred Chatham was suddenly fighting for his life. He would soon be forfeiting that life to Redmon.

Finally, Redmon spoke for the first time when he realized that it was almost over. "Wilfred, I just carved my family's initial in your forehead. I did that to three of your cutthroats. There are not four of your men holding me down now." Redmon used his right hand to open his shirt revealing the brand on his chest. Wilfred's chest was heaving while he tried to regain his breath.

Recognition suddenly came to Wilfred Chatham that he had done the wrong thing by going berserk and trying for a quick kill. He was suddenly exhausted and could do nothing to change that. He was completely out of control now and Redmon cut him several more times as Wilfred tried for hard thrusts. Wilfred had not touched his opponent once with his blade.

Redmon knocked the blade aside each time and scored. Wilfred was losing a great deal of blood now and was growing weaker from that loss and the exertion of the duel. Allison and the others watching were amazed by how swiftly Redmon could move the tip of his sword.

Finally, Wilfred tried one last desperate thrust, which Redmon knocked aside and his sword tip entered Wilfred Chatham's heart. Wilfred stood for a moment looking down at the blade in his chest, then a final time at Redmon's face. As he collapsed, Redmon's blade came free. Everyone stared at the body of Wilfred Chatham. Allison ran for Redmon.

He turned and scooped her into his embrace. "Allison, love, it's finally over. Will you still marry me after what happened here today? I love you."

"Of course I will marry you, Redmon Drury. You are my man. Haven't you figured that out yet? I am so proud of you. You saved the Circle W. I will go anywhere you wish," Allison exclaimed as she held onto Redmon. Everyone suddenly surrounded them.

Franklin kept saying, "Boy, oh, boy, wasn't that something? I never saw nothin' like that before!"

Finally, Franklin remembered the man that rode in with Wilfred Chatham. He looked around and saw that the man was already riding south, pulling the packhorse behind him.

Ralph Maynard and Joe Walsh took the body of Wilfred Chatham out on the prairie and buried it. Neither man could stop talking about what they just witnessed. They had never seen a sword fight and were amazed by the quickness displayed by Redmon Drury considering his size.

No marker was placed where they buried Wilfred Chatham, and neither Redmon nor Allison ever asked where they put the body. Eventually, the grama grasses would take the spot back and cattle would graze there. There was a sigh of relief on the Circle W that it was over.

✿ ✿ ✿

That night, plans were made for Redmon, Allison, and Franklin to go to Santa Fe so Redmon and Allison could be married. Redmon was thinking of something he could give to Allison as a wedding present. He also wanted to take her to Central City and Denver to meet Red and Audrey Brandais. Redmon was proud of Allison and wanted to show her off. Redmon quietly got Henry, Ralph, and Joe to sign an affidavit that stated that they knew Wilfred Chatham to be dead so his land could be filed on.

Four days later, Redmon Drury and Allison Wilbanks were married by a priest in the Loretto Chapel with Franklin looking on. Redmon slipped a beautiful diamond ring on Allison's finger. Redmon was amazed that he was able to find a ring of such quality in Santa Fe. He learned from the merchant that the fine diamond ring came across the Santa Fe Trail from back east. No one else in Santa Fe could afford to buy the ring, so it had stayed in the display case for quite some time.

The La Fonda kitchen decorated a wedding cake for the newlyweds. Everyone in the dining room was invited to join the celebration and share the meal and special cake. During the party in the dining room, Franklin met a widow named Grace Davis. The woman was traveling to El Paso to live with her son. At least she thought she was until she met Franklin Wilbanks. Allison and Redmon immediately saw that Franklin was completely enthralled by the attractive Grace Davis.

At the end of the dinner, Redmon placed an official document in front of Allison. When she opened it, her eyes grew large and she looked at Redmon unbelieving. She threw her arms around his neck and kissed him hard. The document was a deed for sixty-two sections of land under the names Redmon Orrick and Allison Elaine Drury. Earlier that morning Redmon was able to file on the land west of the Circle W, including the Chatham building site. He learned that Wilfred Chatham was the only name on the previous land deed. Fortunately, Wilfred did not name his parents or brother on the deed, so Redmon could file on the land.

Redmon and Allison would head north for their honeymoon so they could spend time alone together on the trail. When they went to their room for the night, Franklin and Grace Davis stayed in the lobby to talk.

Franklin learned that Grace was traveling from Virginia where her husband had died suddenly a few years before. Her son came west earlier and so she decided to sell her house in Norfolk and join him. Franklin was only fifty years of age while Grace was forty-seven. They talked into the night and agreed to meet for breakfast.

⊞ ⊞ ⊞

Redmon and Allison stepped into their room and Allison went into his arms. After locking the door, they shared a passionate kiss. Redmon slowly removed Allison's wedding dress and she shivered with anticipation. When the dress was at her feet, she stepped out of it to stand close to Redmon. Now only in her shift, she helped Redmon out of his coat, untied his tie, and worked the buttons on his shirt, finally pulling it off to expose his broad muscled chest. Redmon could see the swell of her breasts through her shift and it made him almost crazy.

He placed his hands on her shapely hips as she worked at the belt and buttons on his pants. Finally, he grew impatient and finished them for her. He stepped out of the pant legs. Redmon took off his long under drawers and she gasped at the sight of him. She thought she would be prepared for this moment, but seeing Redmon's desire for her almost made her swoon. She reached out and touched him and her legs felt weak. She had waited twenty-two years for the right man and he was standing before her now. She held up her arms and Redmon pulled the shift up and over her head, exposing her body. Her long auburn hair tumbled around her shoulders and down her back. Redmon's eyes traveled from her beautiful face down to her feet.

"Oh, Allison, you are so beautiful and perfect." The words made goose bumps rise on her skin.

He scooped her up in his arms and carried her to the bed. He continued to drink in the absolute beauty of his new wife. Her long auburn hair was loose and arrayed across the pillow. Redmon let his hands rove over every part of her body. When he finally lay next to her, he began kissing her forehead, nose, lips, neck, and then breasts. He kissed her everywhere, drawing sighs from her. From the time she was fifteen, Allison dreamed about what it would be like to be loved by a man. Now, she knew. Redmon's touches and kisses made her skin tingle and want more of him. She wanted him, all of him. Redmon was now hers.

She knew that once they were one, they would be one for all time. She grasped him and begged him to make her a complete woman, and he did. They moved together to a summit that she could never have imagined. She almost screamed out his name at the end. "Oh, Redmon, that was the most wonderful experience of my life. I love you so much. My heart is full because you!"

He responded by loving her again and she responded in kind. She was completely free with him. She possessed so much love to give and he wanted all of it. Redmon thought there were only a few truly beautiful women in the world and he would be married to one of them. To realize that he found her on a ranch in the middle of nowhere was astounding. As he finally lay holding Allison, he thought of Roselind as one of the rare beauties along with Victoria Brownley in Denver. His mother was also one, for she was truly beautiful as well as good to a fault.

Redmon pictured Allison in a beautiful gown at a ball and knew that his new wife could easily hold her own in British society, although he loved having her in her present state of undress. He was still astounded by her perfect form. Her legs were long and shapely, and she had perfect hips and breasts. Her shoulders fit with her slender neck.

"Allison, you are perfect in every way a man could want. I love you!" repeated Redmon.

They made love again, slowly and passionately, as Redmon explored every part of her body and knew he would never have enough of this woman.

When they finally lay together, spent, Redmon expressed his feelings, "Allison Drury, you are amazing. I am the most fortunate man on earth to have found you. I am looking forward to the adventure we will share together."

Allison returned, "Redmon, I did not know what to expect tonight. I dreamed about what it would be like to give myself completely to a man. Your lovemaking was better than I ever dreamed it would be. I am so happy to be your wife. I am your woman alone, and will always be only your woman."

Redmon and Allison entered the La Fonda dining room hand in hand and found Franklin with Grace Davis together as they were the night before. They were laughing and talking, and Allison wasn't sure whether she liked seeing her father flirting with another woman other than her mother. But, she realized that her father was a good-looking man and her mother Corrine was gone now for almost four years. Allison wanted her father to be happy. She thought Grace Davis was very pretty and actually quite nice.

As they enjoyed breakfast together, Redmon observed Allison watching her father and Grace Davis laughing and making eyes at one another. He pinched his new wife on the leg under the table, teasing her about her reaction to her father and Grace flirting.

That gesture made Allison glare at Redmon for only a moment. When he winked, she giggled. She was forced to think about her own blessings with Redmon. She turned those thoughts to wishes of happiness for her father and Grace.

The two couples strolled around the plaza together and Grace walked with her hand on Franklin's arm. She was scheduled to leave on a stagecoach that morning going south, but Franklin asked her to stay with him so they could get to know one another better and she agreed.

Redmon and Allison planned to spend two days with Franklin before riding north for Central City and Denver.

As it happened, Franklin sat Allison down the day after the wedding. "Allie, I want to marry Grace. I won't ask her if you are dead set against it. I loved your mother and you know that. You have been my life since Corry died. Redmon is going to show you a world that I could never do for you. You don't realize it now, but you will get to travel as you always dreamed. I don't want to be alone in the house. Grace is a fine woman and she is a southerner as we were."

Then he held out his hands to her in supplication. Instantly, Allison was up from her chair and into his arms, sobbing. "Oh, Daddy, I love you so much! I have been so selfish. I never stopped to think about what you needed. Redmon has told me that we are going to live an adventure together. I want you to have a woman who will love you. If Grace is the woman you want, then please ask her."

The following morning, Redmon stood with Franklin as his best man while Allison acted as Grace's maid of honor. Franklin bought a very nice diamond ring at the

José Maldonado Mercantile and slipped it on Grace's left hand. This wedding was a complete surprise for Franklin and Grace, as much as it was for Allison. Allison realized however that Grace could make her father happy.

After the wedding, Grace actually took Allison into her arms and whispered, "Allison, thank you for letting me have your father. I promise I will take care of him. When you come home from your honeymoon, I hope we can sit and talk. I want you to know who I am and I want to know all about you. Family is the most important thing in our lives and I want to be a part of yours."

⊞ ⊞ ⊞

Redmon and Allison rode out of Santa Fe pulling two packhorses. Allison was riding the Appaloosa mare that Redmon gave her. Redmon was still riding Lancer, but told Allison that he would have to retire the big stallion after this trip. He took Allison to see the Taos Pueblo and then the Rio Grande gorge on their way north. Each night they camped along a stream, bathed together, cooked their meal, lay in their blankets looking at the stars, and made love. Redmon thought Allison's body was so lithe, shapely, and smooth. In his mind, she was the epitome of what a woman should be.

Allison loved seeing the sights and especially the mountains. She was amazed as they rode along below the high peaks in the Colorado Rockies. Three weeks after leaving Sanda Fe thet rode into Central City and to the Brandais House. Audrey Brandais opened the door to Redmon's knocks.

When she recognized Redmon, she flew into his arms, "Oh, Redmon, you've come home! Red has been worried about you."

Finally, she broke the embrace and noticed Allison. Redmon took Allison's hand and brought her forward. "Audrey Brandais, I would like to introduce my wife Allison Drury. We met on her ranch in New Mexico. We fought some very bad men down there and fell in love in the process."

Audrey embraced Allison, "Allison, if Redmon loves you, you must be special. Welcome to Brandais House. Red is up at one of the mines. There is a saloon man here that has been giving us and other mine owners a difficult time. We have had one gold shipment stolen, but other owners have lost more than we have. There were no robberies until this Marvin La Master came to town. Red is worried because we have a wagon going to Denver tomorrow."

Audrey looked at Redmon, "Well, enough of that, Redmon. You know where your room is. Why don't you get your bags while Allison and I go to the kitchen for a nice cup of tea. That will give us a chance to get acquainted."

Redmon took their bags to the room he used before he rode south. Then he put their horses in the stable behind the house and gave them corn from a bin. He found Allison and Audrey laughing and talking as he entered the kitchen. He got a coffee mug and poured a cup of coffee from the stove. Audrey always had the pot hot for Red when he came home from the mines. Today was no different.

An hour later, Red Brandais came in the back door to the kitchen with a huge grin on his face. He had recognized Lancer and the Appaloosa mare in his stable. Redmon was up instantly, and he and Red were hugging and pounding each other on the back. Allison was impressed that the Brandaises cared a great deal about Redmon. As they sat over their coffee and tea, Redmon told his friends about riding into Santa Fe and discovering Wilfred Chatham. He explained that while sitting near him, he overheard Wilfred order his men to ride south and kill some people named Wilbanks so he could take their land. Redmon described how he followed the men and found them attacking the ranch headquarters of Allison and her father, Franklin.

He told Red and Audrey that he knew he loved Allison from the first time he met her, and even more so as they fought the Chatham hard cases together.

Allison described for Red and Audrey how Redmon took the dead attackers to the Chatham camp and placed them in the cook shack. She described the sword fight between Redmon and Wilfred Chatham when he came to demand giving up their ranch to him. Red hit the table with his fist when Allison described how the duel ended.

Red told Redmon about the saloon owner Marvin La Master who came to Central City along with his gang of thugs. The mine owners were sure La Master's men were doing the robberies. Red said he was worried because they would be sending a good load of gold ore to Denver the following morning.

"Red, I'll be riding along as the guard on that shipment," Redmon said. He saw Allison's look of fear and took her hand. "Allison, that wagon will be carrying our livelihood as well as Red and Audrey's. I'll shoot first and ask questions later, as they say. After all, we defeated Wilfred Chatham and his men. How hard could some saloon owner be?"

Allison helped Audrey prepare dinner for the four of them. While they were eating, Redmon explained how shocked he was in finding Wilfred Chatham in Santa Fe. Chatham's plot to kill the Wilbankses and take over their land had infuriated Redmon, especially with what Chatham had done to Redmon years before. Because he went undetected by his arch enemy, Redmon was able to do away with Chatham's hired killers until eventually killing Chatham himself. The plan to build a Chatham cattle empire had ended with the sword fight.

"So you finally got the bugger that started this whole thing. It's funny that you found him after ten years and so far from where you grew up," Red remarked.

As they finished their dinner, Redmon and Allison told of their wedding in Santa Fe. They related the story of how Allison's father fell in love with and married Grace Davis. All of this happening so quickly before Redmon and Allison left on their own honeymoon trip to Cental City.

✣ ✣ ✣

Back in Santa Fe, Franklin and Grace stayed one more night at the La Fonda Hotel. Grace didn't know what to expect for her wedding night with Franklin. Her first husband, Artimus Davis tended to be an indifferent lover, and after the war he unfortunately was not gentle with her. He came home angry after losing the war and took it out on Grace. He even joined a group called the Ku Klux Klan and rode with a group of former southern soldiers and officers as a nightrider. Artimus would hit her when she asked him why he would ride with such a group. She always felt unfulfilled after Artimus used her. That was the only way she could term what Artimus did to her, using. It hurt Grace deeply that the man she loved could be so harsh with her.

But Franklin was a different man. He took his time undressing Grace, which was new for her. She still possessed a trim body at forty-seven years of age and Franklin was excited when he finally gazed upon her. Their lovemaking was slow, deliberate, and mature. Grace found herself reaching feelings and emotions that she never experienced before. She shivered with anticipation as Franklin moved his hands over her body. She and Franklin reached completion together, which never happened for her before. "Grace, was that all right for you? It has been a very long time for me and I sure didn't want to disappoint you. I know we have both been married, but I think we need to always say what we think to each other. I believe deep love will come for us in time. I want you to be happy on the Circle W."

Tears were freely flowing from Grace's eyes after her new husband's short speech. She suddenly did something she surely would never have dreamed of before. As she moved her body over Franklin and looked down at him, she said, "Husband, you just made me reach feelings I have not experienced before. I never knew what real love should feel like. What you just gave me was wonderful. I will always tell you the truth about how I feel."

She lay on him and Franklin held her, knowing that he just received the ultimate gift of a fine woman. He realized that he could have the love of two women in his lifetime. His Corrine never really liked to be touched, always saying that God only intended the woman's body for making a child. Grace told him that she was filled with much love to give and wanted to feel his hands on her. They made love again, and then slept with him holding her close, which neither ever experienced with their former spouses. This was something new for both of them.

The following morning after breakfast Franklin bought a buckboard to carry Grace's trunks home, and they started south after buying trail supplies. They followed the trail that was now the stagecoach route and supply trail from Santa Fe to Roswell. They camped on the San Cristobal ranch the first night, reaching the Circle W late the following afternoon.

Camping on the trail was a new experience for Grace, but she loved doing it. She cooked their evening meal, and the newlyweds rolled up in their blankets. They looked up at the stars and listened to the coyotes calling in the distance. It was a clear, beautiful night. Grace told Franklin that this night would be one she would always fondly remember.

❖ ❖ ❖

Henry, Ralph, and Joe were there to meet Franklin and Grace when they got home, and it was a good homecoming. They were very surprised that their boss came home with a wife. Franklin also bought supplies in

Santa Fe so Henry took those to the kitchen. Ralph and Joe helped carry Grace's trunks to the master bedroom. Grace was excited by the house, and quickly realized that Franklin and the men would treat her like a queen on the Circle W. She did not have any idea what a ranch was, but looked forward to learning. She couldn't believe that she would not have to cook if she didn't want to.

Grace had written a long letter to her son from Santa Fe and told him of her marriage and where she would be living. She had no idea of her son Brent's negative reaction when learning that she married someone she barely knew. The response that she eventually received from him was hurtful and disappointing for her. Franklin held her while she cried after she read the letter out loud to him. "Grace, I am sorry that your son sent that letter. With some time to reflect, he may realize that his words have hurt you. But, you know I love you, Grace Wilbanks, and will always protect you! Give this wound a little time to heal."

✦ ✦ ✦

Redmon held Allison and kissed her before climbing on the ore-laden wagon seat next to the driver. He was carrying his volcanic carbine loaded and ready along with his pistol. He decided to wear his buckskins even though Allison always told him they smelled bad, and she scrunched her nose when he scooped her up in his arms while wearing them.

The wagon was halfway to Denver when Redmon noticed some movement ahead. He told the driver to get ready for some trouble. Three men came riding at the wagon from around a curve in the road with their pistols drawn. Redmon leveled his carbine and shot one man quickly. He levered and shot the other two so fast they never had a chance. The La Master men were only able to get off one shot and it missed badly. Redmon put so many bullets in and around them that they lost their ability to retaliate until it was too late. The driver was staring at Redmon when the shooting was over.

"Mr. Brandais told us at the mine that you were hell on wheels with that rifle. Now I believe it. Our last driver and guard were killed and never got an even chance. Those were La Master's men all right, Mr. Drury, cause I have seen them with him at his saloon. Thanks fer being with me. I like being alive!" Barney Long said.

The three would-be robbers were left where they lay and the ore wagon went on into Denver to the mill. The ore would be crushed and the gold separated and delivered to the bank.

While in Denver, Redmon checked at the bank and discovered that his account grew substantially in his absence. He put Allison's name on the account as the co-owner and arranged for bank drafts in both their names.

He wanted Allison to be able to spend some money if she saw something she desired.

Late in the day, Redmon and Barney were back in Central City and Allison, Red, and Audrey were waiting for them at the Brandais-Drury mining offices. When Redmon climbed off the wagon seat, Allison was in his arms.

Red was grinning, "Partner, you must have done a job. La Master's toughs were hauled in a few hours ago and ole Marvin is fit to be tied. Also, we got us a new sheriff hired today and he looks to be solid and capable. Man, oh, man, this is goin' to get interesting! His name is Reid Folley and he already braced Marvin La Master in his saloon. Stuck his pistol barrel up Marvin's nose for all to see. Maybe 'our women will be safe on the street again. Boy, oh, boy, this has been some kind of day!"

The excitement wasn't over for the day. As they sat down to dinner, Audrey announced that she was going to have Red's baby in about eight months. Red Brandais, the confirmed bachelor, was going to have a real family. Red jumped up from his chair and swung Audrey around in a circle in the dining room while she laughed along with Redmon and Allison. Dinner that night was a real celebration.

Later, Red quietly thanked Redmon for making him develop the mines in the way they had. Then he took Redmon's hand, "The day you came up that canyon and ran those men off was the best day of my life because you helped me meet Audrey. She has changed my life. I look forward to every day now and what it will bring. Redmon, you are lucky that you found Allison. She is such a good girl. We are both lucky men."

Two days later Redmon and Allison were in a fine room in the Brown Palace in Denver. Redmon was surprised by how much Denver had grown from the last time he saw it. Redmon arranged to have a dressmaker fit Allison for three gowns and accessories to go with them. While Allison was being fitted for her gowns, Redmon went shopping and discovered a new jewelry store close to the Brown Palace. He bought an elegant string of pearls, and a gold necklace with diamonds to match her wedding ring.

After making his purchases, Redmon went to the Brownley Mining offices and renewed his acquaintance with Reece Brownley. Reece invited Redmon and Allison to dinner and then to attend the theater with himself, his wife Victoria, along with their son Chad and his wife Barbara.

That evening, a carriage came to the Brown Palace and collected Redmon and Allison. She was wearing her one nice dress that she brought from home. Allison could hardly wait until the new gowns were ready. She was very excited as they were escorted to the Brownley's home. When Allison saw the Brownley's large, two-story home that she thought was a mansion, not just a house, she blurted, "Oh, Redmon, it is so nice. I'm not sure I belong here! My dress isn't nice enough for this!"

Redmon comforted Allison with his words, "Do not worry, Allison. You will love Victoria Brownley, and she does not put on pretentions. Barbara, the Brownley's daughter-in-law, is also a ranch girl from New Mexico. There is a story you will like hearing about Barbara and what she did to save Chad on her parents' ranch in New Mexico, and then at the theater to stop a killer."

A beautiful young woman met them at the door and held out her hand, "Hello, you must be the Drurys. I am Barbara Brownley. Chad and I just came from the ranch. Mom Victoria is checking on the dinner. Come in, we will all meet in the sitting room for refreshments."

Redmon introduced Allison and then himself. "Barbara, Allison is also a New Mexico ranch girl as you were. I'm sure she would like to hear how you met Chad. Also, I want to hear of your adventure at the theater with the infamous Wilfred Donaldson. I dealt with a Wilfred of my own down on Allison's ranch. She can tell you about that adventure."

Barbara laughed a tinkling little laugh. "I'm sure we will all have some interesting stories to tell. I can hardly wait to hear about your ranch in New Mexico, Allison. My parents' Slash S ranch is located close to White Oaks, a mining town in the south."

"I know where that is," replied Allison. "Our Circle W is some ninety miles northwest of White Oaks. We are located two days south of Santa Fe."

Dinner with the Brownleys was fun. Victoria Brownley was a beautiful woman, but she was also so nice and down to earth. Many stories were told at the table. Allison was amazed when she heard the story of Barbara saving Chad from two gunshot wounds after finding him on her parents' ranch in New Mexico.

Chad related the story of his new young wife carrying a small pistol into the theater and shooting Wilfred Donaldson from across the theater when he was aiming at Reese Brownley from a balcony box.

Redmon told of helping Red Brandais run four of Wilfred Donaldson's men away from what were now the Brandais-Drury mines.

Just before they were preparing to leave for the theater, Redmon brought out a small wrapped package and gave it to Allison. She was wearing a deep purple dress that her mother helped her sew before she died. Allison had been saving the dress for a special occasion, and this was it. The dress highlighted her beauty. Allison's long auburn hair was arranged on the top of her head with strands falling provocatively around her ears. When she opened the package, there was a velvet-covered case containing the gold and diamond necklace. Her eyes grew large and instantly she was in Redmon's arms. "Oh,

Redmon, it's the most beautiful thing I have ever seen. I never dreamed to wear something like this!" Redmon put the necklace around her neck and secured the clasp as the Brownleys looked on.

When the Brownleys and Drurys entered the theater foyer, all conversation stopped. No one in Denver could ever remember seeing three more beautiful women in one place at one time. The locals wanted to know who the new couple might be. Allison, for some reason, did not know just how beautiful she really was. She was somewhat self-conscious because her dress was not as glamorous as those worn by Victoria and Barbara Brownley. Redmon, tall and distinguished with Allison on his arm, told her not to worry for she was beautiful no matter what she wore.

The women in the foyer were concentrating on the new young woman's face, then the dress she was wearing, and finally the beautiful gold and diamond necklace. Some of the young women who were once escorted by Redmon were disappointed when they saw him with the auburn-haired beauty, and even more disappointed as they noticed the diamond ring on her left hand.

The Brownleys introduced the Drurys to many of their friends and fellow mine owners. Most of the people had heard of the Brandais-Drury mines but Redmon Drury was really a mystery man for them. Now they could put a face to the man who recently stopped a robbery attempt on one of his ore wagons coming to Denver. While meeting some mine owners and their wives, Redmon and Allison were invited along with the Brownleys to a soirée at one of the other mine owner's home. For Allison, everything that was happening was like actually living out one of her childhood dreams. Redmon had already exposed her to experiences she never thought she would ever have. The gowns he arranged to have fitted for her would be so wonderful she couldn't imagine getting to wear them. She so wished that she was wearing one of them on this wonderful night. The theater performance was a traveling troop doing Shakespeare's *King Lear*.

That night in their room, Allison took the initiative and made love to Redmon. When they reached the summit together, they called out each other's name. Allison collapsed onto Redmon's chest and he held her. "Allison, love, I am going to want to see you dressed in a fancy dress more often. That was amazing! I will look forward to seeing you in one of the gowns when they arrive. After the soirée, I think we should start south and decide what to do on our land. I have some ideas but we need to make all our decisions together."

The next morning, Redmon woke and watched Allison sleep. He was still having a difficult time with the fact that he found her because of his hated enemy Wilfred Chatham. She was so beautiful with her shinning auburn hair spread around her face on the pillow. The fact that she did not have any idea how beautiful she truly was made her even more attractive to Redmon. He loved every minute they spent together. Redmon had experienced other beautiful women such as Roselind who was beautiful at fifteen years old and he was sure she was even more beautiful now even after having two children. He also lay with a Huron maiden, Pretty Flower, and she was just that, statuesque and pretty. There were others along the way, but none could match Allison. She held his heart in her hands and he wanted to hold and touch her all the time. Then he realized that her bright hazel eyes were staring at him. He pulled her to him and she responded.

A few days later, the first gown was delivered to the Brown Palace and Allison was able to try it on. Redmon simply smiled when he saw her, for he knew it would be like this for her. Allison wore the deep burgundy gown that night and Redmon presented her with the string of pearls, which surprised her again. The Brownleys came for the young couple again in their carriage. The soirée was being held at the home of a mine owner named Samuel Wilkinson. There were buffet tables for the meal, and then dancing. This would be a new experience for Redmon and Allison. They would learn if they could dance together. Franklin taught her to waltz even though her mother Corrine was against dancing. Her father made learning to dance a game and fun. Her father told her that they used to attend box suppers in Georgia when he was a young man, and then dance afterwards.

Allison warned Redmon that she might not be a very good dancer. When the music started they moved to the edge of the ballroom and tentatively swayed to the music. As their confidence grew, they danced along with the other couples. Soon they learned that they danced well together. It began to be fun and they started to whirl around the floor with everyone else. By the time the third dance began, Redmon and Allison were having great fun. They were finally confident enough to change with Chad and Barbara for a dance, but Redmon and Allison quickly realized that they belonged together.

Barbara and Allison went shopping together the next afternoon and shared their stories of growing up in New Mexico and how they found their men. Barbara was mesmerized when Allison described the sword fight between Redmon and Wilfred Chatham. Barbara was amazed with the story of how Redmon found the man in Santa Fe that had hurt him ten years earlier.

Allison's other new gowns were delivered to the hotel within the week. Barbara Brownley was there to help Allison try them on. Wearing the purple gown, Allison's creamy shoulders, neck, and the swell of her breasts were shown to perfection. Both Barbara and Redmon could only say, "My goodness!" when they observed Allison in the gown. That evening Allison wore the deep purple gown with her diamond necklace to a dinner party.

The morning after the dinner party, Redmon and Allison rode back to Central City. When they reached the Brandais House, they learned that things were changing quickly after Reid Folley took over and was hired as sheriff. Marvin La Master engineered the murder of a mine owner named Stephen Grayson. Sheriff Folley was forced to shoot and wound Marvin La Master who was now in jail awaiting trial for murder.

Redmon and Allison rode south with a promise to return in one year once their ranch headquarters was built.

⸎ ⸎ ⸎

The letter came by ship to Gretna Green and then to Drury Manor. Joselyn Drury was so excited to get another letter from Redmon. She was relieved to know he was alive for there was no word from him for more than a year. She opened the letter, stunned at first, then amazed, as tears flowed freely down her beautiful face. When Red Roland found his wife crying and holding the letter to her breast, he moved to her side. "What has happened, Joselyn? Why are you crying so?"

"Oh, Roland, Redmon is alive and he is married. It's all here in the letter," Joselyn answered.

So she read the letter again for Red Roland, but more slowly this time. Redmon told them of his partnership with Red Brandais and of their striking a rich vein of gold in the mountains of Colorado. He explained that once he was sure his partner was secure and the mines were running smoothly, he grew restless. He decided to head south from Central City and finally arrived in Santa Fe where he discovered none other than Wilfred Chatham. He described sitting close to Wilfred and listening to him plot the deaths of a ranch family so Wilfred could take their land. That drew a snort and grumble from Red Roland. When Redmon explained that Wilfred never realized who was sitting next to him, they both laughed. Redmon told of deciding to follow Wilfred Chatham's cutthroats and being forced to kill one who was firing down on some ranch buildings. He explained that that was when he met Allison Wilbanks and her father Franklin.

Redmon went through the rest of the story of fighting the Chatham men and finally the sword fight with Wilfred Chatham. His written words were, "Father, I carved a capital D on Wilfred's forehead and exposed to him the brand he gave me so he would finally know who he was facing before I killed him. He never knew until that moment."

Redmon went on to explain that he and Allison fell in love during the months they spent fighting the Chatham men who were trying to take the Wilbanks' land. "Father, an old acquaintance of yours is now with us. He was the cook at the Chatham camp but became disgusted with Wilfred Chatham and came over to our side. He told us his name was Amos Sudder until he learned my name. Then he revealed that his real name was Henry Sudderth, and that you and mother helped him when you were both young men. Henry is now part of the Circle W, the ranch owned by my father-in-law. Allison and I were married in Santa Fe a week after the final fight with Wilfred Chatham. Mother and Father, you will be proud of Allison for she is everything you would want in a daughter—intelligent, wise, and honest to a fault."

Redmon did not describe Allison's beauty for he was formulating a plan that he would not even reveal to Allison until their ranch headquarters was complete. Then Redmon told his parents that he filed on part of the land that Wilfred Chatham once held, including his building site. When Redmon explained that he and Allison now owned some forty thousand acres of land, the Drurys were stunned. They did not understand the Western concept of ranching, and certainly did not understand the idea that one person could own that much land. To learn that you could file on land and own it was unbelievable to his parents. This America must truly be an amazing place. First, the gold mines and now this revelation about the amount of land that their son and new daughter-in-law owned. It was astounding for the Drurys when they just hoped that their son would somehow survive in North America. It was abundantly clear that their son did far more than just survive in that faraway land. Redmon wrote that he would write again once their ranch house was finished so he could describe it to them.

A week later another letter came to Drury Manor and it was from Allison. Allison, in a flowing hand, described in detail everything Redmon did for the Wilbankses after reaching the Circle W. It seemed that Redmon downplayed most of his deeds, which did not surprise Red Roland and Joselyn. Allison told them everything in great detail and they realized that the tale could be made into an adventure story. She even told them some of the things that Redmon told her about his adventures in Canada, Montana, Wyoming, and Colorado, which made clear that Redmon also down played those adventures in his previous letters. Joselyn loved reading Allison's wonderful flowing handwriting. She seemed to be able to describe the action so vividly that you felt as though you were actually there with Redmon and then Allison.

At the next Drury family gathering Joselyn read both letters for Roddrick, Roselind, Madeline, and Rory MacDougal, Madeline's new husband and the son of a Scottish nobleman. The family hung on every word in Redmon's letter.

When he wrote of his marriage to Allison Wilbanks, Roselind's eyes misted and everyone at the table noticed. When Redmon described the amount of land that he and Allison owned, the family was again astounded. In his letter, Redmon humbly said that when Wilfred Chatham finally came to the Circle W, he challenged him to a fight with swords and that Redmon won.

When Joselyn read Allison's words, a change came over the table. The family was completely spellbound with the tale Allison wove. Allison's writing actually told a story that they could see in their minds, as Red Roland and Joselyn were able to do when they read the letter for the first time. Her descriptions of Redmon's trials on the trails from Canada to New Mexico were brought to life for all of them. She told of the fistfight and shootout in Helena, Montana. They laughed when she related Redmon's stories of Rosie, the Morgan mare, attempting to bite Redmon, and pulling off the saddle blanket with her teeth and throwing it on the ground when Redmon tried to saddle her. They gasped at the tale of Redmon fighting off the Sioux Indian brave, but laughed at how Rosie protected Redmon by kicking another brave in the head. They marveled when Allison described the beautiful spotted Nez Percé horses Redmon acquired in the Indian attack. They liked hearing about gold mining and the partnership of Redmon with Red Brandais in Colorado.

The Drurys were astounded when Allison described the Colorado Rockies with peaks that reached fourteen and fifteen thousand feet and were covered with snow year around. They roared when Allison told the tale of Redmon taking the dead cutthroat Nate Burleson and sitting him at the table in the Chatham cook shack as if staring off into space, only to be discovered by an old friend of Red Roland.

Allison told the story of Redmon entering the pantry at the Chatham cook shack and cleaning it out twice, bringing the food to the Circle W where they had been under siege for months until Redmon came and helped them. They laughed when Allison told the tale of Henry Sudderth coming to the Circle W and offering to cook for them since they already took all his food anyway. The description of the sword fight between Redmon and Wilfred Chatham was described in much greater detail in Allison's letter and they hung on every word. She told of Redmon lightly using the tip of his sword to carve a capital D in Wilfred Chatham's forehead, and then telling Wilfred what he just did and revealing the brand on his chest for Wilfred to see. She said that Wilfred never knew whom Redmon was facing until that very moment. Roddrick jumped up, threw out his fist, and yelled, "Yes!"

Then Roddrick sat, looked at Roselind, and said, "I'm sorry dear. I know this must be difficult to hear that your brother is dead."

Roselind replied, "Rod, do not fret, for my brother died that night in the stable at Chatham. He ordered the deaths of our new sister-in-law and her father. Wilfred finally received his reward in this life. I told him ten years ago that he would eventually reside in hell and that he would be put there by Redmon's hand. I believe my prophecy came true and he is suffering the fires of hell at this very moment!"

Allison described the wonderful gowns that Redmon commissioned a dressmaker to fit her for, and the gold and diamond necklace and beautiful string of pearls he bought for her. She told of Red and Audrey Brandais and their house in Central City, Colorado, that Redmon helped build. She described their friends, the Brownleys, and the absolute beauty of Victoria Brownley who was from England, and the theater performances they attended together. They liked hearing about the soirées, and dinner parties that Redmon and Allison attended, and the dancing. They laughed when Allison said that she and Redmon were not sure that they could even dance together the first time without falling down.

All the ladies loved hearing about the clothes, the soirées, and the theater events that she and Redmon attended in the place called Denver.

The letter finished by describing Santa Fe and the La Fonda Hotel along with her and Redmon's wedding in the Loretto Chapel with its wonderful free-standing wooden staircase. When the letter was finished, they all sat for a moment. Then Rory blurted, "I would be wonderin' if this lass Allison would be ugly fer yer Redmon never was tellin' what she might be lookin' like." To which Madeline punched him in the shoulder. "What, Maddie? I was jist wonderin' if she be a bonnie lass like yerself or no. One thing is clear. Redmon's wee wife is a bloody fine letter writer," which caused a good-natured laugh around the Drury table.

✿ ✿ ✿

During the trip to Central City and Denver, Redmon and Allison decided to call their ranch the 'R bar A'. When they reached Santa Fe, they ordered a branding iron made for that brand. While in Santa Fe, Redmon met an army surgeon and asked him if he could perform a task for him. Redmon showed the brand on his chest to Dr. Charles Lacey and asked if he could remove the C. Hours later the hated C was gone from Redmon's chest. Doctor Lacey told Redmon and Allison that he had been a regimental surgeon in the Union Army during the Civil War. He wanted to see the west when the war ended. The surgeon actually did a miraculous job of cutting, rearranging, and sewing the skin to remove the hated brand. Allison insisted that she be there with her husband during the operation. She was amazed by his tolerance for pain as he refused the surgeon's offer of laudanum to dull the pain while he performed the surgury. Redmon's explanation was that he endured the pain when the brand was put on his chest, so he could endure it when it was removed. Allison held his left hand as Dr. Lacey worked with his scalpel first and then his sewing needle and cat gut.

Redmon insisted on giving Charles Lacey a hundred dollars for the surgery. Holding five twenty dollar gold pieces, Charles Lacey watched as the tall, broad-shouldered man walked across the plaza holding the hand of the beautiful young woman. He would have liked to hear the story of how the man received the brand. No explanation was forthcoming, so the doctor let the matter drop. It was clear to the Army doctor after seeing it that this Redmon Drury carried this C brand on his chest for quite a number of years, probably from boyhood.

The doctor turned and flipped one of the gold pieces in the air and caught it. He thought he did an excellent job removing the C brand from Redmon's chest. He was as amazed as Allison by Redmon's tolerance for pain. In a few months, there would be some scarring but the brand would no longer show.

Redmon and Allison bought supplies at the José Maldonado Store and asked the storeowner if he knew of any men who might want to work on the building crew for a house south of Santa Fe.

"I know of some men who would like to work. They were on the building crew down there before. Señor Drury, were you the ghost they spoke of?" asked the storeowner.

Redmon smiled. "Señor Maldonado, I was at the camp twice and left some deposits for them, but I know nothing of a ghost. If the men want to work for a fair wage, have them come to see us." Redmon spoke in Spanish.

José Maldonado was surprised, and then he grinned. "Señor Drury, I think you will have all the workers you need. I will see to it."

Because Allison was completely impressed with the water closets in the Brownley house, Redmon made the decision to order four sets of porcelain fixtures along with all the pipe needed to plumb two houses and a bunkhouse. When they left the store, Redmon noticed something that caught his attention. He took Allison's hand and pulled her down the street.

A man was standing next to what looked like metal scaffolding on wheels with four mules harnessed to the thing. It was a drilling rig for a water well, the man told them. Redmon asked some questions about how it worked and the man explained the process to him. He turned to Allison and asked, "What do you think about having some wells drilled on the ranch?"

"We always go through some dry periods each year. Wells could save our cattle when we get into drought times." She replied to his question.

So the Drurys arranged to have Lewis Thompson bring his rig to the R bar A and drill three wells. That night after leaving Santa Fe, they camped at the same creek on the San Cristobal ranch where they camped before. Redmon was sore from his surgery but never complained. Allison knew that he was hurting. She changed the bandage and applied some medicinal salve that Doctor Lacey had given them. There had been some bleeding into the original bandage, but again Redmon never said a word.

They rode into the Circle W and Allison immediately noticed the change in her father. He appeared to be so happy, and it was apparent that Grace already made a difference for him. After hugs all around and taking care of the horses, Redmon and Allison told everyone about their trip to Colorado. The following morning they would all ride to the former Chatham building site and decide if that was where they wanted to build their new house using the existing structure.

Henry cooked an excellent dinner that night, and the conversation around the table was enjoyable. Redmon and Allison described for her father and his wife their trip to Central City and Denver.

Early the following morning the whole Circle W crew rode out. Even Grace rode with them, wearing pants, shirt, boots, and a hat that Allison provided. Henry packed a picnic lunch. When they reached the old building site, the cook shack and builders' tents were still there with tent flaps whipping in the breeze. Franklin chuckled when Henry pointed out the bullet holes that Redmon had put in some of the tents.

⁂

Redmon looked around and wondered why Wilfred Chatham had picked this site. It was wide open and would be blown by the wind from every direction. Redmon already figured out that the wind blew hard during different parts of the year, especially in the spring.

Henry spoke up, "I tried to tell that Chatham fellow once when he was here that this was the wrong spot to build, but he said he wanted everyone in the area to know where the Chatham cattle empire was located. I tried to tell the man that there was a better place only a half mile from here but he wouldn't listen."

"Let's go have a look at this place you are talking about, Henry," Redmon said.

They found the opening to a shallow valley. There was the escarpment above on three sides much like on the Circle W. Redmon spotted green grass up at the head of the valley. They rode and found a good spring located there.

Redmon and Allison walked the valley hand in hand as the others watched. Suddenly, they saw Allison jump into Redmon's arms. When they came back to the spring, Redmon asked Henry, "How hard would it be to move the cook shack and tents to the mouth of this valley? Allison is going to have her house built here. We're going to use all that quarried block to build on this spot!" Suddenly, everyone was talking at once making suggestions.

A week later, wagons were hauling the stone blocks from the dismantled Chatham house to the valley. The night of the picnic in the valley, Redmon and Allison sat and designed the house they would build. She could not believe the size of the house Redmon planned to build for her. As it happened, Grace was an outstanding artist. She saw the rough sketches Redmon was making and asked if she could help. Soon she was making detailed drawings from Redmon's rough sketches. When Grace was finished, they all stared at a completed plan for the two-story house. Allison hugged Grace, thanking her, and then threw her arms around Redmon's neck because the house was going to be wonderful.

The crew from Santa Fe came out and went to work. A cousin from the original crew came down the Rio

Grande, and most of the workers from Socorro also came back. One crew went to the Gallinas Mountains to the south and cut more logs, hauling them back to the new building site. More supplies were brought from Santa Fe and the cook shack was moved with Henry in charge. Henry would cook for the crews while Grace cooked at home. She confided to Allison that having Henry as the cook really spoiled her.

One afternoon Grace and Allison sat and talked. Grace confided that her former husband did not treat her very well during their marriage. She just did not know any better until she married and was with Allison's father. She told Allison that her first husband, Artimus, always made fun of her wanting to draw and paint so she did it in secret and hid her work. Grace grew excited when she told Allison that Franklin encouraged everything she wanted to do, and she already loved him almost to distraction.

"Allison, the day your father found me in the La Fonda dining room was the best day of my life. I have never been as happy as I am here! I am disappointed to say this, but my son is much like my first husband."

Allison thought back to the years she was growing up with her mother, Corrine, and suddenly remembered the times that her mother put down her father's enthusiasm. Her mother often refused to do things that would have been fun for Franklin and Allison.

Her mother was constantly quoting the Bible and the excesses of mortal man. Her mother actually warned her before she died to beware of men because they believed that women were only put on this earth to be used only for their carnal pleasures. Allison realized how wrong her mother was when she thought of Redmon and the pleasure he gave her.

Allison took Grace's hand. "Grace, I have come to realize that my mother, although a good woman, never loved my father in the way that he deserved. I only ask for my father to be loved the way he should be, whole-heartedly."

The two women held one another and Grace whispered, "You are the daughter I always wished for, Allison. Your father has made me into a complete woman for the first time in my life."

⊞ ⊞ ⊞

As the house went up, it exceeded all of Allison's expectations. It was going to be big and nice. Redmon designed a huge living room, study, and dining room next to a big kitchen that Henry helped design. There were pantries, also. A large master suite with bedroom, dressing room, bathing room, and closets would be included. A curved staircase would lead to five bedrooms and a bathroom on the second floor. Redmon and

Allison worked alongside the crew and talked to them in Spanish, which gained their respect and loyalty.

Franklin and the ranch crew pitched in. At night Franklin went home to Grace, and she often rode to the worksite and helped Henry feed the building crew. Franklin was proud that Grace and Allison seemed to be growing close during their time together.

With the number of men they were able to put to work, the new house went up quickly. Two months after starting, the roof beams were put in place. As it was going up, Allison thought the house was an engineering wonder.

Redmon, Ralph, and Joe dug out the spring. They built in a spring box and buried pipe from the spring box to a large tank that would gravity feed water to the house from further up the valley. There were two fine carpenters on the crew who built the kitchen cabinets, and a kitchen table and chairs. Franklin took Grace and Allison to Santa Fe so they could buy or order all the furniture for the new house. Allison bought all the window glass needed for the house and a bunkhouse which they would build with the leftover block from the original Chatham house. Three months after beginning the building, the house was completely finished.

Allison ran from the kitchen to the bedrooms to the bathrooms, trying all the faucet taps and flushing the toilets, clapping her hands to the delight of Redmon when they all worked. The curved staircase that Redmon and the carpenters built was beautiful. The craftsmanship throughout the house was outstanding.

Franklin wanted to know what Redmon planned for the extra set of bathroom fixtures he had ordered. Redmon had begun the habit of calling Franklin "Pop" as Allison always did. "Pop and Grace, the extra set of those fixtures is going to your house. We're going to bring you into the modern world. And besides, I believe Grace is tired of that old outhouse." Instantly, Grace was hugging both Redmon and Allison.

The building crew began construction of the bunkhouse while Redmon and the Circle W crew built and plumbed a large bathroom in the Circle W headquarters. They also built in a spring box and tank to get water to the plumbed kitchen and new water closet. Grace and Franklin were beaming from ear to ear when it was all finished. Redmon had discovered something in José Maldonado's store in Santa Fe and bought three of them. It was a coal-fired water heater invented by a couple that owned a ranch to the southeast near the county seat of Lincoln. The couple, named Talley, was marketing the water heaters through their company in St. Louis. Redmon built one of the heaters into the new house, and they built a small room on the side of the Circle W house to hold another water heater. The new

R bar A house and the Circle W house would have hot and cold running water, a rarity in the West for the time.

The Brownley house in Denver was the inspiration for the plumbing and bathrooms. As it turned out, there was a coal mine located to the southwest of the two ranches at a place called Carthage. Carthage was along the stagecoach route from Socorro, located on the Rio Grande River, to Lincoln, the new county seat. The coal for the water heaters was supplied by that Carthage mine.

Redmon and Allison moved all their belongings to the new house and took up residence. It was agreed that every Sunday, dinner would be shared at one of the ranch houses. The Drurys had shared this same tradition in England.

❖ ❖ ❖

Their first night in their big new bed was amazing for Redmon and Allison. They gave themselves over completely to their lovemaking, followed by bathing together in the big porcelain tub. Redmon marveled again at the beauty of his wife as he carefully explored her wonderful body. Allison responded in kind to every touch from her husband. When they finally came together, they moved as one, giving in to their passion.

During their first month in their new home, the bunkhouse was going up quickly. Redmon figured out that there would be enough block left to build a springhouse to store meat and keep it cool. Allison wanted a chicken coop for fresh eggs so Redmon built one for her, bringing the chickens in from Santa Fe. When the bunkhouse was almost completed, part of the crew began building a rock barn using rock from the escarpment.

Redmon wanted to bring his horses home from the Circle W, so he began building a set of corrals, taking a crew to the Gallinas Mountains to cut posts. Winter was coming and Redmon was everywhere helping the crews to finish the headquarters. Allison told Redmon that the short, cedar wood from the trees on the ranch was good for winter fires, so a crew went to the low hills and cut wagon loads of that wood for the house fireplaces and bunkhouse stove. Lewis Thompson drilled the three water wells in various locations on the R bar A, and built windmills over them with tanks to catch the water pumped from the wells. With water on the ranch, the R bar A was ready for cattle.

One of the Spanish workers told Redmon about the Spanish cattle along the Rio Grande and where he could buy them. With a wagon that Henry Sudderth turned into a chuck wagon, Redmon, Allison, and the Circle W crew made the trip west to Socorro and bought cattle. They worked their way up the Rio Grande and bought more. Franklin also bought some of the Spanish cattle to put with his longhorns. The Spanish cattle were a more compact, shorter breed than the rangy longhorn. A month after the Rio Grande trip, the Drury's R bar A was finished and there were cattle on their range wearing the R bar A brand.

The Drurys settled in for the winter. Henry Sudderth decided to stay and cook for Redmon and Allison. They also hired two vaqueros, José Ruiz and Joseph Alvarez, as ranch hands. Both young men were jovial and easy going. The time around the meal table was always enjoyable. José and Joseph could still not believe how well they were treated on the R bar A. The bunkhouse with its bathroom was amazing. It was a luxury they were not accustomed to enjoying on other ranches.

✸ ✸ ✸

Lord Reginald, Lady Lydia, and Mortimer Chatham now called the former Dudley Manor and its lands, Chatham Hall. Doctor Seth Jenson, who was the Dudley's family physician for many years, accused Wilfred Chatham of murdering both Sir Thomas Dudley and Melissa Dudley Chatham. She was only twenty-six years old and in perfect health until she married Wilfred Chatham. Doctor Jenson had soon noticed that Melissa's skin displayed the same odd-colored tint that Sir Dudley exhibited when he died so quickly. Doctor Jenson was sure Wilfred used some kind of poison to do away with them both. Unfortunately, he could prove nothing against Wilfred

Chatham, but he speculated openly when Reginald, Lydia, and Mortimer quickly moved into Dudley Manor directly after Melissa was buried. When the Chathams immediately changed the name of the manor, it fueled the beliefs of the local nobelmen and townspeople that Dr. Jenson was correct about the murders. Mortimer was the Chatham who was sent to deal with the doctor.

Before Seth Jenson realized that he was being baited and challenged, he was fighting a duel with Mortimer Chatham. Mortimer goaded Seth Jenson into calling the Chathams murderers in front of two noblemen. Mortimer chose swords because he was considered an expert with the blade, as was Wilfred. Mortimer dispatched Dr. Seth Jenson quickly, but the rumors of murder remained. The Chathams found themselves with a cloud of suspicion over them that would remain for years to come. There were also those that termed the duel as murder, set up to quiet the good doctor and keep him from talking about Wilfred Chatham. The killing of the doctor did not help the Chathams' reputation in middle England.

Then Wilfred went off to America and wrote to his family that he was in the process of setting up a cattle empire in a place called the New Mexico Territory. Englishmen were investing large sums of money in cattle operations in the western United States. Western Colorado, Wyoming, and Montana had large cattle spreads funded by English noblemen. He also described the house he was building that would look just like the original Chatham Manor which had been built close to the Eden River.

Then for some reason, the British Chathams received not a single letter from Wilfred for well over a year. He usually kept them apprised of his efforts to build a manor house and a cattle empire in the western United States. They finally wrote to the last address he gave, which was a place called the La Fonda Hotel in Santa Fe, New Mexico Territory, but received no reply for a another year. Finally, a short letter came informing the Chathams that Wilfred Chatham left the hotel suddenly. He did not come back. The short letter said that it was rumored in Santa Fe that Wilfred Chatham died on land well to the south of Santa Fe. The letter was signed by the manager of the hotel. Sir Reginald now considered himself as the new lord of Chatham Hall and its lands. However the Chathams did not know that members of the family of the late Sir Thomas Dudley and Melissa were working behind the scenes to wrest the former Dudley lands away from the Chathams, who they considered to have stolen those lands by murder.

⌗ ⌗ ⌗

In Castle MacDougal, Madeline Drury MacDougal was not happy. Rory MacDougal was dashing in the beginning of their courtship and had made so many promises to Madeline before they were married, but as time passed the relationship deteriorated between the young married couple. Rory became abusive toward her. He used her hard when she gave herself to her husband, but she always felt unfulfilled and mistreated afterward. Rory left bruises on her body and always made her think it was her fault afterward. Madeline was just thankful that no children resulted from her union with Rory. She never said anything to her family when they got together, which was becoming less and less frequent.

Rory finally refused to take her south to Drury Manor to see her parents. Then Madeline learned that Rory was using one of the MacDougal chambermaids. Madeline was now twenty-three years old but felt older. She was losing weight and did not look well. She decided that she was slowly sinking as low as she might possibly go. Madeline was never truly accepted by the MacDougal clan because she was English. Some even called Madeline the "Stinking Sassenach."

The chambermaid, Moira MacLean, was constantly reminding Madeline that she was taking Madeline's man from her. This development was actually good, Madeline decided, because Rory was not beating on her if he was with Moira and bedding her. Thankfully, Rory did not use her any longer because he seemed to be satisfied with Moira. The problem was that Madeline felt like a prisoner in Castle MacDougal.

Another real problem for Madeline was that one of the MacDougal men, Shamus MacDougal, seemed to think that he could use her. After all, Rory was lying with Moira MacLean. Then one day, the MacDougal men brought the body of Rory back to the castle. He was shot and killed by one of the MacDonald clan while trying to steal their cattle. Soon after Rory was buried, his parents made it clear that they wanted Madeline gone from the castle unless she was willing to take cousin Shamus into her bed. She refused so Enis provided a poor palfrey to ride for Madeline to return to Drury Manor.

With a few clothes that she could carry in two large sacks, Madeline started south early on the morning after the burial of her husband. Moira MacLean was there and screamed at Madeline that she was the one that caused Moira's man to be killed. The chambermaid called her a witch and wished Madeline ill luck as she rode away from the castle.

The MacDougals did not know that Madeline carried a small pistol that Roddrick provided for her when she first came north as a young bride. He taught her to load and shoot it. She was dropping through a pass out of Scotland when she realized that she was being followed. When she knew that she was well into England, Madeline rode into some trees next to a brook that flowed from the highlands. She tied the palfrey up to a tree. Kneeling, Madeline dipped her cupped hand into the brook and drank deeply. Then she moved her horse closer to a tree she could use for cover. With her pistol cocked and ready hidden in the folds of her skirts, she waited. Madeline heard the approach of the horse and suddenly there was Shamus MacDougal grinning when he finally located her next to the tree. "Well, well, there ye be, wee lass. Ye almost escaped me. I was planin' te have ye at the castle don't ye know. Maddie lass, ye know ye'll be goin' back te Castle MacDougal te be me woman. First, though, I'll have ye right here te teach ye how twill be between us."

He climbed off his horse and walked toward her. He was wearing the kilt and cap displaying the MacDougal tartan colors.

Madeline waited until she knew she could not miss, raised the pistol, and shot Shamus MacDougal. The surprise on his face was something she would never forget. His look changed from one of leering satisfaction to that of fear in an instant.

He stood for a moment looking at Madeline, and then crumpled to the heath. Madeline waited long enough to make sure he didn't move then climbed on the palfrey and rode away south. Half a mile later she broke down and cried for having killed a man, even though she knew that she just saved herself from the brutality of Shamus MacDougal, a reputation he earned among the women of the MacDougal clan.

Dusk was descending when Madeline reached Drury Manor. She gave the palfrey to one of the stablemen who greeted her, but he gave her a questioning look when he saw her alone and on such a poor horse. Her good Morgan mare was one that the MacDougals kept and refused to let her ride home. With her sacks of clothes in tow, she made her way to the back door of the manor house.

When she entered the kitchen, there was a squeal from her old nanny Agnes Gates. Madeline ran to her, sobbing with relief. Agnes was the first to notice how thin Madeline was under her cloak and held her away to look at her face. Suddenly, Lady Joselyn was there and wrapped Madeline in her arms.

An hour later, Madeline had told the entire story as the family sat at dinner. Red Roland was seething with anger to learn that his little girl suffered and was abused by Rory MacDougal. He was angrier still when he learned that another MacDougal followed and planned to attack his daughter and use her. Joselyn bathed Madeline and saw all the fading bruises on her daughter's body. Joselyn could not believe how thin her beloved daughter had become. When Madeline slid between the sheets in her own bed, she felt clean and safe for the first time in a very long time.

Madeline was glad to let her mother hold her while she cried her relief of being home. She and Rory were married for five years, thankfully she never became pregnant with his child. She knew that if there was a child in the marriage, the MacDougals would never have let her go, and the Drurys would not have seen her again. She knew she was home and safe as she drifted into a dream of how it was on Drury Manor when she, Redmon, Roddrick, and Rodney were all together as children before that night of the branding. That one fateful night seemed to change everything for the Drurys.

✿ ✿ ✿

Shamus's horse drifted back to Castle MacDougal three days after the shooting. When Madeline had fired the shot, the horse bolted and took off back north. Enis MacDougal blamed the MacDonald clan. They retaliated for their son Rory's death by killing Aierie MacDonald.

A MacDougal tracker found the return trail of Shamus's horse back from the south. They found Shamus's body lying in the heather near the brook. He was shot through the heart. Jamie MacDougal also found the tracks of the palfrey that they had put Madeline on to send her home. The MacDougal clan laughed about the poor horse Madeline was sent south riding and that they kept the fine Morgan mare that she owned. Now it seemed that Madeline did some damage of her own to the MacDougal clan.

Enis MacDougal bellowed out in frustration, "That Sassenach slut murdered our Shamus!"

They loaded the body of their kinsman on his horse and headed back north. Enis MacDougal intended to return and deal with the Sassenach slut, as he thought of Madeline. He never approved of his son's selection of Madeline from the very beginning. He had already selected a good Scottish lass for his son. Rory had found the Sassenach on a trip south. He continued to court the Sassenach until he finally brought her home as his wife. Enis thought it only right when Rory discovered his wife to be frigid and barren that he sought Moira MacLean for his pleasure. He would never admit that the trouble might have been his son's, even though Moira MacLean did not become pregnant by his son, either.

Back at Castle MacDougal, there was mourning for Shamus at the burial, although there were some young MacDougal women there who were actually relieved that he was dead. Shamus had been brutal with them, too. The man seemed to think that any unattached female in the MacDougal clan was fair game for his use.

Enis MacDougal was planning to go south to deal with the Sassenach slut when the MacDonalds hit a group of his herders and carried away three MacDougal lasses. The trip south was put aside for a time to deal with the MacDonalds. In revenge, they would take MacDonald girls to make up for the loss of their own.

❖ ❖ ❖

The winter passed quickly on the R bar A. For Allison it could not be called anything but idyllic. She and Redmon worked on the ranch by day and loved one another at night. Allison developed the habit of running her fingers over the healing scar tissue on Redmon's chest when they lay together. Now that the brand was gone, Redmon allowed her to touch the spot. As much as he loved her, Redmon would not let her touch the hated C when he still wore it. Now he told her that her touching it was bringing the feeling back to the repaired skin.

The nights were always an adventure for the new couple. They seemed to never have enough of one another. Allison's only regret now was that she was not getting pregnant. She wanted to present Redmon with a child from their love, but unfortunately, it was not happening. It was Redmon who broached the subject that he was thinking about for quite some time. "Allison, Love, what would you think about a trip to England? I would like to see my family at least one more time. They are so far away and this could be the last time I ever see them.

You are my life and this is our home. We will be here until we are old and gray, but I would like one more chance to see them. We would be gone at least a year and a half, maybe a little longer."

Allison jumped into Redmon's lap with her arms around his neck. She was crying as she held her husband, "Sweetheart, I told you when we were married that I would follow you anywhere and that includes to England. In truth, I love what we have built here. I love this house you have built for us. The thought of the trip scares me a little, but I would love to see and meet your family. I can't imagine going across the country and sailing across an ocean, but I would love to see where you grew up. When I was growing up, I dreamed of traveling and seeing the world, so you would fulfill my childhood dream. Redmon, I love you and will be proud to go with you!"

✚ ✚ ✚

After a few weeks of preparation, they were riding for Central City. They would take the train east from Denver. Red and Audrey Brandais took Redmon and Allison to Denver in their new carriage to catch the train. Audrey would have her baby any day but insisted on going to Denver with them. Franklin Wilbanks agreed to oversee both ranches while they were gone.

Franklin was not happy that he wouldn't be seeing Allison for well over a year, but understood Redmon's desire to see his family for the first time in eleven years. Grace convinced him that the trip would be good for Allison. Franklin knew that many bad things could happen, and some of them dangerous, on a trip that long and arduous. Storms at sea could take ships quickly. He was afraid for his daughter who he loved so much, but he also knew that Redmon would protect Allison with his very life if it came to that.

The Wilbankses had come from Georgia in a covered wagon to find their land and build the ranch. So, Allison was excited to ride the train as it would be a new experience for her. Upon arriving in Chicago, Redmon and Allison decided to stay for a few weeks before heading east again. Packed in their luggage, were Redmon's swords and carbine along with the Sioux knives and bow and arrows he took during the attack on the Green River. The weapons were secured in a long wooden case that Redmon arranged to have built and lined with velvet. Allison raised an eyebrow when he commissioned the Denver carpenter to build the wooden case. "Allison, you never know," Redmon explained, "We might want to shoot rabbits on the heather."

They would also have some gifts for his father, mother, Roddrick, and Roselind.

"Rabbits on the heather my eye, Redmon Drury!" Allison knew he was carrying his volcanic pistol under his coat in a side holster he found in Denver.

Chicago was an amazing sight to Allison, but New York astounded her. She thought the seemingly endless plains were a wonder, but the large cities were something else altogether. At the train station, they asked about a good hotel and were taken, along with their trunks, to the Regis, one of the best hotels in New York at the time. They made arrangements to attend the theater, with the help of the concierge who procured tickets for them. When they were bathed and dressed, a hansom cab arrived at the hotel to take them to the theater.

Redmon and Allison enjoyed several singing and musical acts, but the featured performer was Jenny Lynn. She received three curtain calls. Allison couldn't stop talking about it after the performance, which made Redmon chuckle at her enthusiasm.

They were outside the theater waiting in line for a horse-drawn cab to take them back to the hotel when a man stepped next to Redmon. "Give me yer money or I will be shovin' a knife in yer ribs. Now make it quick!"

Suddenly, the would-be thief found the muzzle of a huge pistol shoved up his nose.

"I believe you have picked the wrong people to assault," Redmon countered. "If you make a move, you will find something running up your nose that could ruin your day."

A man standing nearby watching the confrontation laughed. "Well done, man. These street ruffians get away with some money all too often. What is your name? I would like to know the man who could handle this street ruffian so easily and quickly."

"My name is Redmon Drury and this is my wife Allison. We own a cattle ranch in the New Mexico Territory." Redmon pushed the muzzle harder into the thief's nose. "You are very fortunate tonight, for the last man who tried something like this is buried on our ranch. Run along before I change my mind."

The man turned and ran off to the jeers of many nearby theatergoers who had seen how Redmon handled the situation.

The next morning in the *New York Daily News,* there was a story about the New Mexico rancher named Redmon Drury, and his wife Allison, who produced a huge pistol outside the theater and stuck it up the nose of a street thief who attempted to extort money at knifepoint. The story told of how the thief ran for his life from the big ranch owner. With that, Redmon and Allison became honored guests of the hotel, even receiving special treatment from the maître d' when they enjoyed their meals in the dining room.

It took a couple of days to find a ship that would sail into Solway Firth and Gretna Green. It would not be departing for another week. Redmon and Allison used the time for shopping as she added to her number of gowns and accessories. These were in addition to the ones she had found in Chicago.

Before sailing, Redmon looked over the *Fair Wind* to be sure it was a clean ship for Allison. After talking to Captain Turner, Redmon booked passage and the Drurys would have a nice cabin. All of Allison's gowns were packed in new trunks that Redmon bought and were brought aboard the *Fair Wind.*

Allison was excited by the activity along the dock. Seeing the masts of all the ships in the harbor was something she could never have imagined. The salt-tinged air was distinctive, another new and unusual experience for her.

They watched as a number of crates were loaded into the hold along with a great deal of pipe and tool box for the trip to England. The *Fair Wind* cast off and worked its way out of the harbor on the evening tide.

❖ ❖ ❖

Allison enjoyed the spectacle of leaving the New York harbor amongst the other ships, but when the ship hit the open ocean, seasickness came. At first she wondered if she could finally be pregnant and held some hope for that. Redmon held her head throughout the night, and helped her to the chamber pot in their cabin. "Oh, Redmon, I'm so sorry," she repeated over and over again.

Mercifully, the sickness passed by morning and she was able to bathe, dress, and go on deck for fresh air. Captain Turner greeted her and hoped that all was well, for the crew had reported hearing her in her misery during the night. An embarrassed Allison assured the captain that she would survive. When she made the comment that if she could survive shooting outlaws, she could surely survive a little seasickness, her comment drew a strange look from the captain, causing Redmon to chuckle. Later, he explained to Captain Turner that Allison and her father were forced to fight off land grabbers and shoot five of them to keep their ranch intact.

Allison suddenly became a star on the *Fair Wind* when the captain passed the story on to the rest of the crew.

Allison thought the Great Plains, which the train passed through, were vast, but nothing could compare to the Atlantic Ocean with water as far as she could see. After that initial bout of seasickness passed, Allison enjoyed the voyage. To see the ship at full sail was really something in her estimation. She thought the *Fair Wind* fairly flew across the ocean. Allison clapped when a pod of whales swam along with the ship for a time. She loved how they surfaced, blew, and then went back under the waves, resurfaced again, and blew their spray. The immense size of the animals was amazing for a Western girl to see. When their huge tails came out of the water, Allison almost squealed in delight. She had loved seeing some of the remaining buffalo on the plains, but seeing the whales was an experience she would keep in her mind for a lifetime. The captain and crew enjoyed watching Allison in her enthusiasm as she stared up at the billowing sails and clapped at the sight of the whales. When they were on deck, the seamen often stared at Allison for she was truly beautiful. She never failed to have a cheerful word for the men when they were near her.

In their cabin at night, Redmon and Allison loved and held one another, drifting off to sleep listening to the ship creaking and groaning as the water could be heard passing the hull.

One evening during the meal at the captain's table, Captain Turner mentioned in passing that he fenced. The next morning, he and Redmon began their daily fencing sessions. It quickly became apparent to Captain Turner that Redmon was a true master of the sword. The captain was surprised when he learned that Redmon Drury learned the sword and foil under a French master in Canada.

The first mate and seamen watched the sessions and quickly realized that Redmon Drury was not a man to trifle with. His quickness and moves were amazing for a man his size, and none could ever remember seeing a left-handed swordsman. They also found it intriguing that Redmon wore a pair of moccasins when he fenced with Captain Turner. Allison also watched the sessions and was accustomed now to the idea that Redmon handled the foil and blade well. She was always impressed by how fluid her husband's actions were when he moved.

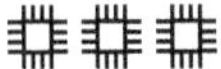

Six weeks after sailing from New York, the *Fair Wind* docked at Gretna Green. Allison could see the excitement written on Redmon's face as he looked at the town and the countryside beyond. He hugged her close as they prepared to leave the ship. Captain Turner said farewell to Redmon, and especially Allison, telling them how much he enjoyed their company. Redmon and Allison would spend one night at the same inn where Redmon stayed before he took the ship to Canada as a fifteen year old.

During their ocean crossing, the couple talked about how much they missed their bathrooms. Redmon made sure Allison received a bucket of hot water each night so she could wash, but it just wasn't the same. They would have a surprise for his parents as well as Roddrick and Roselind when they reached Drury Manor. Redmon arranged for a coach to take them to the manor house the following morning.

Redmon was wearing his suit, wide-brimmed western hat, and the high-heeled cowboy boots he had become so accustomed to wearing as he and Allison entered the inn. Allison was attired in a nice dress with her long auburn hair hanging loose around her shoulders. What set her apart was her tan complexion from being in the sun out west. She did not shy away from the sun as most high-born English women did. She was tan, beautiful, and healthy looking.

The new couple drew curious stares from the collection of seamen and locals sitting in the low-ceilinged common room. When Redmon signed the register as Mr. and Mrs. Redmon Drury, Henry Williamson took a double take.

"Would ye be any relation to the Drurys of Eden?" the older clerk asked.

"Red Roland is my father. I stayed here some twelve years ago before I took ship to Canada," Redmon answered the clerk.

"I knew it. Ye be the boy I remember. Welcome home. I think yer family will be needin' ye." The innkeeper's last statement worried Redmon somewhat. Now he was anxious to get to the manor and learn if there was a problem or trouble with his family. Immediately, the Chathams came to mind. Redmon was restless that night and Allison, who now knew his moods so well, was worried also. Later, during their evening meal in the common room, all eyes were on the tall, handsome couple. Word was passing around the room that the man was the long-lost son of Red Roland Drury along with his beautiful wife from America.

Allison loved seeing the strong, smoke-stained beams and the large fireplace at one end of the room. The smells of the room were distinctive. Redmon had described the inns where he stayed during his travels, now she was actually getting to live that experience herself. The men in the room noticed the strange high-heeled cowboy boots Redmon wore. These men had never seen anything like them before. A few men saw the butt of a huge pistol at Redmon's side. They all knew that Redmon was an Englishman, but he did not act like the son of a nobleman, and his wife was a sight to behold. What a beauty! She looked like none of the sallow, simpering English noble ladies they were accustomed to seeing.

There were two other men sitting in the corner of the common room also carefully watching the couple. These were hard men who made their living along the roads of northern England. They looked for people coming from ships who might have the promise of money on their persons. They heard the name Drury and knew that meant money. The Drurys were the largest landholders along the Eden.

Redmon noticed the men when he and Allison first sat down. From the corner of his eye, he saw that the men continued to study him and Allison. He recognized these men even though he didn't actually know them. Redmon knew they would be on the road the following morning. He even believed he knew where an attempt at robbery would come because he knew the countryside. He would have Allison prepared as well as their driver. That night, Redmon and Allison held one another and talked about what the innkeeper might have meant by his statement that his family needed help.

Just as Redmon thought, the men were there during breakfast and watching them again. He chuckled because the men were so predictable. As the driver Liam Crosswait and Redmon loaded the trunks, the men were outside the inn watching. Before they rolled away from the Eden Cross Inn, Redmon warned Liam about the men and where he thought the attack would probably take place. Redmon gave Liam some instructions before he climbed up to the driver's box. Both Redmon and Allison were ready with their pistols inside the coach. As they approached a bend in the road lined with trees, Liam Crosswait popped his whip over the horses' backs and they increased their pace into a near run. The highwaymen had ridden hard away from the inn to get in position. The riders now spurred their mounts into the road, finding themselves almost being run over by the coach horses.

They had expected the coach to travel along the road at a leisurely, stately pace, presenting no problem for them. They just managed to get out of the way as the coach and horses thundered past, and then gave chase, firing over the driver's head to scare him into stopping.

Redmon leaned out the window of his door and began shooting, levering and shooting his volcanic. He decided to shoot at the hooves of the horse on the left. His third shot struck a fore hoof, forcing it to pull up lame and limping. Allison leaned out the back window on the other side of the coach. With her hair streaming, she aimed her pistol and wounded the other robber through the arm with her second shot, causing the man to pull up and also drop back.

Allison sat back on the cushions and began repairing her hair. Redmon sat down himself, looking at his wife with respect. "Allison, Love, did you shoot that man?"

"Well, sweetheart, he was shooting at us. He might have shot Liam, and we couldn't have that now, could we? I didn't want one of us to have to drive the coach to your parents' house. That would have been a poor way for us to show up." He leaned over and kissed her.

❖ ❖ ❖

Red Roland, Joselyn, and Madeline were just sitting down for their noon meal when they heard the coach rumbling along the drive to the manor house. They moved from the dining room and along the long hallway to the double front doors where they waited. The coach pulled to a stop.

The door opened and a tall, bearded man stepped out wearing some kind of wide brimmed hat. He reached into the coach and a tan, slim arm took his offered hand. When the young woman was handed out, the arriving couple turned towards their greeters. Joselyn screamed and ran forward. Redmon let go of Allison and scooped his mother up into his arms and swung her around in a circle. Red Roland and Madeline were joined in hugging Redmon.

When they finally broke apart, Redmon took Allison's hand. "Mother, Father, Madeline, I wish to introduce my wife Allison Elaine Drury. You would be proud of her for she just stopped some highwaymen from robbing us by shooting one of them."

Joselyn put out her hands and Allison took them. "Allison, we have enjoyed your letters so much. What is this about highwaymen? I hope Redmon was jesting."

"It wasn't as dramatic as all that. Redmon shot the hoof of one man's horse. I was fortunate to hit the other one in the arm." They heard Liam Crosswait snort, "Mum, that was the finest shot I have ever seen."

Redmon laughed. "That's my wife. She always downplays how brave she is."

Liam Crosswait unloaded the trunks and bowed to Allison. "Mistress Drury, I turned and looked back when you made the shot. Even with the coach rocking, you made one of the finest pistol shots I have ever seen. I would be proud to have you in my coach again." Then Liam Crosswait bowed to Allison again.

After the coach rolled away, Redmon pulled Allison to him. "Mistress Drury, I believe you have made a conquest," causing Allison to punch him.

Joselyn took Allison's arm and led her and Madeline into the house while Redmon, Red Roland, and a houseman carried the trunks to Redmon's old room. They all sat at the large dining room table and, at first, it was somewhat awkward after the initial excitement of seeing their son for the first time in over twelve years. Then the conversation began to flow and, suddenly, everyone seemed to want to talk at once.

One of the stablemen was sent to Eden Hall to inform Roddrick and Roselind that Redmon and his wife just arrived at Drury Manor. Joselyn would also send a letter that afternoon to inform Rodney in Sheffield that Redmon and Allison had arrived home to Drury Manor.

Red Roland stumbled over the words but tried to say that they should never have let Redmon get on the ship.

Redmon held up his hand. "Father, Mother, it was what needed to be done. You know that if I had stayed here, I would have gone after Wilfred immediately and probably be hanged as Mortimer said. I was able to have experiences that few men get. I gained skills in Canada and the West that saved my life several times over."

Then he took Allison's hand, "And, I met this woman that I love beyond my own life. We are partners in every way as are you and Mother. Leaving gave me the skills to deal with Wilfred Chatham in the way he deserved. He was evil and died as he lived, trying to hurt others. He finally paid for the evil deeds he wrought. Allison and I have built a fine home on land we own. We will raise our children there as you raised us here. To be honest with everyone, my going to America gave me the love of my life! We have pictures to show you of the land and our home so you can see what we have done. We will also have some surprises for you, along with Roddrick and Roselind as well. ”

The conversation flowed freely, and Redmon learned why Madeline was home at Drury Manor and without her husband. Madeline was honest and talked of the bad marriage, the abuse at her husband's hands, his death, and finally given the choice to bed Shamus MacDougal, who was worse than Rory, or leave the castle. She told of being followed from Castle MacDougal by Shamus and being forced to shoot him or be ravaged by the Scottish clansman after being cast out of the castle. So this was the cause of the strange statement by the innkeeper, Henry Williamson.

Enis MacDougal and his men had come to Drury Manor wanting to take Madeline back for punishment for the killing of Shamus MacDougal. They were now harassing Drury Manor by stealing cattle and taking two young women from the manor lands. The British army refused to go into the Scottish highlands to retrieve the two girls.

Both girls were the daughters of Drury yeomen. Enis MacDougal threatened to keep coming at them until Madeline was returned to the MacDougal clan.

Allison was dismayed to learn that Madeline could be cast out, and then expected to be punished for defending herself.

✦ ✦ ✦

When word came to Eden Hall that Redmon had come home, Roselind was shocked. She honestly thought she would never see him again because he was so far away in America. Now, he was here with his new wife. Would she be ugly as Rory predicted? Roselind thought she could handle that more easily than if the woman was pretty. After all, Redmon was her first man and her first true love. She loved Roddrick, but always wondered what a life with Redmon would have offered if her father had allowed them to marry. Then she realized that Redmon was handsome and would somehow find a woman that matched him. Redmon's wife lived in the wilds of the West. She had never met an American. Would she be wild as well? She read all the letters reliving Redmon's adventures. When she read the flowing hand of Redmon's wife she could actually visualize, through Allison's narrative, Redmon fighting what they called outlaws, riding the wild land, and with it how the wonderful scenery came to life. Roselind realized if Allison looked as good as she could write, she would be something to see.

The description of the sword fight between Redmon and Wilfred was so graphically worded by Allison, you could almost hear the clang of the blades jump off the written page. Roselind's own brother had betrayed her, so his death did not hurt her as a brother's death should have. She was now a Drury through and through. She was well-read and could speak French.

Roselind did not stop learning and studying when she and Rodderick married. Joselyn made sure that she finished her education.

Roselind knew that she was also well-loved by Rodderick. Now she prepared herself to meet the woman that Redmon had found and married in that distant land. What Roselind expected did not prepare her for what she found at Drury Manor.

Roddrick had a groom harness horses to the carriage while Roselind gathered the children, Clendon and Clarissa. They packed some clothes because they expected to stay over at Drury Manor. Roddrick realized that Roselind was nervous and took her hand. The carriage ride seemed to take hours even though it was only some fifteen minutes.

As they walked through the front door, they could hear laughing coming from the sitting room. When they entered, everyone stood, and Roselind focused her attention on the tall, bearded figure who was holding the hand of an absolutely beautiful woman.

Redmon pulled her forward. "Allison, love, I would like you to meet my brother Roddrick and his wife Roselind. This must be my nephew Clendon and niece Clarissa."

Roselind could only stare, for Redmond Drury was an absolutely imposing figure of a man. Redmon hugged Roddrick and they pounded each other's backs. The hug for Roselind was a good one, but without a great deal of emotion as she expected. He did not hold her overly long.

Allison put out her hand to Roddrick first and then to Roselind. "Redmon has told me so much about you both. It is such a pleasure to finally meet you." She knelt, still holding Redmon's hand while reaching out her other hand, "Clendon, you are so handsome, and Clarissa is so beautiful. I believe we will become fast friends as well as family."

Roselind and Roddrick both heard Redmon's endearment for Allison and knew he was completely committed to her. Roddrick would have expected nothing less knowing his brother. Roselind had not seen Redmon for twelve years. They were really no more than children when that fateful night occurred and her brother branded him. He was now a tall, confident, strapping, handsome man. His beard and mustache were perfectly trimmed and made Redmon Drury look dashing as well as distinguished. Roselind wanted to dislike Allison for having him, but she could not. Allison Drury was truly nice as well as very beautiful.

Soon they were all looking at the mementos that Redmon and Allison brought to show the family. They liked seeing his buckskins and moccasins, and hearing his story of how the Huron Indian maiden named Pretty Flower had made them for him. They were obviously used and well-worn by Redmon. The stories of Canada, Emile Boushard, and Long Bow were fun to hear again. Redmon told his family that he had long since written to Emile and told him of his travels and where he finally settled. He even told his mentor of the sword fight that occurred on his new father-in-law's ranch that finished his nemesis from his youth.

"Redmon tries to hug me when he is wearing those buckskins and they stink. They smell like wood smoke and dead animals, and probably some other unmentionable things if you can imagine," Allison told the group.

Immediately, Clendon and Clarissa wanted to smell the leather outfit. Clarissa scrunched her nose, causing everyone to laugh. "Uncle Redmon, how can you wear these things?" Redmon suddenly picked Clarissa up and swung her around, and she squealed in delight. Both Clendon and Clarissa had hung on every word of the letters from Redmon that came from the exotic place called America.

They loved seeing the fine drawings done by Grace of the Circle W and the R bar A, and even of the curved staircase in the new house. She had drawn pictures of the longhorn and Spanish cattle, and Red Roland and Roddrick laughed and enjoyed seeing them compared to their English cattle. When Redmon described how large and heavy the tall, rangy longhorns were, they were amazed. It was hard for them to believe how wide the horns on some of the animals could be. Redmon and Allison would have a surprise for Red Roland in one of their crates that was on the ship.

There were also drawings of the mesas and mountains around Santa Fe as well as the adobe buildings in Santa Fe. Redmon described how the late afternoon setting sun turned the adobe buildings to red gold.

Roselind, Joselyn, and Madeline were in awe when Allison described the bathrooms that Redmon installed in both the R bar A house and the Circle W ranch house. The Drurys were hearing that some of the finer hotels in London were now installing them. Redmon winked at Allison, for they had bought four sets of fixtures and pipe in New York, along with two of the coal-fired water heaters they found in Chicago, and everything was loaded on the *Fair Wind*.

Wagons would bring everything to Drury Manor in a day or two from Gretna Green. Both Roddrick and Roselind noticed the wink between Redmon and Allison. Roselind realized at that moment that there was a close bond between Redmon and Allison that could never be broken. She actually fantasized in her quiet moments over the years about Redmon. She and Redmon shared so much during their time together and it was always in her mind in spite of her love for Roddrick. She realized quickly that fantasy was not reality.

The Drurys loved to hear about the Rocky Mountains that contained peaks rising fourteen and fifteen thousand feet in Colorado. Allison told them of the antelope that populated the ranch as well as the mule deer that they often hunted for a different flavor of meat. They even brought a large bag of piñon nuts for the Drurys, and explained that they grew on some of their pine trees at the ranch. They explained that the Indians and Spanish people of the area often roasted the nuts to give them a slightly smoky flavor.

Redmon told of the huge elk of the Colorado Mountains that were far larger than the English stag. He described buffalo on the plains, and the vast sea of grass in the middle of the United States. Clendon wanted to see Redmon's volcanic pistol and carbine that he described in the letters, along with the Sioux Indian knives, and the bow and quiver of arrows. Red Roland and Roddrick wanted to hear about the Morgan and Nez Percé horses that Redmon was raising. Joselyn, Roselind, and Madeline wanted to know more about the house on the R bar A from Allison.

Allison explained that most of the furniture, and all the dishes, linens, and bathroom fixtures came from back east over what was called the Santa Fe Trail. It was explained that long trains of wagons, pulled by teams of six mules and loaded with the luxuries and goods that Westerners wanted, traveled for two thousand miles over rough, rutted roads. These long wagon trains carried the goods and supplies into Santa Fe and then on west and south from there.

Allison told the women how her father Franklin met and married Grace in Santa Fe when she and Redmon were getting married themselves. Redmon made the comment that good women were often in short supply in the West. His family all saw him wink at Allison. "I was just fortunate to find one of them out in the middle of nowhere."

Redmon wanted the opportunity to talk to Madeline and learn about the MacDougal clan and their threats to Madeline and the family. He was finally able to get his sister alone before dinner. She told Redmon everything about Rory MacDougal, the abuse she suffered and his infidelity with the chambermaid. She told Redmon that she was forced to fight off Shamus MacDougal twice when he caught her alone in the castle, and Rory actually laughed and did nothing about it. Madeline told Redmon how frightened she was when Shamus came after her on the route home. She said having to shoot and kill Shamus was the most difficult thing she ever thought of doing in her life, but she refused to be raped by Shamus MacDougal. "Redmon, I am so proud of you and what you have accomplished, and I think Allison is wonderful. I have to tell you that I am afraid for Momma and Poppa. The MacDougals are hard and dangerous people. They are constantly feuding with a family named MacDonald near their lands. Killing, retribution, and kidnapping are part of their lives. The MacDonalds are the ones that killed Rory when he was caught stealing their cattle, which is a sport in the highlands. Enis MacDougal is a hard man and he would think nothing of hurting Momma and Poppa to get me back as punishment for killing Shamus. He might even hurt Rod and Roselind to send a warning to me. If the MacDougals ever got their hands on Clarrisa, we would never see her again. That possibility scares me to death, for she is so sweet and innocent. My being here now is a danger to everyone on Drury Manor. I may have to leave and go to Sheffield and live with Rodney to protect our family. I simply don't know what to do."

Madeline was crying now and Redmon took her into his arms and held his little sister. "Maddie, we were both young when I went away. I have gained experience against hard men and will not allow you or our parents to be hurt. We are family, and that is what matters."

The next morning the wagons that were loaded with all the plumbing supplies arrived. Red Roland and Joselyn were overwhelmed that their son and new daughter-in-law would provide such a luxury for them, and bring everything all the way from America. When they noticed four sets of fixtures, they looked at Redmon. "Well, Allison and I thought both houses could be brought into the modern age. Besides, I think Rod needs to bathe more often." He punched his brother in the shoulder. They told the family about the hot water heaters, and explained that they were actually invented by a couple that owned a ranch south of theirs and the couple founded a company to manufacture them. Immediately, Joselyn and Roselind were hugging Redmon and Allison.

"Well, don't get too excited yet. You are getting ready to work very hard helping Allison and me install these bathrooms. We consider ourselves plumbing experts now, but it is very hard work," Redmon said.

That afternoon, they laid out where the two bathrooms would go in Drury Manor. One would be in the master suite of bedrooms, and one down a hallway among the other bedrooms on the second floor of the house. The following morning the men figured out where they could build a large tank upstream from the house on a raised platform so water would gravity feed down into the house to provide the pressure needed to make everything work. Red Roland ordered the oak wood.

There was a woodyard in the town of Carlisle close by where the wood could be obtained quickly. A group of workers from the manor dug the trench in which the pipe would be buried. The plumbing holes were cut in the floor of the bathing room in the master suite. All the piping was run through the house and to be hidden in the walls and floor.

The larger sewer pipe was plumbed to a large pit that was dug for the waste and covered with thick boards. The turf was then replaced. Part of a large bedroom was converted into the other bathroom, plumbed, and the fixtures installed. Redmon taught Roddrick and his father as they did all the work, as well as the Drury blacksmith who was helping them. Everything was installed in less than two weeks because they had so many men to help do the work.

When all was ready, they let water into the big oak tank from a screen-covered pipe that was buried and put into the river. With Allison's suggestion, they built a charcoal filter box that would clean the water before it entered the water tank. The tank leaked from all the seams until the thick planks swelled and sealed. Red Roland could never remember seeing Joselyn so excited.

When Redmon knew the tank was full, he slowly opened a valve and water ran through the charcoal filter and then to the house. Redmon checked each connection. They were all tight with no leaks. The blacksmith, Albert

Abney, would be able to maintain the system if there were any problems later. Redmon complimented the blacksmith and dubbed him as a first-rate plumber when all was finished. Albert beamed, and was actually excited to have been part of doing something so new.

Redmon put coal in the firebox and lit the water heater. An hour later there was hot and cold running water in the kitchen and two bathrooms. The Drury cook was as excited as everyone else to have hot running water in her kitchen. The toilets flushed and everything else worked. Joselyn must have hugged Redmon and Allison ten times.

The carpenters closed up the walls and ceilings when they were sure there were no leaks in any of the plumbing connections.

"Hot baths all around tonight!" Redmon yelled, causing everyone to cheer.

Dinner that night was fun. Madeline whispered to Allison that this was how it used to be at Drury Manor before Redmon left. Allison asked Clarissa to sit next to her at dinner and soon the little girl was chatting with her new Aunt Allie as she began to call Allison. Clarissa told everyone that she liked to hear Aunt Allie speak Western. That drew laughs and Allison hugged the little girl. The family commented about Redmon losing much of his British accent when he spoke. As dinner ended, they planned to go to Eden Hall the following morning to plumb that manor house.

After talking to Madeline about the situation with the MacDougals, Redmon broached the subject with Allison that night in bed. A plan was beginning to form in his mind. Redmon sat with Roddrick after dinner and learned of the mean letters that Roselind received from her mother. Roddrick also told him of some of Wilfred Chatham's deeds before he left for America. One nice thing he learned from Roddrick was that Roselind had completed her education.

Then Redmon said, "Allison, I finally talked to Madeline. She told me all about these MacDougals and what it was like for her living in their old castle. I would like to propose a solution."

Allison threw her leg over and straddled her husband. "Sweetheart, I think Madeline should go home with us. We can protect her and we might just find some good cowboy for her. That was what you were going to propose, wasn't it?"

Redmon grinned in the moonlight as they enjoyed each other. "I love you, Allison Drury."

The following morning after a hearty breakfast, two carriages, along with wagons loaded to the brim with supplies and men, headed for Eden Hall some six miles away. Redmon chose to ride one of the Drury Morgans as did Allison. When she came to the breakfast table that morning wearing her pants, boots, shirt, and vest and carrying her Western hat, Allison's long auburn hair was tied into a ponytail.

The British Drurys could only stare until Madeline laughed and clapped, "Oh, Allison, I only wish I could wear something like that. It looks so liberating."

"Madeline, I have some you can try on, Allison told her. "We also wear what are called split-riding skirts in the west. I suppose the people here would be scandalized, for they expose the woman's knees and lower legs, but they are so comfortable for working and riding on the ranch."

A gasp came from both Joselyn and Roselind, but then they giggled at the thought.

"Are women actually allowed to get away with such a thing in your West?" Joselyn asked.

"The women often work and brand cattle next to their men on some ranches. You can't very well wear a dress doing that work, at least I can't," Allison said. "After our ranch hands were run off or killed by the Chatham men, I often worked alongside my father until we were forced to fight them off from behind the barricades we built on our porch. I'm sorry, Roselind, but those men were very hard on us," Allison replied.

Redmon came into the dining room carrying his pistol, holster, and carbine, setting them by the door. "Just a precaution," he explained when he drew curious looks from his family. "We might meet some scallywags as Pop Wilbanks calls them."

The wagons and carriages were some three miles from Eden Hall when a group of riders swooped down on them from a stand of trees along the route. Redmon and Allison were riding in the van of the procession facing the riders. Redmon made sure his volcanic was loose in his holster. Allison reached into a bag she had tied on the saddle, drew out her pistol, and held it next to her leg.

The obvious leader of the riders surveyed the cavalcade. "Well, laddies, it appears we will be doin' well teday. We'll be havin' the treacherous Sassenach slut back, and two more fine lasses and one little lassie fer the future in the bargain. This one a wearin' men's clothes is a comely bonnie lass."

Redmon made a quick study of the big man that was Enis MacDougal. The man sported a full, somewhat scraggly beard, and wore the traditional kilt with his knees showing. He also wore a soft-looking bonnet with a feather on one side. It was obvious that the patriarch of the MacDougal clan was accustomed to intimidating people by his size alone. There was no doubt in Redmon's mind that the man was a fierce fighter. Redmon quickly assessed the other men and thought one in particular looked very capable.

He quietly told Allison, "Watch the one behind the leader and to the right of us. I'll take care of the leader and any others."

Finally, Enis MacDougal turned his attention to Redmon. "Who might ye be, laddie? What would that getup be that ye be wearin? Ye wouldn't be thinkin' that ye could face us by yerself would ye now, laddie?"

Redmon laughed. "You're quite a talker for a Scot. I thought Scottish men let their weapons do their talking. You'll be lucky if my wife doesn't shoot one of your ears off. As to your question, we are the Drurys from the New Mexico Territory in America, and I have just talked far more than I intended."

Enis roared with laughter and kneed his horse forward, putting his huge hand on the butt of a pistol in his belt. Redmon's draw of his big volcanic was so quick and smooth that most of the men, both Scottish and in the Drury cavalcade, didn't even see it happen.

Suddenly, a shot rang out and smoke was curling away from Allison's pistol. The man behind Enis MacDougal that Allison was assigned to watch tried to pull his pistol and was going to aim at Redmon. Allison never hesitated. She raised her pistol, aimed, shot the man's hand, and his pistol flew away onto the bright green turf.

The Scots sat on their horses in stunned silence, staring at the beautiful young woman wearing pants and a wide-brimmed hat who just shot Angus MacDougal.

Angus was one of the clan's most fearsome fighters. He was holding his hand, which dripped blood. He was staring into the eyes of the beautiful woman whose pistol was still pointed in his direction.

Enis MacDougal stared into the muzzle of the pistol held by Redmon. "MacDougal, I believe you are probably a good man, but I will shoot you if you pull that pistol. My wife and I killed nine seasoned gunfighters that wanted to take our land. My sister, who does not lie, has told me that your man Shamus tried to rape her when she was on her way home from her own husband's funeral after being cast out by you. Now, if you want to die, go ahead and draw that pistol." Suddenly, Redmon saw another man attempting to draw on him. He moved his aim and shot the feather off the man's bonnet. Then the muzzle was back on Enis MacDougal. Again the action by Redmon was so sudden and unexpected that the MacDougals were left stunned.

Enis MacDougal finally let his hands drop. "Laddie, ye and yer lass seem te be quite good at shooting yer pistols. Yer lass is bonny as well. I kin ye are tough with the pistol. De ye fight any other way?"

Redmon replied, "I learned the sword from a French master in Canada, and also hand to hand fighting with knives from a Huron Indian brave on the Great Lakes in Canada. Fighting is not what I want, but I will kill to protect my wife and my family. I understand the

MacDonalds killed your son. It seems that you have foes aplenty without the Drurys to add to them."

Enis MacDougal roared. "Right ye are, laddie, right ye are, but we mean te have the lass Madeline back in the clan. I have another son that needs a wife. We'll be watchin' fer her. Ye'll be loosin' her te us one day. She canna stay in the house fer ever." Then the MacDougal men turned their horses and followed their leader north.

✸✸✸

Redmon and Allison were off their horses and hugging, and were soon surrounded by the rest of the family. Madeline held tightly onto Allison, as Red Roland grabbed Redmon's arm shaking his hand up and down. "Son! That was quite something! Rod and I would have fought to protect our women, but you and Allison made the difference. How did you learn to do what we just witnessed?"

"Twelve years of rough experiences fighting some tough men across Canada and the western United States," Redmon explained. "In the west right now you must handle a pistol because there is very little law and order. The closest law enforcement to our ranch is over a hundred miles away. It will come in time and we will be able to put our guns down, but not yet."

Three weeks of hard work found Eden Hall plumbed and working perfectly. On one of their first nights at Eden Hall, Redmon presented Roddrick and Red Roland with wrapped packages. Roddrick received a six-shot Colt revolver and holster. They once belonged to Nate Burleson, but they were in excellent condition. Red Roland received an almost new Winchester lever action rifle that belonged to Wilfred Chatham. It had been on his horse when he came to the Circle W to attempt to buy out Franklin Wilbanks. Redmon and Allison thought it appropriate to give something that came from Wilfred Chatham, the man who had branded Redmon. Redmon also gave Chatham's sword to Henry Sudderth. Both Roddrick and Red Roland were excited by the gifts.

There was also a long box hauled on the plumbing wagon that was brought into the house. When it was opened, the Drurys stared. Redmon pulled out two long sets of horns that still had white skulls attached. Both sets of horns were at least ten or eleven feet in length. The horns were polished and the skulls perfectly white. Redmon explained that the horns were from Texas longhorns that roamed the Circle W ranch but were killed by the Chatham crew for food.

Redmon had each set prepared for hanging, one at each of the Drury manors. Immediately, everyone wanted to run their hands along the horns and touch the skulls. Red Roland and Rodderick could not believe how large and long the horns were. Now they could actually place an image in their minds from the stories they had read in the letters from Redmon and Allison.

Then Allison asked some men to bring in a crate that was also loaded in the plumbing supply wagon. Everyone thought it was plumbing supplies that Redmon never opened. When the men opened the crate, Allison presented Joselyn and Roselind each with large oil paintings of landscape scenes from the area around the R bar A. Both were in nice wood frames and ready to hang. They were pastoral scenes of mountains, pastures, and cattle grazing in the distance, with clouds and blue sky above. Grace Wilbanks had done the beautiful paintings. The painting for Joselyn included the new house that Redmon and Allison built, which could be seen in the distance. The painting for Roselind showed the Appaloosa horses grazing near a mesa. Both paintings showed some of the spring wildflowers that bloomed on the ranch.

Neither Joselyn nor Roselind could believe that Redmon and Allison brought the crate all the way across the country and then over the ocean just for them. The women hugged Allison and thanked her many times over for the extraordinary paintings. The other drawings that Redmon and Allison brought would eventually be framed and hung in Drury Manor.

Roselind suggested hosting a party for the local gentry that would introduce Redmon and Allison. Eden Hall contained a large, window-walled room that could be cleared for a ballroom, and may have been designed for that purpose at one time.

Redmon was completely amazed when he saw the transformation that Roddrick and Roselind had made to the old Chatham Hall. Redmond remembered the room they would use for dancing as never having been used for much of anything. All the window frames were painted in a light blue. The inside of the manor house was redone into a bright white and comfortable atmosphere. It certainly was not the dreary place that Redmon remembered where he and Roselind snuck around in their youth. There was comfortable furniture everywhere, along with bright Persian carpets. Eden Hall contained enough bedrooms for guests who might need to stay over after the party.

The new bathrooms just installed and freshly painted made Eden Hall an imposing and fine home. Roselind hugged Redmon and Allison repeatedly just as Joselyn did at Drury Manor House when the bathrooms there were finished. All of the plumbing worked perfectly, making the family appreciate the luxury they would have in the Drury Manor houses. Both Drury Manor and Eden Hall were now two of the finest homes in northern England.

Plans were made and invitations sent to the local noble class of the Eden River area. There would be dinner and dancing. Musicians would be brought from Carlisle for the occasion. Allison chose to wear the deep burgundy gown because it was a perfect complement to her auburn hair and complexion.

Because Madeline had resided in Castle MacDougal for five years, her gowns were out of date and faded, so Allison insisted that Madeline wear her dark purple gown. Few alterations were needed to the gown. While they worked on it, Madeline confided to Allison that the elegant gown made her feel *pretty* again, a word that had not been part of her vocabulary for a very long time. Allison thought Madeline would be beyond pretty with the right dress and makeup. After all, she was Joselyn's daughter. Both Allison and Redmon noticed that Madeline had a haunted, weary look about her. She was just beginning to gain some of her weight back. Joselyn, Roselind, Allison, and Madeline made quite a collection of beauty.

There were actually some stories circulating around the neighborhood now about the American Drurys and their deeds on the highroad from Gretna Green to Drury Manor. Liam Crosswait was very profuse in his praise of Redmon, and especially Allison Drury for leaning out a coach window, with her long hair streaming, and shooting a highwayman that was attempting to stop and rob his coach. The story grew with each telling how the beautiful American woman and her English husband thwarted the highroad robbers. Then the Drury yeomen who were with the plumbing wagons, told the story at two different local taverns, of her shooting the pistol out of the hand of Angus MacDougal. All of which took place in a confrontation with Enis MacDougal, making him turn tail and run for Scotland. As that story spread from tavern to tavern and into nearby manor houses it also grew with each telling.

Now the local gentry and their ladies could hardly wait to meet this American sharpshooter as Allison was being termed. Noblemen also frequenting the taverns for a tankard of ale liked hearing the stories being told of the American Drurys. The English Drurys never hosted a gathering, or the Chathams before them. The yeomen who helped on the water and plumbing projects told of the wonderful bathrooms installed in both Drury Manor and Eden Hall that now actually contained hot and cold running water, and of all things, toilets that flushed. All these stories combined to pique a great deal of interest among those invited to see for themselves the former Chatham Manor house and meet these American Drurys.

When they weren't working, Redmon, Red Roland, Roddrick, and Allison rode the Drury manor lands. Redmon was able to see and learn about all that his father and Roddrick had done in his absence to make the land productive.

Both Red Roland and Roddrick found it interesting that a person had to have a great deal of land in the West to run cattle because of the semi-arid climate. Redmon explained that they drilled three water wells on their ranch and put what were called windmills on those wells in order to pump water to the surface for their cattle.

❖ ❖ ❖

On the day of the party, carriages and coaches began arriving from as far south as Darlington. Sir William Nelson, and his wife Ofelia, would have a room on the second floor of the manor next to the bathroom. Then Roddrick and Roselind learned that the first cousin of Queen Victoria came with the Nelsons, so he was assigned a bedroom also close to the bathroom. Lord William, Lady Ofelia, and Sir Albert Stuart were amazed when they used the bathroom to freshen up after their coach ride. Allison made sure there was a full-length mirror in each bathroom so the women could look at their dresses and hair before leaving the room.

The Drurys stood in a reception line and introduced themselves to the guests as they arrived. Most of the guests focused their attention on Redmon and Allison. Redmon had lost much of his British accent after twelve years in Canada and then in the western United States. With his well-trimmed beard and mustache, Redmon Drury, at almost six feet four inches tall, was very handsome. Allison was wearing her deep burgundy gown, with the gold and diamond necklace. She was absolutely beautiful with her auburn hair done up. Allison asked Clarissa to stand with her and help her meet the guests, which put the little girl over the moon. Clarissa had already became quite attached to Allison during their time together. One of Clarissa's favorite things to do with Allison was to ride double as partners on one horse as they roamed the Drury lands.

The Drurys were an attractive family and all the visitors noticed. The Drurys, it seemed, were almost a mystery in the neighborhood for they were always a very private family. That mystery was now being revealed to the local gentry and they liked what they were seeing. Roselind, standing between Roddrick and Redmon, was ravishing in a sea-green gown from London. Joselyn and Red Roland presented the picture of a distinguished nobleman and his lady, as Joselyn was also quite beautiful. She was not widely known in the neighborhood, as she was always content to remain in the background and take care of her home and children over the years. The women guests wanted to know where to find gowns like those worn by Allison and Madeline. When asked, Allison simply replied, "Denver, Colorado, by a French designer there," causing Redmon to chuckle. These

British aristocrats would have no idea where Denver, Colorado might be located.

Madeline was curious about Allison's riding clothes. The day before the party, she tried on Allison's pants, boots and shirts. She thought them comfortable, making her feel so free. Madeline would love to try riding a horse astride in them rather than riding side saddle as noblewomen were expected do in England. She had tucked her long dress around her legs and rode astride when she came south from Castle MacDougal, but the circumstances prevented that experience from being much fun. All she could think about at the time was that she needed to get home safely. Madeline and Allison, with Clarissa there, laughed together as she walked around the bedroom in Allison's boots and clothes. She even strapped on Allison's holster and pistol and giggled when she looked in the mirror at her full reflection.

Once all the introductions were made, drinks were served, giving the guests an opportunity to mingle. The men wanted to meet Redmon and Allison, and especially to hear about their handling of the highwaymen.

The British men also wished to learn about the Drurys' American ranch. When Redmon mentioned that their ranch comprised sixty-two sections of deeded land, those standing around them were shocked. Redmon recounted the story for the men on how his wife, leaning out the coach window with her long hair streaming, shot one of the highwaymen who was chasing them. The noblemen roared with laughter when hearing the tale. Redmon also told the story of Allison and her father fighting off outlaws who attempted to take their ranchland in America. They could not imagine that one family would own forty thousand acres.

Roselind was able to show her home to the ladies before dinner was announced. The oil painting by Grace Wilbanks was now displayed in the sitting room for all to see. Everyone was told that it was a pastoral scene from the cattle and horse ranch owned by Redmon and Allison Drury in the western United States. It showed green grass, wild flowers, and blue sky with Appaloosas grazing and mountains in the background.

The men marveled when they saw the longhorn skull and horns that were now hanging in Roddrick's study. When the Englishmen learned that the horns were from the kind of cattle that roamed the West, they roared with laughter. Redmon told the men that he had seen some longhorn bulls with wider racks than the set hanging on the wall.

The women in attendance were all wealthy and high-born who lived in fine homes. The pressure was now on the noblemen to install bathrooms in their manor houses such as they were seeing and using. Roselind enjoyed showing the women how everything worked. The aristocratic women were amazed when hot water ran from the tap on the lavatory sink. They gazed at themselves in the long mirrors, making a final check of their gowns and hair before leaving the bathroom. "What a luxury," they all commented.

Dinner was announced and everyone found their places in the crystal chandelier-lit dining room. The conversation around the table was lively. Roselind was quite worried that she and her house staff would be unable to entertain the guests properly, but the dinner went off perfectly. Madeline remained close to Allison throughout the evening. For Madeline, Allison was becoming much like a sister and a lifeline. The thought of Allison and Redmon leaving her and going home was devastating. She had been terrified when the MacDougals stopped them on the road, thinking the Scotsmen might actually take her away. But, Redmon and Allison defeated the highlanders and she was safe. Redmon had always protected her as a little girl.

The dancing began in the ballroom and Redmon took Allison into his arms for a waltz. Queen Victoria's cousin, Sir Albert Stuart, asked Madeline to dance and she moved with him around the ballroom floor. The man was quite a talker and Madeline began to relax and enjoy herself. After three dances with Allison, Redmon was paired with Roselind, while Allison danced with Roddrick.

They never really sat together and talked since he came home, and Redmon realized that he actually felt uncomfortable with Roselind in his arms. She was more beautiful now as a mature woman than when he left England so suddenly twelve years earlier. Holding Roselind now was not the same as it was long ago. They were married adults, and so many years had passed between them that being this close was not the same as when they were teenagers.

They made two turns around the floor when she shocked him. "Redmon, I have never stopped loving you. I love Roddrick with my complete heart, but you were my first love. I would have gone with you to Canada. My parents and brothers treated me terribly after we were found together. What they did to you was the worst thing I had ever experienced. I ran away from here the night you were taken away from me in the stable. I died a little when Wilfred branded you.

I hid in our cotter's cottage for four days, and then went to your parents to be with you. I learned when I arrived at Drury Manor that you had already gone to Canada on the ship. I was so devastated when I realized that you were gone and I had lost you. I know I just bared my soul to you. I also realize now that it was never in the stars for us. Roddrick has been completely wonderful to me, and Clendon and Clarissa are a godsend. Allison is wonderful and you are a fortunate man."

Redmon was uncomfortable with the intensity of Roselind's revelations and realized he needed to be brutally honest. "Roselind, I did love you very much, but time passed and I was learning how to survive in a harsh land. You found an outstanding man in Roddrick. In the end, I was fortunate to find my soul mate in Allison. She is my woman in every way, and that is the way I want it to be. We were good together when it was our time, but that was twelve years ago. You have a wonderful family, and I will have the same in New Mexico with Allison. Roddrick was always my best friend as well as my brother. He loves you, and will protect you for all time. We are family, and I am thankful for that. Roselind, you are a wonderful woman and mother, and I am very proud of you for what you have accomplished. You, along with Rod, have turned Eden Hall into a wonderful home." The dance ended and they parted. Redmon gathered Allison in his arms and told his wife how much he loved her.

"I love you, too, mister, but what brought that out of you? I think it's our turn for a dance now," replied Allison.

Roselind watched Redmon and Allison together and knew she just bared her soul for nothing. She had carried those thoughts for so long, and now that they were out she realized they were finally finished. In her heart she knew that she had the most wonderful man, and she was where she needed to be. Redmon had been a dream since she was five years old.

Now she knew that that was all it ever was, a dream. The guarded thought was always there, hidden away in her mind. Now she finally realized that she was fortunate that Roddrick loved her. She and Redmon were clearly different people now. She possessed the perfect home, a good man, and children she loved with all her heart. She knew that Redmon would never repeat what she had just said to him, because he possessed that kind of character and honor.

Roselind had worked hard from the time she came to Roddrick to make Eden Hall a happy home after her experiences growing up in the always-strained dreary Chatham Manor. That is exactly how she wanted it to be. Clendon and Clarrisa were being tutored in French and learning other subjects from a hired tutor much as the Drury children were taught. Eden Hall was no longer the dreary, forbidding Chatham Manor it once was. Back then, nothing she did was ever good enough for her parents. Her brothers were indifferent to her until that fateful night when they found her with Redmon in the stable. It was always about what kind of marriage they could arrange for her to further their aims. She was never going to be given a choice in the matter by her father. She found Roddrick, told him of her love, and asked him to do the same thing Allison asked of Redmon.

❖ ❖ ❖

Redmon danced with Clarissa and bowed to her after each dance and told her what a fine dancer she was. Clarissa beamed from ear to ear and curtsied to her uncle. Redmon also danced with Madeline and his mother during the evening. Joselyn wanted to know where he learned to dance so well, and he replied, "Allison and I learned together in Denver at a mine owner's soirée."

The evening was very successful for the Drurys. Red Roland and Joselyn bid their guests farewell when the evening concluded. The noblemen and their ladies talked about the wonderful Eden Manor house on their way home. Lady Olivia Nelson earlier had confided to Roselind that it was wonderful to enjoy a hot bath without needing to have hot water hauled from the kitchen.

In their room that night, Redmon and Allison made love with abandon. When they were lying in each other's arms afterward, they both agreed that it was time to head home.

"I would like to see Rodney, however," Redmon told his wife. "We can take a trip to Sheffield to see him before we take ship for home." Then they laughed and hugged.

Allison decided to broach the subject she was contemplating and thinking about for weeks. "Sweetheart, what would you think about taking Madeline home with us? I know that we discussed it before, but now it is time to get serious about it."

He pulled her closer. "Oh, thank God! Allison, Love, I have been thinking the same thing. I know we talked of it, but I believe it is what needs to be done to protect Madeline, as well as the rest of the family. I don't believe that Enis MacDougal will leave her alone as long as she is here. We could protect her."

The following morning, the guests who had stayed over at Eden Hall were having breakfast with the Drurys before they traveled home. The couples and their families who lived near to the manor left the night before after the dancing. Redmon planned to tell his family that he and Allison intended to sail for home after a trip to see Rodney. They would bring up the subject of taking Madeline with them when all the guests had left. Allison had already talked to Madeline about going to New Mexico with them. Her reaction was to throw her arms around Allison and reply, "Yes, yes, yes!"

The plan changed unexpectedly when Sir William and Lady Ofelia Nelson invited all the Drurys to Darlington Manor for a party that would include dinners, a foxhunt, and dancing. Sir Albert Stuart insisted that they come. No one refused an invitation from Lord William and Lady Ofelia Nelson, or Sir Albert Stuart. This was a singular honor given by the Nelsons that no noblemen in their right minds could refuse.

After the departure of the remaining guests, Redmon brought up the subject of their leaving after the Nelson soirée and foxhunt. Redmon stated that he and Allison wanted to see Rodney before beginning their trip home. When he mentioned that they would like to take Madeline with them to New Mexico, there were protests from the family members.

Madeline was finally able to break into the spirited family discussion as she spoke, "Momma and Poppa, I want to go with Redmon and Allison. The MacDougals will never leave me alone as long as I am here. Drury and Eden Manors will always be under threat from the MacDougals if I stay. Roselind and Clarissa could very well be in grave danger if I remain here. I have been married to a Scotsman, so I am not marriage worthy in most Englishmen's eyes now and you well know it, certainly not in the north of England by any noble families who know of my background. I love you all, but I must leave here for your protection and mine. Besides, Allison has promised to introduce me to a nice cowboy!"

Redmon laughed, but then after a great deal of talk and tears by her mother and sister-in-law, it was finally agreed that Madeline would go to America. So, Red Roland, Joselyn, Redmon, Allison, and Madeline set off for Drury Manor to make preparations for the journey to Darlington Manor. Roddrick, Roselind, and the children would come in their coach and all would leave from there for the trip south to Darlington Manor. The Nelson party would be a three-day affair with the foxhunt, along with dinners, and dancing on the final evening. In preparation for the trip, Redmon, Allison, and Madeline wearing pants, rode the Drury Manor lands. Allison and Madeline practiced riding sidesaddle for the foxhunt.

The two young women put together riding habits in the Drury colors of purple and gold. They helped Roselind gather her riding clothes to make a perfect oufit for the foxhunt.

The Drurys did not have any idea of the number of noblemen and their ladies who would be converging on Darlington Manor. They were pleased to learn that Lady Ophelia had rooms set aside for them. The Drurys were unaware of the fine impression they made on Lord and Lady Nelson. Ofelia Nelson was completely impressed by Joselyn, Roselind, and Allison. Lord William Nelson was already making arrangements to have bathrooms installed in Darlington Manor after seeing and using those at Eden Hall. He even asked Red Roland to allow the Drury blacksmith, Albert Abney, to come to Darlington Manor and direct the installation of the plumbing. Red Roland readily agreed, which impressed Sir William Nelson. Albert would be paid a tidy sum for helping to plumb Darlington Manor. He studied the coal-fired hot water heater and thought he could build a temporary one for Sir William and Lady Ofelia to use until they could order one from St. Louis. Redmon told Sir William that he would make arrangements for the water heater to be shipped when he reached America.

❖ ❖ ❖

Duplicate coaches rolled south pulled by fine Morgan coach horses. The coaches displayed the Drury crest on their doors, and both were polished to a fine shine. Their horses for the foxhunt were being pulled behind the coaches. All their trunks of clothes and saddles were loaded and tied down on the top of each coach.

Joselyn decided not to ride in the hunt, although she was capable. She giggled when she said that she would stay behind at Darlington Manor and wrangle the children, a term she heard Allison use when talking about herding cattle in the west. Allison practiced riding a sidesaddle along with Madeline for a few days before the trip south.

Roselind did the same at Eden Hall. Allison told Redmon that it made her feel silly riding that way, but she was up for the challenge. She decided to make a game of the riding and have fun with it, as she did most things. All of their trunks packed with clothes and saddles were loaded on top of the coaches. Redmon included his case of weapons. When Allison questioned him, he simply replied, "I might need to shoot a rabbit or a skunk," which caused her to shake her head.

Only Redmon realized that the Chathams' stolen manor was near Darlington in Leeds. The sworn enemies of the Drurys could very well be present for this gathering of noblemen and their ladies.

For the first night of their trip, the Drury coaches stayed over at the White Horse Inn. As the coaches approached the imposing three-story Nelson Manor house, Red Roland exclaimed, "Oh, my! The queen's banner is flying from the roof of Darlington Manor. Do you see it?"

In the other Drury coach, Roselind suddenly took Roddrick's hand. "Rod, there is my parents' coach ahead of us. I saw the Chatham crest at the curve in the lane. What am I going to do? I never thought about them being here. I never wanted to see them again!"

Roddrick pulled her close on the cushions. "You are a Drury as you have always been. We protect our family. I suppose we could have Allison shoot their ears off, as they say in America."

"Rod, what if they learn that Redmon killed Wilfred? Mortimer is as evil as Wilfred ever was," Roselind asked with concern.

"Well, as Redmon says in his Western vernacular, 'We will cross that stream when we come to it.'" Roselind hugged him and finally laughed, pulling his face to her and kissing him, which caused Clendon and Clarissa to say, "Ew, ew!"

The activity in front of the huge manor house was bustling and organized. Trunks were unloaded from the coaches that traveled a far distance. As it happened, a house steward was assigned specifically to the Drurys when they arrived, and men were ready to take charge of their trunks and carry them to their rooms. The Drurys were given a suite of rooms next to one another on the second floor of the manor. As it happened, the Chathams were given two small rooms on the third floor of the manor house. That did not set well with them. They thought their station in British society was greater than that.

The Drurys received their next surprise when they all walked into the large foyer of Darlington House. There stood Rodney Drury waiting for them with a huge grin on his face. They noticed that he seemed to be with a very pretty young woman. Immediately, there were hugs all around. Redmon had not seen his oldest brother in fourteen years, and the reunion between the two was something to see as they hugged and pounded backs.

Rodney was somewhat amazed when he saw his little brother who was no longer little. All the Drury men were tall and handsome, but Redmon was imposing. He was slightly taller than Rodney, but both brothers were handsome and quite dashing. Rodney then introduced his companion. Her name was Jane Chadwick, the middle daughter of Earl Thomas and Lady Elizabeth Chadwick of Chadwick Manor near Chesterfield. Jane Chadwick was a cousin of Sir William and Lady Olivia Nelson. It was clear to his family that Rodney and Jane were a serious couple.

Allison was then introduced to Rodney and Jane. Rodney was amazed by the sheer beauty of Allison. He had read the letters from Redmon and Allison that his mother had sent to him, but there was never any mention in the letters about what Allison looked like. Jane could only stare, for she thought Allison made the other women pale in comparison to her beauty.

She absolutely loved reading the adventures of Redmon Drury, especially those written by Allison. The story of how Allison shot the highwayman and the Scottish highlander made her laugh out loud. Jane thought those stories and the other adventures made quite a tale. She was happy now that she was getting to meet them all.

❖ ❖ ❖

All the coaches were taken and parked while the horses were put in a paddock. Redmon noticed the Chatham coach with three fine horses tied behind it. Evidently, Sir Reginald, Lady Lydia, and Mortimer planned to ride to the hunt. Redmon quietly warned Allison that they might have to help Roddrick protect Roselind from her former family. Roddrick told Redmon of the nasty letters that Lydia Chatham had sent to Roselind. It seemed that Lady Lydia sent several over the years as stories of the remade Chatham Manor circulated. Each of Lydia Chatham's letters spewed venom.

When Redmon got the chance, he quietly told Roddrick, "I saw the Chatham coach, Rod. We will stay close and help you protect Roselind. We will not allow her to be abused by those people. If they have any respect for the Nelsons, nothing will happen here."

Redmon also alerted Rodney and asked him to help protect Roselind. Rodney knew everything that had happened between the Drurys and the Chathams, and was forthcoming with Jane Chadwick about the history between the two families, so Jane was also prepared for any trouble that might occur.

After washing up and dressing carefully, the Drurys went down the wide staircase together and entered the ballroom. Because the queen was present, the Drury women were dressed in fine gowns and the men in their best suits. Clarissa placed her hand in Allison's so she could be close to her. Each family was introduced and their names were called as they entered the room. They heard the names of Sir Reginald and Lady Lydia Chatham announced ahead of them along with Mortimer and Anne Chatham. All the couples were moving toward a dais to be presented to the queen, who was sitting in a very fine cushioned chair. The Drurys could see Sir Albert Stuart standing close to the queen, helping identify each couple or family for her.

When each couple entered the ballroom, they handed a card to a uniformed steward who spoke out in a booming voice. When the Drurys entered, they handed over their cards to the steward and the man announced so all could hear, "Sir Roland and Lady Joselyn Drury, and Madeline Drury, of Drury Manor, Eden. Roddrick and Roselind Drury, Clendon and Clarissa Drury of Eden Hall. Rodney Drury of Sheffield and Mistress Jane Chadwick of Chesterfield. Redmon and Allison Drury of the R bar A Ranch in the New Mexico Territory, United States of America."

When the Drurys were announced, especially the names Roselind, Redmon, and Allison, and where they were from, many heads turned to look. Some in the room did not even realize there was a Rodney Drury and knew nothing of him. The fact that he was with one of the most sought after and wealthiest young women in Jane Chadwick was quite something.

The Chathams' heads whipped around when they heard Roselind's and Redmon's names announced. The looks on their faces could have frozen water. When the Drurys stepped to the dais, the men bowed and the women dropped curtsies. Sir Albert Stuart spoke in a clear voice for most in the room to hear. "Your Grace, these are the Drurys, your loyal subjects on the Eden River. This is Sir Red Roland and Lady Joselyn, and their daughter Madeline of Drury Manor. Now I wish to introduce Roddrick and Roselind Drury and their children Clenden and Clarissa. I recently spent a wonderful few days at their beautiful Eden Hall. They were the finest of hosts.

They have bathrooms in their manor houses with hot and cold running water engineered by one of the next couples you will meet. Your Grace, I wish to introduce Rodney Drury, who is now an accomplished barrister residing in Sheffield and his companion, Mistress Jane Chadwick of Chadwick Manor, whom I am sure you know. You will remember that Jane is a cousin of Sir William and Lady Ofelia, our hosts."

"Now, this next couple you will enjoy meeting. Your Grace, I would present Redmon and Allison Drury who own a cattle and horse ranch of some forty thousand acres near the former Spanish capital called Santa Fe in the western part of America. Redmon and Allison thwarted two highway robbers when they reached our shores. You might find it interesting that Allison shot one of the robbers while leaning out a window of the moving coach while it was taking them home to Drury Manor from Gretna Green. Then she shot the pistol from the hand of a Scottish Highlander who intended to attack and harm the Drurys. It has become quite a tale."

Allison was embarrassed by the attention because all the noblemen and their ladies gathered around the queen and heard the praise heaped on her by the queen's cousin. The queen seemed to study the Drurys. She acknowledged Sir Roland and Lady Joselyn and told them how much she appreciated their loyalty.

Then the queen focused her gaze on Allison and smiled. "Young lady. That is quite a tale as my cousin Albert says. Personally, I abhor violence, but I am terribly sorry that you were forced to defend yourself in our land. I hope the remainder of your stay in our land is pleasant with no further high adventures." Then the queen actually put out her hand to Allison, which drew a gasp from the assembled gentry.

Allison took the offered hand and curtsied. "Thank you, Your Grace. Coming to your beautiful country, as well as meeting you, is an experience I will remember and treasure for the rest of my life."

The Drurys moved away from the dais to make way for more couples. Immediately, they were surrounded. Noblemen and their ladies wanted to meet the people who made such an impression on the first cousin and favorite of the queen. To be singled out in such a way by Sir Albert Stuart was quite something in these noblemen's eyes. Redmon and Allison answered questions about their ranch in New Mexico. Red Roland and Roddrick answered questions from those interested in the plumbing. Some even asked if they might come to Drury Manor and Eden Hall to see the bathrooms that had made such an impression on Sir Albert Stuart.

Roselind was carefully watching her mother, father, and brother stare at her from across the room with looks filled with utter hatred. She took Roddrick's hand for reassurance and he squeezed it. She had not seen her family for twelve years and it was obvious that there was no forgiveness in them for her running away and then marrying a Drury. The letters that her mother sent to Eden Hall always hurt Roselind a great deal. She had called Roselind every nasty name imaginable.

The visiting continued as some old friends of the Chadwicks met Rodney and Jane. They were trying to determine if the couple was serious about each other. Finally, the Drurys were able to move to a refreshment table in an adjoining room where other couples were gathered.

It was there that Lady Lydia Chatham came at her daughter with Reginald and Mortimer behind her. "Well! If it isn't the traitorous daughter of a true British noble family. You are no more than a cheap prostitute for moving in with these people. You have been used by two of them, which makes you even worse."

Roselind's hand shot out so suddenly that few people that were actually listening to the vicious tirade by Lady Lydia Chatham even saw the motion. Roselind slapped her mother so hard that Lydia Chatham's head was turned to the side, and a red mark was left instantly on her pallid cheek. The slap however was heard throughout the room. There were gasps of shock from women standing near the scene who saw and heard the slap. Immediately, the Drury family closed ranks. Roddrick put Roselind behind him to shield her from her former family.

Joselyn and Madeline gathered the children, and Redmon and Rodney quickly stepped next to Roddrick. Red Roland lined up next to his sons. Allison moved next to Redmon, but reached and took Roselind's hand in hers and pulled her close for support.

Jane Chadwick initially seemed shocked by the suddenness of this confrontation, but then stepped to support Roselind. Jane Chadwick's first fiancé was killed during a highroad holdup by robbers, much like those who attempted to stop the coach when Redmon and Allison reached England. Jane actually resigned herself to becoming an old maid until she met Rodney in Sheffield and they decided to become a couple. They were both now twenty-nine years old. Jane decided that the Drurys were a fine family including the adventurous long-lost brother named Redmon. Rodney told her everything that happened to Redmon and Roselind some twelve years earlier when they were only fifteen years old. There were no secrets between Rodney and Jane. She was also impressed when she saw Allison instantly support Roselind. She might have expected some tension between Roselind and Allison, but obviously there was none.

To everyone's surprise, Roselind suddenly spoke in perfect French. "You have no idea what a noble family is, or what it should be. I received a complete education while residing at Drury Manor. I have been treated with respect as a Drury. I am a Drury, and am very proud of that fact. You people have committed unspeakable acts as a so-called noble family! Lady Joselyn has been more of a mother to me than you ever were. The Drury name is one to be honored, as I do!"

There were gasps from the people standing nearby that understood French. Redmon laughed out loud, for it was clear that the Chathams understood nothing that Roselind said. "Well said, Roselind. You are a credit to the Drury name!"

The Chathams were somewhat stunned that Roselind learned to speak French while she was with the Drurys. They were sure that their daughter just said some bad things to them in that language. They stared at Roselind with surprise and loathing written on their faces.

Reginald Chatham turned red and looked as though he was about to explode. "You Drurys are no better than London street urchins. You stole our land and you well know it. That woman who we once called daughter is no better than you. She belongs with you. We washed our hands of her when she betrayed us with him." Reginald Chatham pointed at Redmon.

Red Roland spoke quietly. "Chatham, your arrogance was your undoing. Drury honor is something your sons could never understand. Roselind has always possessed that kind of honor. We are proud to have Roselind as a part of our family and we will protect her. You people never deserved to have such a fine daughter. Now do not approach our daughter again."

Mortimer, standing behind his father, was sneering at Redmon, who simply looked back at him with an expression that could not be read. Allison stepped close to her husband, still holding Roselind's hand. "So that is the other coward that ordered you held down by other men so he could watch. He looks just like Wilfred, the coward who tried to have my father and I murdered so he could steal our land," Allison said in an unconcerned tone.

The sneer on Mortimer's face turned to one of shock, and then to pure hatred. "You people clearly had something to do with my brother's death," Mortimer bit out.

Allison laughed. "Your brother tried to steal my father's ranch by having us murdered by the nine men he hired. Then he came to murder us himself. In the

West where we live, cattle, horse, or land thieves are either shot or hanged. My father and I shot several of your son's hired outlaws. When he finally showed up, we got him. Your land-stealing brother is buried somewhere on the Circle W, which my father still owns. As to your remarks about Roselind, you people have no idea what a fine woman she is, and you could not even carry her water, as we say in the West." Roselind squeezed Allison's hand in response.

The look of shocked dismay on the Chathams' faces could not be described, and Redmon laughed and squeezed Allison's other hand. Allison was trying to divert the Chathams' attention away from the Drurys to her. She would take the blame for killing Wilfred to help her family. Mortimer stepped toward Allison and raised his hand as if to strike her, but she never flinched. Instead, Allison stared into Mortimer Chatham's eyes, daring him to finish his swing.

Redmon stopped Mortimer cold and said, "Mortimer Chatham, twelve years ago you and Wilfred ordered me held down by four men, and Wilfred put a brand on me. Two years ago, Wilfred tried to murder my wife and her father for their ranch land. If you attempt to strike my wife, you are a dead man. Your father spoke of us as the dregs of society. Look to your own house for what your own family has done to others. Murder and mayhem seem to be family traits of the Chatham brand. Cattle now walk over the ground where your brother is buried on my father-in-law's ranch. Wilfred will rot in hell for his evil deeds. If you require satisfaction, I will gladly oblige your wishes. Your mother and father have insulted a member of our family and you have attempted to strike my wife. I will even give you the opportunity to select the place, time, and weapons, because you seem to think so much of yourself. I believe the queen frowns upon the practice of the manly art of combat of honor.

In the West, where we live, the practice still takes place with pistols, face to face. A man is not held by four stout yeomen as you and your brother did to me, lo, those many years ago. By the way, I no longer wear the brand you gave me that night. I was able to have it removed in Santa Fe by an army surgeon after we buried Wilfred on the ranch he was attempting to steal.

Suddenly, Mortimer Chatham tried to strike Redmon, and there was a gasp from the watchers who were gathered around to listen to this extraordinary and unbelievable confrontation between two British noble families. Redmon caught Mortimer's wrist in an iron grip. "I will have satisfaction, Redmon Drury. You and your American slut of a so-called wife will pay for this outrage. You Drurys have never been worthy of licking Chatham boots," Mortimer spat.

Sir Albert Stuart was suddenly standing next to Redmon and Allison. "Mortimer Chatham, you embarrass yourself and your family. You have insulted my friends and two fine ladies. I heard everything said here, and I believe you owe the Drurys, and expressly Lady Roselind and Allison Drury, an apology. If you refuse that apology, I will personally see to it that you do get your wish and face Redmon Drury man to man. Will you, and your father and mother, apologize to the Drurys for your comments toward them?"

Mortimer spoke through gritted teeth. "We will never apologize to these people. They deserve nothing but our distain."

"Very well then. Redmon, you may choose the weapons, but I will choose the time and place for this contest of honor," Sir Albert instructed.

Redmon spoke evenly, but he still held Mortimer's arm in a hard grip and looked into his eyes. "Sir Albert, I will allow Mortimer to select the weapon of his choice since he seems to be so offended by our presence here. I could choose pistols, but shooting him down quickly would be far too easy. I should probably choose knives in hand to hand combat in the Huron Indian way, but that would also be much too easy. So I will allow Mortimer to choose." Then Redmon displayed a smile that Allison recognized instantly.

Mortimer suddenly smiled for the first time. "I choose the sword. Redmon Drury, you will die by my hand, as you should have died twelve years ago. My sister and this slut of yours will be welcome to your dead remains after I am through with you."

Sir Albert Stuart spoke. "The Nelsons have invited us here as their guests. I will not allow this feud between the Chathams and Drurys to disrupt these festivities, which our hosts have planned. Redmon and Mortimer, you will not under any circumstances confront one another here. You will meet on the field of honor the morning after these festivities are concluded. The queen will be leaving this very afternoon to return to London. If she hears of this, you will both be arrested. Redmon Drury, have you a second with whom I may converse?"

Roddrick spoke up. "I will stand with my brother as his second."

Rodney also spoke. "I will also be proud to stand with Redmon in this matter of honor. I do however question whether my brother's opponent has enough honor to participate after his insults toward two fine women." Jane Chadwick, who was standing next to Allison, suddenly laughed, which caused Allison to join in.

"Very well. Mortimer, who will stand with you?" Sir Albert Stuart asked.

Reginald stepped forward after giving Rodney a hard look and said, "I will stand with my son," and then gave Redmon what he thought was a knowing look.

"I observed that this confrontation was initiated by Lady Lydia Chatham toward her daughter. I will warn both families that I will tolerate no further embarrassment for the Nelsons during their planned activities. This trouble between your families will be concluded, and I mean completely concluded, four days hence. Am I understood by both parties?" Sir Albert looked at the Chathams first, specifically Lady Lydia who was as red as a beet. She nodded. Then Sir Albert looked at the Drurys. Red Roland spoke for them. "Sir Albert, there will be no trouble from the Drurys, I can assure you. We wished for none of this to occur here. If we had realized that something like this dispute might have occurred, we would not have come."

"Sir Roland, I, along with the Nelsons, invited your family here because we enjoyed your party and company so much at Eden Hall, so I suppose this confrontation might be my responsibility. Lady Chatham, as I observed, initiated this unfortunate episode and will bear the brunt of the dishonor demonstrated here!" Then Sir Albert looked hard at Lydia Chatham. She blanched and shrank back.

Redmon squeezed Mortimer's wrist so hard he winced, and then he released him. The iron grip should have given Mortimer a premonition of what was to come for him. Mortimer, in his arrogance, gave Redmon a scathing look, but the Chathams turned and retreated from the room. The Chathams, because of their hatred for the Drurys, displayed little respect for the Nelsons who had invited them for the planned festivities.

Sir Albert watched the Chathams leave the room, and then turned to Redmon and Allison. "Redmon, you must know that Mortimer is considered as a master of sword as was his brother Wilfred. I have heard it said that Mortimer is more accomplished than his brother was. I will also tell you that Sir Thomas Dudley and his daughter Melissa were close friends of my family. Their doctor Seth Jenson told me that he was almost certain they were poisoned but could not prove it. Mortimer challenged the doctor, who was a good man, to a duel and killed him easily. I believe the Chathams have much to answer for in their next life. Redmon, beware of Mortimer for I believe he will be devious."

"Sir Albert, we are sorry that this happened here. We did not realize that the Chathams would be here when we accepted the invitation of the Nelsons' hospitality. We certainly didn't want trouble with anyone. The trouble between the Drurys and the Chathams began some fourteen years ago, or maybe even before that time. Roselind was treated terribly by her family. She has been our daughter from the time she came to us for protection. We are fortunate to have her as part of our family," Red Roland said.

Tears were flowing from Roselind's eyes when she heard her father-in-law speak of her and when he defended her to her own mother and father. Roselind realized that she was loved and would be protected by the Drurys. Roselind was immediately in Roddrick's arms and surrounded and supported by the Drurys. Allison turned to Jane Chadwick and smiled. "Jane, as we say in the West, I think you will do to ride the river with. I look forward to our getting acquainted."

Sir Albert looked at Redmon and Allison. "I realize it may be a sensitive subject but I would very much like to hear about what happened to Wilfred Chatham in your New Mexico. I know it can't be proven, but I believe what Doctor Jenson said about Wilfred doing away with my friends in order to get Dudley Manor. Also, Redmon, I would like to hear of this branding if you would consider confiding in me."

Joselyn and Madeline took Roselind to her bedroom so she could calm down. Clendon and Clarissa wanted to know why that woman had talked in such a harsh and mean way to their mother. They did not know that Lydia Chatham was actually their grandmother. Roselind never spoke the names of her parents or brothers in her children's presence. As far as Roselind was concerned, that chapter of her life was a closed book. The letters she received had steeled Roselind against her mother. Joselyn Drury was her mother now.

Sir Albert, Redmon, and Allison walked in the gardens together, and Redmon explained that he and Roselind grew up together on adjoining manors. "We planned to marry at fifteen. Then Wilfred and Mortimer caught us together one evening. They ordered me held by four of their men in the stable and Wilfred branded me on the chest with a C. They threatened my life if I stayed on the manor. I took ship to Canada to protect my family. In a place called North Bay, Canada, I learned the sword and fencing from a French master. I also learned weapons and hand-to-hand fighting from a Huron Indian brave. He taught me forest craft and how to survive in extreme conditions. Sir Albert, no one here in England understands what it is like living and surviving in the wilderness of Canada, and then in the West. You learn many skills out of necessity there."

"Ten years after leaving England, I discovered Wilfred Chatham in Santa Fe. He was plotting to murder Allison and her father Franklin, and take over their ranch land so he could establish a western cattle empire, as he called it. Allison and her father held the land with a legal deed, but that did not seem to matter to Wilfred Chatham. He sent men to kill them because he knew it would be easy to do with the law so far away. I followed his cutthroats south from Santa Fe to Allison's ranch. We all fought them and Chatham's men died."

"Finally, Wilfred came to the ranch and I noticed he carried a sword that was hanging from his saddle. We fought with our blades and I killed him. During our time fighting Wilfred's men, Allison and I fell in love and married. I wanted her to see England one time before we settle on our ranch. Now this confrontation with the Chathams here has hurt my family and I am sorry for that. I am terribly sorry if Lord and Lady Nelson have been embarrassed by what occurred here today. Especially with the queen being here.

The Chathams carry a great deal of hatred for the Drurys and I have no idea why. That hatred goes far beyond what Roselind and I did as children and young people. Reginald Chatham completely mismanaged their lands and was in debt to lenders. My father bought those loans and acquired the former Chatham lands. Maybe that is part of their hatred for us. Sir Albert, I can tell you that Wilfred Chatham was completely evil, and I believe Mortimer is much the same. He laughed and spit on me as I was being branded. When I challenged him to face me afterward, he said that his father would have me arrested and hanged if I came after them for what they did to me. Well, now we have come full circle and we will finally meet as Wilfred and I finally met. Wilfred seemed to think he was an outstanding swordsman, but he was not."

"Redmon, how well do you handle the blade?" Sir Albert Stuart asked. "You are telling me that Wilfred Chatham was considered to be a master but you defeated him. I have heard that Mortimer is a master. He and Wilfred learned from Sir Henry Tanney, who was once the best in England during his military years."

"Sir Albert, I suppose we will learn how well Mortimer learned the sword in four days when we meet. Wilfred was also purported to be a master of the blade and was taught by the same man that taught Mortimer. Wilfred was clearly not the swordsman he seemed to think he was when we met. My master, Emile Boushard, was an excellent teacher, and I believe he taught me well. I have been fortunate to find military officers with whom to practice since leaving North Bay, Canada." Redmon was confident with this response.

⛭ ⛭ ⛭

That evening there was some tension in the dining room as the guests gathered and sat down for dinner. All the guests now knew of the trouble between the Chathams and the Drurys.

They also knew of the impending duel that would be fought between Mortimer Chatham and Redmon Drury.

Earlier that afternoon, Allison went to the rest of the Drury women and told them that when they all walked into the dining room, they must present a united front and look as though nothing concerned them. They must all look their very best for the assembled noblemen and their ladies. They would all help one another to dress and do their hair and makeup. Roselind went into Allison's arms and thanked her for holding her up against her former family that afternoon. Jane Chadwick even came to the Drury rooms so she could prepare for the meal and get to know the Drury women better. Soon all the girls were laughing together as they did each other's hair. Allison kept the mood light and Jane Chadwick told the other women what a good time she was having being part of the group.

The Drurys walked into the dining room with their heads held high and proud. When Allison came into the dining room on Redmon's arm, there were gasps from the women. Allison was absolutely beautiful. She was wearing a dark blue gown that Redmon had bought for her in Chicago. What everyone in the room noticed was the tan, healthy complexion that Allison Drury displayed. Next came Red Roland with Joselyn, and she was stunning in an ivory gown. At fifty-two, Joselyn was still very beautiful as well as regal. Rodney came into the room with Jane on his arm, and the Nelsons, along with the Chadwicks, were amazed. Allison and Roselind had helped her with her hair and makeup, and Jane was stunning in her purple gown. Jane Chadwick was always quite pretty, but never spent much time trying to look pretty. On this night, she was quite stunning.

Roddrick stepped into the room with Roselind on his arm and there were gasps again from the women. Roselind was a picture of beauty wearing Allison's deep burgundy gown that fit her like a glove. Joselyn and Allison had carefully arranged her long, dark-blonde hair and makeup to perfection. She held her head up and was as regal as any queen.

Edward Benford, the man who was supposed to marry Roselind if the marriage contract had been completed, could only stare when he saw Roselind. He had eventually married quite a plain young woman named Julia Mansfield, who sadly displayed very little personality. The Chathams could only stare at Roselind. Her beauty was enthrawling. They hated that she seemed to be quite proud of being with the Drurys. They were shocked when she spoke out to them in perfect French. One of their few friends who understood French told them after the confrontation what Roselind had said to them. Reginald Chatham would never admit that he had only seen his daughter as a pawn to be used to gain advantage when she was fourteen and fifteen years old. His plans were completely ruined the night she ran away after being ruined by Redmon Drury. The Chathams hated to admit it, but they also recognized that Clendon and Clarrisa Drury were extremely handsome children. It was clear that Clarrisa would be beautiful when she grew older. Madeline followed, holding the hands of Clendon and Clarissa. She presented quite a picture of beauty, wearing one of Allison's American gowns from Denver.

The Drury family was placed at one end of the long table while the Chathams were seated at the other end. It was clear to all that Lady Ofelia Nelson was warned of the trouble between the two families and acted accordingly. The men in the room were openly admiring the Drury women for they were all quite beautiful, but clearly Allison and Roselind were in a class by themselves. Some of the men who knew Mortimer's skill with a sword, thought it unfortunate that Allison would soon be a widow. Two of the younger noblemen present planned to court Allison after Mortimer Chatham killed Redmon. They both thought Allison would look stunning on their arms in London and hosting parties at their manor houses.

None of these people knew the journey Redmon Drury had traveled to reach this point in his life. None of the men present, especially Mortimer Chatham, could have any idea just how dangerous Redmon Drury actually was when confronted with danger.

Allison noticed a young woman that was quite pretty, but she was always standing behind the Chathams and appeared to be cowed by them. Allison learned that the young woman was Anne Chatham, Mortimer's wife of three years. To Allison, the young woman looked so sad and unhappy.

Allison was apprehensive about Redmon facing Mortimer. She knew, however, that he was strong and resourceful. She prayed that her man could survive the coming test with Mortimer Chatham so they could go home and resume their lives. She knew Redmon possessed far more character than Mortimer Chatham after her experiences with Wilfred. The confrontation in the refreshment room also demonstrated the Chathams' lack of character as far as Allison was concerned. Madeline, who was watching Allison and took Allison's hand under the table, said, "Allison, it will be all right. I believe Redmon will take us home to America. I trust you both with my life."

The conversation around the table was light, but the specter of the coming duel was the topic of the subdued conversations. There were many furtive glances toward Redmon and Allison during the meal. Sir Albert Stuart now knew that Redmon easily dispatched Wilfred Chatham with a sword, but kept that knowledge to himself. Allison actually described the duel in detail for him during their walk and he chuckled at the details.

After the meal the couples strolled the gardens, and many wanted to meet and learn more about the American Drurys. Jane Chadwick brought her parents Sir Thomas and Lady Elizabeth to meet the Drurys. Rodney suddenly surprised everyone when he knelt before Jane and proposed. Rodney had already asked Sir Thomas for permission and it was granted. Sir Thomas and Lady Elizabeth were afraid that their daughter would never find a good man to marry. Sir Thomas took the time to investigate the Drurys and discovered a well-established family who were large landholders in northern England. Sir William Nelson and Sir Albert Stuart also gave ringing endorsements of the Drurys.

Jane immediately accepted Rodney's proposal. She went into his arms and whispered in his ear, "I was wondering how much longer you would wait. I was afraid that I was going to be forced to ask you! I love you, Rodney Drury." Rodney slipped a beautiful diamond ring on Jane's left hand. Congratulations were the order of the day for the couple. Her parents hugged her and admired her ring. Then the Drurys surrounded the newly engaged couple.

The Chathams were watching the proceedings and wondered what the Chadwicks were thinking, allowing their daughter to marry into such a family. They said some very unkind things about the Chadwicks' lack of character for allowing such a match. Those comments would get back to Sir Thomas and Lady Elizabeth Chadwick. The Chadwicks were also friends of Sir Thomas Dudley and Melissa Dudley before she married Wilfred Chatham. Sir Albert Stuart gave Sir Thomas

Chadwick the details he had learned about the demise of Wilfred Chatham, and of his attempt to take the land belonging to Allison's father.

All who met and conversed with Redmon and Allison were impressed with their straightforward manner. Some of the noblemen and their ladies wanted to talk to Roddrick and Roselind and learn what they were doing at Eden Hall after the descriptions of their wonderful house by Sir Albert Stuart. Several of these people asked if they might come to see what Roddrick did with the plumbing. Roselind invited them.

The Chadwicks came to Rodney and Jane and told their daughter how wonderful she looked. After the glowing remarks Sir Albert Stuart made about the Drurys, they were excited that Jane might have finally found her man. Then the proposal came along with the wonderful diamond ring. They were now excited for their daughter in spite of the trouble looming between the Drurys and Chathams.

The Chathams heard all the glowing descriptions of the wonders wrought by Roselind and Roddrick at the former Chatham Manor and were seething with anger. Their anger grew as each nobleman who was in attendance sang the praises of Roselind Drury as a wonderful hostess and to the wonders of her home. They lurked in the garden and watched their former daughter holding court. Lydia Chatham spewed venom at the injustice of how such lowly people were being held in such high regard by people the Chathams considered to be their peers.

Before the evening ended, the Drurys and Chadwicks sat on the terrace at the side of the large manor house so both groups could learn more about one another. It was clear for both families that Rodney and Jane would be well matched. Jane Chadwick decided that she enjoyed being with Allison Drury and the rest of the Drury women. She looked forward to traveling to Drury Manor and Eden Hall.

🎛 🎛 🎛

No one knew that the Chatham hatred for the Drurys went back four generations. Orrick Drury was a young man that had fought in the king's army and on a battlefield in France found himself fighting at the back of Edward, the king's son. Orrick saved the young knight and heir to the throne twice from being impaled from behind during the battle. Edward knighted Orrick Drury there on the battlefield, and his father gave Orrick the lands along the Eden River in northern England for his deeds. As it happened, the lands that the king presented to Orrick Drury were near those held by another noble family named Chatham. Manfred Chatham was also on the battlefield that day, but rather than show bravery, he slinked from the field showing cowardice. Because of his family's standing as noblemen, Manfred was not brought before the king for punishment. However, part of the Chatham lands were taken from them and given to Orrick Drury. From that day forward there was a deep-seated hatred for Orrick Drury who was a foot soldier who attained knighthood through bravery. The Chathams referred to him as no more than a boot lackey. There was a stain on the Chatham name because of Manfred's cowardice on the battlefield that was forgotten in time, except in the minds of the Chathams. The name Manfred was never given to any future Chatham son. They resented the fact that the king would take part of their land and give it to a man they considered below them in station.

Then the ultimate insult came when Orrick Drury was able to marry the daughter of a nearby nobleman. Her name was Elizabeth Fairfield. Orrick was able to win her hand only because he received a title and lands from the King of England. Manfred Chatham had also coveted Elizabeth Fairfield, but her father chose Orrick Drury for his daughter, which was a slap in the face of Sir Walter Chatham, the patriarch of the Chatham family. Where Orrick Drury was tall and handsome, and honest to a fault, Manfred Chatham was considered a coward by the crown.

Orrick and Elizabeth built the original Drury Manor. The worst part for the Chathams was that Drury

Manor was only a stone's throw from Chatham Manor. Manfred's hatred for Orrick and the Drurys was passed down through four generations. Each father told his sons that the Drurys were no better than stable hands that received their title by trickery and deception. The Drurys always managed their lands well, and Orrick realized that an education would be the key to their continued success. He made sure his sons, and their sons, would have an excellent library and the best tutors. Where the Drurys were humble and glad for what they had, the Chathams were arrogant and always envious of others.

The Chathams seemed to feel as though they had to tell others that they were of noble birth. The story of the Drurys' lowly birth was passed down to Wilfred and Mortimer Chatham by their parents from the time they were little boys. When Roselind came along, she was largely ignored by her brothers until that fateful night in the stable. The Chatham hatred ran deep, except in Roselind.

※ ※ ※

That night after the dinner, Redmon and Allison made love slowly and carefully. She wanted to be as close as she could possibly get to her husband and never wanted her time with him to end. They had grown so close and loved each other more than ever.

In their small bedroom, Mortimer was abusing his young wife Anne. He was taking his frustrations of looking the fool by Redmon Drury out on his wife. Anne whimpered and begged Mortimer not to hit her anymore.

✳ ✳ ✳

The morning of the hunt there was a swirl of activity around the horse paddocks. Redmon and Roddrick saddled all their horses. "Rod, we need to stay together when we ride. Mortimer or Reginald may try to hurt Roselind or one of the other girls to get at us. I know I haven't said it, Rod, but I am proud to have you as my brother. Now we need to protect our women. We'll warn father to keep his eye out and stay close to Madeline, but we need to watch his back also. Now that Reginald and Mortimer have declared their hatred for us openly and know that I killed Wilfred, they may try something underhanded before tomorrow morning.

If I know Allison, she will have that little pistol hidden somewhere on her and will shoot either Reginald or Mortimer if they try anything…and ask questions later." They both laughed.

Roddrick slapped Redmon on the arm. "Redmon, you are a good man. I know you always loved Roselind, and then that night happened. You found Allison and it is easy to see that you belong together. When I saw the two of you, I was honestly relieved. I wish that night never happened, but it brought Roselind to Drury House and to me. I love Roselind and thank my lucky stars every day for her. I feel as though I might have let you down when you were forced to leave home all those years ago. I thought afterward that we could have faced Mortimer and Wilfred together, along with father. You don't know it, but father challenged Reginald Chatham with the sword, but the man declined. Reginald knew what a fine swordsman our father is and that he would have died. Then Roselind came to hide with us. I fell in love with her and wanted her for myself. I know that she has always loved you, and I can live with that because she is my wife. I was afraid what her reaction might be when we learned you came home, but it has worked out for the both of us. Now I know that we can face the Chathams as a family and never waiver in our strength. We have Rodney with us like it was when we were young. Redmon, you have an amazing woman, and she has supported Roselind completely since we came here to Darlington Manor. She has become a stalwart friend of my wife. Clarissa would probably go home with you if we let her. She keeps saying she could become a cowgirl like her Aunt Allie." Then they laughed together and slapped shoulders again.

Rodney and Jane joined them just then, and Redmon asked his older brother and Jane to ride on the hunt with Red Roland and Madeline to help protect them. Jane was dressed in a traditional riding habit. Rodney had taken her into his arms when he saw her and told her how proud he was to have her as his fiancé.

At that moment, Red Roland, Roselind, Allison, and Madeline walked to the horses. Red Roland cleared his throat. Redmon had seen Allison in her riding habit in their room, but in the morning sunlight she was stunning. The skirt was in the Drury deep purple with gold trim, while her jacket was also purple with a gold blouse underneath. She sported a pointed cap also in purple, with a feather sticking out from one side. "I thought the feather Enis MacDougal wore looked cute, so I fixed all us Drury girls up with one," Allison said, causing them all to laugh.

Roselind and Madeline were wearing matching outfits in the Drury deep purple and gold. Redmon gathered Allison into his arms, as did Roddrick with Roselind. Redmon swung Allison around in a circle while she rested her hands on his shoulders and giggled. When he set her down, they stepped behind a horse where she pulled his head down, and kissed him hard. Roddrick planted a kiss on Roselind's lips in full view of the nearby noblemen and their ladies. The Chathams also saw the gesture.

Roselind responded excitedly, "Oh, Rod! Just wait until I get you to the room tonight. I am so proud to be a Drury. I heard what you told Redmon. It seems that our stars are aligned, for I have the finest man in all England. I love you, Roddrick Drury, and I will show you just how much tonight."

Madeline watched her brothers and hoped for the same kind of treatment one day from a good man. Red Roland beamed as he watched his sons and their wives, and then helped Madeline to mount her horse, as did Redmon and Roddrick for their wives. Red Roland told Rodney how good it was that he came, and quietly told his son how much he and his mother liked Jane Chadwick and were proud of their engagement.

Allison commented to Roselind and Madeline, "I wish we were all riding like the men. Girls, we would show these men how riding should be done. When we get back to Drury Manor, all three of us are going to put on pants and go riding together. If a MacDougal shows his face, we will shoot his ears off!" The men laughed and the women giggled.

Roselind reached for and took Allison's hand and looked into her eyes. "I look forward to it. Just the three of us before you, Redmon, and Madeline begin your journey home."

Madeline explained to Jane Chadwick that Allison was going to dress them in pants when they arrived back at Drury Manor so they could all ride astride. Jane looked at Allison and then giggled when she thought about being able to ride like a man. Jane had heard all the stories about Allison shooting the highwayman and then the Scottish highlander and thought Allison to be so daring. She rode close to Allison. "Allison, I wish that I could have known about your outfits in time. I would have loved it if all four of us matched."

The duel with Mortimer was looming in all their minds and the women didn't want to think that Redmon could be killed. The men did not know it, but the three Drury women got together earlier and all three were carrying their loaded pistols, ready just in case of trouble from Mortimer Chatham. Redmon stepped into the saddle and rode next to Allison.

Looking around the stable yard, Redmon found Mortimer and Reginald Chatham. They were glaring at him with looks of pure hatred on their faces. Redmon decided to prick their egos a little, so he smiled and doffed his hat to them. Then he noticed the small, sad-looking figure sitting uncomfortably on a horse that was dancing excitedly next to Mortimer. Redmon could clearly see that the horse was the wrong mount for the young woman. She should be riding a more docile mare. The young Anne Chatham appeared to be completely miserable and unhappy about being there. The swirl of activity in the stable yard was something to behold. The noise was clearly making the horse Anne was riding harder to control.

All the noblemen and their ladies were either wearing the traditional red and black riding jackets with white pants or skirts and black hats, or the colors of their respective manor lands. The baying of the hounds being held by Nelson huntsmen rose above the whinnying of horses and the excited chatter of the riders anticipating the ride to come. Sir Thomas Chadwick joined the Drurys and would ride with Rodney and his daughter Jane.

Suddenly, the hunt horn was blown and the hounds were released. The riders closest to the running hounds spurred their horses into a run after the retreating hounds and the rest of the riders followed. The Darlington huntsmen had dragged a scented skin with a fox smell away from the paddock earlier for the hounds to follow. A fox would be released by a huntsman along the route of the chase. The Drurys stayed together as they pounded out of the stable yard.

Redmon noticed that the Chathams were riding well ahead, so he relaxed, enjoying riding next to Allison. They rode across a wide green meadow, jumped a brook, and then entered some woods. Allison laughed when they jumped a downed log together. Redmon looked behind and the rest of the family had successfully jumped the log and were right with them. They broke from the woods into another wide meadow and saw the hounds and a number of riders approaching a low stone fence. The dogs went over the fence, and then the first riders were jumping their horses. A group of riders, including the Chathams, came to the fence and jumped. Both Redmon and Allison saw one horse balk and throw its rider over the fence. Redmon recognized the horse and realized the fallen rider was Anne Chatham.

Redmon called to Allison to stop and help the young woman. Redmon looked back and motioned the rest of the family to ride on. Redmon and Allison pulled their mounts to a stop at the stone fence. The rest of the family jumped the stone fence and rode on.

The couple could see the young woman lying on the turf on the other side of the stone wall and she was not moving. Her horse was standing nearby trembling. Mortimer and Reginald continued to ride on, leaving Anne behind. Another rider came back who had jumped the fence, turned immediately, and came riding up. He was a young nobleman named Alistair Worthington. "I saw Anne thrown and came back as quickly as I could. I stayed close to ensure her safety."

Redmon lifted Allison out of the saddle and they quickly climbed over the fence and knelt next to Anne Chatham, along with Alistair. They gently rolled her over and she moved slightly. Allison asked Redmon to go to the nearby brook and wet a kerchief she pulled from her skirt pocket. Allison bathed Anne's face and she began regaining consciousness. Finally, she was able to sit up but was clearly groggy. Allison thought it fortunate that the girl did not break her neck in the fall, and continued to dab her face with the cool cloth.

"Thank you, mistress, for helping me," Anne whimpered. "Thank you all. My stallion refused the jump and I lost my seat."

Then Anne saw Alistair. "Oh, Alistair, you are here! I am so sorry that you have to see me like this, but you came!" It was immediately apparent to both Redmon and Allison that the two young people cared a great deal for one another, and wondered how Anne came to be with Mortimer Chatham. A horse came pounding up and all three saw the fear register on Anne's pretty face when she recognized the rider.

Mortimer Chatham looked down at the people attending his young wife. "I should have known one of these people would attempt to hurt us. Which one knocked you from your horse?" Anne tried to speak but Mortimer cut her off. "Drury, I will take great pleasure killing you in the morning. Anne, stand up and get on your horse. You are embarrassing me!"

Alistair spoke up. "Chatham, no one knocked the lady from her horse. It balked at the fence and threw her. That stallion is clearly not the proper mount for Anne to be riding. You make your accusation falsely."

Anne tried to stand but was unable. "Anne, I told you to get up and mount. Now do it!" Mortimer climbed from the saddle and walked toward her with his quirt raised as if to strike his wife, and she cringed back from him. Allison quickly rose and stood over Anne to protect her. Alistair immediately moved in front of the women.

Mortimer pointed his quirt at Anne. "I told you to get up, you dumb little wench. You are worthless! You are embarrassing the Chatham name by your actions."

Redmon stepped next to Allison to protect her. Alistair Worthington was young, but he never flinched when Mortimer tried to quirt him. "Mortimer Chatham, if you attempt to strike me, you will regret it. I would challenge you for what you just said to your own wife, but you seem to already have an appointment in the morning. However, I will not allow you to abuse your wife. She has done nothing wrong."

"Mistress Drury, may I stay with you? Mortimer will beat me if I am forced to go with him!" Anne whispered from behind.

Allison knew that she should never get involved in a marital dispute, especially with it being Mortimer Chatham, but the young wife sounded so desperate.

Redmon heard the girl's request and already knew what his wife's response would be, and chuckled. His wife would protect the young Anne Chatham completely, and probably shoot Mortimer if the need arose. It was a stalemate until more riders began arriving, including Sir Albert Stuart. "I would be interested to hear what is occurring here," he said as he looked down from the back of his hunter. Anne was still sitting on the turf behind Alistair Worthington and the Drurys.

"These people are attempting to keep my wife from me. I was going to help her back to her horse, but the Drury woman is keeping me from her," Mortimer replied.

Redmon laughed and Alistair spoke. "Not true, Sir Albert. Mistress Anne was thrown from her horse and rendered unconscious. We were helping her recover when Mortimer arrived and ordered her to mount her horse on her own, even though she was unable to stand. Sir Albert, Mortimer Chatham was attempting to quirt his own wife as well as calling her terrible names. I, as well as mistress Drury, offered our protection to her."

Sir Albert looked down at the frightened Anne Chatham. "Mistress Anne, I will ask you. Are you well enough to ride now, and with whom do you wish to leave here? Your husband or Mistress Drury."

In a frightened voice Anne Chatham replied, "Sir Albert, I wish to stay with Mistress Drury. My husband will surely beat me if I am forced to go with him." Anne realized that this might be her only opportunity for the protection that she craved for three long years now.

Mortimer exploded. "You treacherous little bitch. After I deal with the Drurys, I will teach you a lesson you will not forget. You are no better than my sister."

Sir Albert made his decision. "I have heard enough. Mistress Drury, are you agreeable to taking Mistress Anne

Chatham under your protection pending the outcome of tomorrow's contest of honor?"

"Yes, Sir Albert, I will gladly do that, and I believe Alistair Worthington would also agree to be a protector for Mistress Anne," answered Allison.

"I will gladly agree, for I will see no woman abused," Alistair chimed in.

"So be it. Mortimer Chatham, you will not attempt to approach your wife for the remainder of this day. Remember you are a guest of myself and Lord and Lady Nelson. After all I have seen and heard from you, I would challenge you myself, but it seems that there are many ahead of me." All knew that Sir Albert Stuart was a renowned swordsman and duelist in his own right. "Tomorrow morning will determine what occurs next. Is that clear? I may very well decide to place Mistress Anne under the protection of the queen no matter the outcome tomorrow, for I will never see any gentlewoman abused."

Mortimer sneered. "After I dispatch this buffoon tomorrow, I will go to the queen myself. You will be finished as her advisor for your highhanded actions here today." Mortimer climbed into his saddle, but pointed at Redmon before riding away. "You are a dead man walking."

Everyone watched as Mortimer rode away stiff backed along with his father. Anne sobbed as she fell into Allison's arms. "Oh, thank you, Mistress Drury. I have never felt such relief in my entire life. Living with the Chathams has been a complete and utter nightmare."

Sir Albert Stuart heard Anne's comment and spoke to her. "Mistress Anne, if you would agree, I would like very much to converse with you this afternoon." Anne readily agreed to speak with Sir Albert.

Alistair helped Anne to mount her horse, as Redmon did Allison. "I had my pistol ready and would have shot him if he was stupid enough to attack us. Sweetheart, he is as evil as Wilfred, maybe even more so. I think he may even be a little crazy. He challenged Sir Albert, the advisor to the queen, so he must be unstable. He could be completely unpredictable when you fight him."

"Of course the Chathams are crazy and evil, everyone in the neighborhood around Eden knew that. I was always amazed that Roselind somehow escaped their affliction," he replied, and grinned at her as he climbed into the saddle.

A large group of riders made their way back to Darlington Manor. Before they reached the manor stables, Red Roland, Roddrick, Rodney, Roselind, Jane, and Madeline caught up with the cavalcade. Roselind and Madeline gave Allison a questioning look when they saw Anne Chatham riding next to Allison. "I will need your help when we reach the manor," she told Roselind.

Grooms were there to take care of the horses so the noblemen and their ladies could move to the terrace at the side of the manor house for refreshments. Allison took Anne Chatham's hand for reassurance as the Drurys climbed to the stone-flagged terrace. Alistair Worthington was there next to Anne. The men went to procure the refreshments, while the women found a place to sit on the wide terrace. All their fellow noblemen and ladies were watching the Drurys with Anne Chatham.

The drama seemed to be never ending. Joselyn came from the house, along with the children, but she appeared flushed as she told of what happened after the riders left on the hunt. "Lydia accused Redmon and Allison of murdering Wilfred in New Mexico to take his land. Lady Ofelia Nelson stepped in and stopped the accusations. She reminded Lydia that she was a guest in the Nelson home. Lady Ofelia told Lydia Chatham that she would tolerate no further outbursts from the Chathams during these festivities or she would ask them to leave the manor immediately after the foxhunt. Lady Ofelia apologized to me and told me again how much she enjoyed being at Roddrick's and Roselind's home." Then Joselyn noticed Anne Chatham sitting next to Allison and exclaimed, "Oh dear! You are Mortimer Chatham's wife. I am terribly sorry, but that was how it all happened."

"Lady Drury, I am sorry that woman accosted you. I hope Lady Nelson put her in her place. I will tell you that this is the safest I have felt for over three years. I will explain how I came to be with the Chathams if I may stay with you. I would rather disappear than be forced to go back to Mortimer Chatham," Anne replied. The men came back with refreshments and Anne Chatham launched into her story as Alistair sat next to her. "Alistair, I am glad you are here to learn why I married Mortimer so suddenly. I am embarrassed by the story, but I want you to hear all of it. My parents, Sir Edwin and Abigail Bradbury, owned a manor located next to the Dudley's Manor, which you well know. I was a young girl of thirteen when Melissa Dudley married Wilfred Chatham. A year later, Sir Thomas Dudley died suddenly. Within a year after Sir Dudley's death, Melissa was dead. Doctor Seth Jenson, who was our local doctor, suspected that Sir Thomas and Melissa were both poisoned by Wilfred Chatham. Then Dr. Jenson was forced into the duel by Mortimer and killed easily."

"I never knew, but my father overextended our manor with lenders. Three years ago when I was fifteen, Mortimer bought my father's loans and forced me to marry him by threatening to put my parents off the manor if I refused him. He lied to me, because once we were married, the Chathams made my parents leave the manor anyway. They are living with an aunt in London now but are almost destitute. The last three years with the Chathams has truly been hell on earth. They are the most evil people you could ever imagine. They talked constantly about how much they hated the Drurys."

Then, Anne continued, "Mistress Roselind, I am sorry but they have said terrible things about you. Since I have lived in the Dudley Manor House, they have constantly blamed you and your family for causing them to lose Chatham Manor. I thought they were going to go crazy when your names were announced to the queen. I know many things that are terrifying about them, but I know they would have killed me if I revealed what I knew while still living with them. I cannot go back to Mortimer for I know he will beat me! I would rather be dead than be forced to go back to him!"

✿ ✿ ✿

Buffet tables were set for a late noon meal. After, the ladies would go to their rooms to rest and then prepare for the dancing to come later. Alistair asked Anne if she would allow him to escort her for the dancing that evening and she agreed. "Alistair, I always hoped we would be together, but then Mortimer blackmailed me into this terrible marriage. Do you think Redmon has a chance against Mortimer?" Anne asked. "All I have heard is that he is a master of the sword and would kill Redmon easily. I am praying for Redmon Drury to prevail tomorrow morning. Mortimer Chatham is one of the most evil men you could ever imagine."

"I certainly hope Redmon can prevail for our sakes. Redmon seems to be a good man. I learned that he dispatched Wilfred Chatham rather easily and he was supposedly a fencing master. I have the fervent hope that we might be together as we were meant to be," replied Alistair.

The Drury women surrounded Anne Chatham as they passed the glaring Chathams along the terrace. They heard Lydia call Anne a traitorous little bitch as they passed. In their rooms, Allison was able to get a hot tub of water for bathing. When Allison and Roselind stripped Anne to get her in the tub, they were both appalled. Anne Chatham was covered with many new bruises on her slender body. There were many fading marks that were obviously nasty bruises at one time. It was clear that Mortimer beat and abused her often, treating her harshly at times.

Anne cried when Allison and Roselind stared at the bruises on her body. Immediately, the two women gathered the young woman into their arms and held her while she cried. They assured Anne that not all men hit and abused their women.

Allison and Roselind looked at one another over Anne's head and had tears in their eyes as well as being angry. Seeing Anne simply reaffirmed for Roselind what her older brother was like. When Anne was washed they found one of Allison's gowns that she could wear. With a slight amount of alteration it fit well. By shuffling around rooms, all the Drurys were able to wash and dress for the dancing. Alistair came up to meet Anne.

The Drury women quietly told their men about how badly Mortimer abused Anne. She was still a child at eighteen and Mortimer was thirteen years older. Allison told Jane Chadwick that it absolutely made her sick to see all the terrible bruises all over the young Anne Chatham's body. Jane would in turn relate this story to her mother Lady Elizabeth Chadwick.

Rodney and Jane Chadwick were there so they could accompany the family downstairs for the dancing. Allison invited Jane Chadwick to be part of their group. While they were doing each other's hair, Allison related how Redmon Drury followed Wilfred Chatham's cutthroats from Santa Fe and helped Allison and her father fight off attacks. She described for Jane how Redmon took the dead Nate Burelson to the Chatham building site and left him sitting at a table to be discovered later. Then Allison described the sword duel between Redmon and Wilfred to save the ranch.

There was anticipation for the dancing because all the guests now knew that Redmon and Allison Drury rescued Anne Chatham, and everyone heard of the second confrontation between Redmon and Mortimer Chatham in which Mortimer was separated by order from his young wife. They heard the words that Mortimer said to Redmon Drury about being a dead man walking.

More and more drama kept unfolding between the Chathams and the Drurys with each event at the Nelson party. Quietly, Red Roland and Joselyn went to Sir William and Lady Ofelia Nelson and apolgized for any embarrassment that they may have caused, and offered to leave Darlington Manor immediately if it would help ease the tensions. Sir William spoke for himself and his wife. "Sir Roland, you have done nothing to lose our respect. It is an honor to consider you and Lady Joselyn as our dear friends. We hope to be invited to Drury Manor some time in the future to continue our friendship. Olivia, as well as I, hope that we might spend time together in the future. You, along with Joselyn, clearly have honor, and we respect that very much. In our estimation, the Chathams are clearly the perpetrators of all these difficulties you are encountering. We wish for you, Lady Joselyn, and your entire family to stay. I will be there in the morning to assure that your son Redmon is treated fairly in his confrontation with Mortimer Chatham."

Now the assembled noblemen and ladies waited in anticipation for the Drurys to come into the ballroom. Each entrance by the Drury family was always quite something, so the noblemen and their ladies waited for them to appear. The Chathams were already there in the ballroom and appeared to be none too happy. The Drurys finally entered as a family and made an immediate impression. The women in the room focused their attention on the gown Allison Drury was wearing. It was a beautiful shade of blue green that was completely different, and the style was unique. Around her neck was a silver and blue stone necklace that matched the color of the gown perfectly. What was amazing was the emerald on the necklace. The emerald was fit for the queen, and the women in the room sighed when they saw it. Everyone thought the American Drurys must be wealthy beyond all comprehension. The four Drury women, along with Jane Chadwick, were all stunning as they came through the doors on their men's arms. Then came Anne Chatham on the arm of Alistair Worthington and the women gasped. Immediately, all looked at Mortimer Chatham and he appeared to almost explode with anger. Some expected smoke to come from the man's ears. The dress that Anne was wearing was far better than anything the Chathams ever provided for her. Also entering the room with the Drurys was Sir Thomas and Lady Elizabeth Chadwick, with their daughter Jane on Rodney Drury's arm.

All present now knew of the engagement of Rodney Drury to Jane Chadwick, so those two families would now be aligned. The Chadwick name was well respected in England and by the Crown. The Chathams found their family position suddenly shrinking in importance even though they lived in the former Dudley Manor house, and controlled the appendant lands.

The orchestra began playing and the couples moved onto the ballroom floor to waltz. Redmon and Allison remained close to Alistair and Anne just in case Mortimer attempted a move against his wife. To this point, Mortimer and the Chathams seemed to have not cared or shown any respect for Sir William or Lady Ofelia Nelson by following instructions to stay away from the Drurys.

At the refreshment table, the ladies wanted to know about Allison's gown and her necklace. They learned that the color was called turquoise and was designed and fitted for her in New York. The stone was mined and shaped in New Mexico where they lived, as was the emerald mined by Indians. Redmon took the large native emerald and arranged to have it properly cut and polished by a jeweler in New York and set on the turquoise necklace. The British noblemen and their ladies were amazed when they heard the story of the necklace and the emerald. This New Mexico, where Redmon and Allison lived, must be quite an amazing place if silver, the blue stone, and emeralds could be mined there. Word was being circulated that Redmon and Allison Drury also owned gold mines in a place called Colorado.

Earlier that afternoon, Anne Chatham escorted by Alistair, sat with Sir Albert Stuart and told him how she was forced to marry Mortimer Chatham by blackmail. Then she revealed that she accidentally overheard Mortimer and Reginald discuss the fact that Wilfred murdered Sir Thomas Dudley as well as Melissa. "They were talking about Wilfred not writing for quite some time. They were deciding if they could take over Dudley Manor if Wilfred was dead. Then Mortimer admitted that he goaded Dr. Jenson into a duel so he could kill him to silence him. Lydia caught me listening to them. Mortimer gave me a beating, and to make him stop, I had to promise not to tell anyone. Sir Albert, do not trust them in the morning for they will do anything to gain an advantage and protect themselves. They are the most evil people you can possibly imagine."

❖ ❖ ❖

The evening passed and the Chathams didn't cause any problems. Redmon and Allison danced together but traded with Roddrick, Roselind, Red Roland, and Joselyn a few times. Redmon danced with Clarissa, which she loved. The Drurys were ever vigilant to protect Anne Chatham. Redmon, Allison, and Anne quietly slipped away from the dancing early so Redmon could rest for the confrontation with Mortimer the following morning. Redmon drank very little of the champagne that was being dispensed. They arranged to have a small bed placed in their sitting room for Anne. Allison sat with Anne that night and caressed her forehead until she finally went to sleep. Anne kept thanking Allison over and over for taking her in and being her protector. Allison so wanted to walk down to the ballroom and shoot Mortimer between the eyes for what the man did to that sweet young woman.

Surprisingly, Redmon slept well, but Allison and Anne did not. Redmon was up and dressed before dawn. He dressed carefully in pants and a shirt that gave him free movement. Then he put on his moccasins. He retrieved his sword from his wooden weapons case. Before he left the bedroom, Allison clung to him finally letting him go. He went down the stairs and found Sir Albert Stuart and Sir William Nelson, along with Roddrick, Rodney, and his father, waiting for him. None of his family appeared to have slept.

They went to the stable where horses were waiting for them, already saddled. Some of the noblemen noticed Redmon's footwear but made no comment. They also noticed the unique quality of the decorated leather sheath containing his sword that he carried. These English noblemen thought Redmon would have no chance against a man they knew to be a master swordsman. Some had even observed Mortimer fight a duel and felt badly for the beautiful wife of Redmon Drury.

They were mounting their horses when Mortimer Chatham swaggered to the stable along with his father Reginald. "Let us conclude this farce quickly so I can take my wife back and then go to the queen and inform her of the misdeeds of Sir Albert and Sir William," Mortimer said. Redmon never said a word, but realized that Wilfred had used the same words before they fought on the Circle W.

Redmon did not know that Allison, Roselind, Madeline, Jane and Anne arranged to have their horses saddled and were planning to follow behind the men. Roselind's face displayed an almost sick, worried look as they rode after the men they could see in the distance. There was a tree-lined meadow not far from Darlington Manor where they dismounted and tied the horses. "Allison, are you certain that you want to be near for this? The outcome may be difficult to witness," Roselind asked.

Allison looked straight at Roselind. "I know you have always loved Redmon. You have been able to love two men, but I have only one. If Redmon is to die here today, I will be here for him because he is the love of my life. If he does not survive, I am going to shoot down Mortimer Chatham for myself and for Anne, who deserves a chance at life. I will gladly suffer the consequences for my man."

The women rode into a stand of trees on the opposite side of the meadow from the men. Then they moved to a position where they could watch. All five women held hands as they watched the men assembled across the meadow. Allison was on one end so she could be ready with her pistol. Roselind was holding Allison's left hand in hers. Jane Chadwick placed her arm around Anne Chatham's waist to protect her.

When Redmon and the others rode to the meadow, there was already quite a group of men present. All the men must have ridden early from Darlington Manor. Redmon handed the leather-sheathed sword to Roddrick, climbed out of the saddle, and took it back. Then he heard Mortimer ask, "Well, Drury, were you required to borrow a blade from Sir William? I am sure no rustic such as you have become could possibly afford a decent weapon as will be required today."

Redmon chuckled. "I have carried my own blade now for a number of years. You never know when you might need to do away with a polecat, as we call them in the wilds of Canada and America," Redmon returned.

Red Roland, Roddrick, and Rodney flanked Redmon, and Alistair walked behind as Red Roland asked quietly, "Son, are you sure you can handle this?"

"Yes, Father, I believe I can. We shall see soon enough, won't we?" Redmon answered confidently.

Sir Albert addressed the group. "This contest of honor will be fought between Redmon Drury and Mortimer Chatham. All know that the queen has forbidden the practice of the duel. I will take responsibility for this contest taking place today. Gentlemen, when the first sight of drawn blood is seen, I will call a halt to the contest to ascertain if that first wounding is sufficient to satisfy honor. If not, the contest shall continue. If anyone attempts to interfere with the combatants, I will shoot them down without hesitation. If that is understood by both parties, then gentlemen, you may take your positions."

Mortimer walked out into the meadow whipping his blade through the air from side to side as if to intimidate Redmon. Redmon watched and chuckled at the display. Wilfred had tried doing the same thing, seemingly to scare Redmon. Redmon finally unsheathed his sword from its decorated leather sheath and there was an audible sigh from the men who were near and looking on. It was one of the finest French blades they could ever remember seeing. Suddenly, these noblemen wondered it there might be more to Redmon Drury than they first thought. None of them thought that a man who lived in the wilds of America for twelve years could be trained for the sword. The sword had been Emile Boushard's personal blade when he was the master of sword in France. Redmon gave a small bow and nodded to Sir Albert Stuart and Sir William Nelson, which was proper, and then he bowed to his father and brothers.

Mortimer never acknowledged either of the noblemen or his own father, and the men standing near noticed the obvious slight given to Sir Albert and Sir William. It was obvious to the gathered noblemen that Redmon Drury was properly trained as to the etiquette of the duel. Finally, Redmon turned and walked toward the waiting Mortimer but uttered not a word.

As for Mortimer, he sneered, "Drury, after I kill you as you well deserve, I am going to have that slut of yours arrested for the murder of Wilfred. I am going to take my wife back and beat her as she richly deserves for making me look foolish before my peers."

Redmon decided not to appear untrained as he had done with Wilfred, but go on the defensive early until he determined Mortimer's style and training. Immediately, Mortimer attacked, attempting to bring a quick end to the duel.

Redmon countered every move and determined that Mortimer and Wilfred learned from the same instructor. Mortimer expected to finish Redmon easily, but when Redmon repelled every move, a bit of doubt began to creep into Mortimer's mind. The noblemen standing and watching were astounded, for they immediately recognized the superior skill with which Redmon Drury fought with his blade.

Soon Mortimer found himself on the defensive, being backed across the meadow. He could not understand how it happened. Redmon retreated early and Mortimer thought he surely had the man he hated above all others. He tried a thrust to finish Redmon, but his blade was knocked aside and he was cut on the right shoulder.

Red Roland, Rodney, and Roddrick stood still and concentrated on every move that their son and brother made. Never had they seen such mastery of the blade. They had lived the adventures that Redmon lived through his and Allison's letters. To see him in action now on this field was almost to see him as in the wilds of America. Every move was quick, precise, and calculated. He was so effortlessly quick that it was amazing. Red Roland and Roddrick had told Rodney of the confrontation with Enis MacDougal and how easily Redmon handled that situation. Rodney was amazed when they described how fast Redmon drew his huge pistol to protect them. Now they were seeing Redmon in a fight where he was clearly the master.

Rodney also noticed the five women across the field and recognized Jane Chadwick among them, and was proud of her for being there to support his family. She was clearly no shrinking violet and he was proud of that fact. His future father-in-law, Sir Thomas Chadwick, was also there to witness the duel of honor. He and Sir Thomas Dudley had been friends from childhood, and heard the sneering comments about his and Elizabeth's low character for allowing their daughter to marry a

Drury. He learned that this was a deep-seated rivalry going back many, many years.

"Halt!" Sir Albert called out and Redmon, who had drawn first blood, stepped back but remained ready with his blade poised. "Mortimer Chatham, Redmon Drury has drawn first blood. Will you retire from the field of honor?"

"No, I will never retire as long as this man stands and I live and breathe!" Mortimer replied, and the contest resumed.

Sir Albert Stuart, after watching the contest to this point, knew what the ultimate outcome would be so he began watching Reginald Chatham carefully. He could see the complete look of shock registered on Reginald Chatham's face when the man realized that his son was going to lose his life fighting Redmon Drury.

Mortimer attacked with wild abandon, attempting to bring a quick end to the contest. That would be his ultimate undoing, for he was expending a great deal of energy and lost some technique in the effort. The clang of the blades could easily be heard across the meadow. It was now clear to the men watching that Redmon Drury was far superior to Mortimer Chatham and was a true master of the sword.

Allison and the other women gasped with each attack that Mortimer made, but Allison soon realized that Redmon was the superior swordsman. She watched in fascination as Redmon went on the offensive as he did with Wilfred. Every move was quick and smooth. They saw the first draw of blood, and Anne spoke up, "Mortimer will not quit. His ego will not allow it. He has boasted too often that he would kill his hated enemy easily."

Redmon still had not uttered a word, but was now tired of the contest and realized that Mortimer was tiring quickly. It was clear that Mortimer was not in the physical condition needed for an extended contest. Redmon however was in top physical condition from work and fencing on the ship with Captain Turner. He began to cut Mortimer in several places and blood was staining his shirt. Redmon wanted Mortimer to suffer for what he did not only to him, but to Anne. He continually cut Mortimer, so there was more blood flowing from the many cuts Redmon was giving him. All of a sudden, Redmon flicked his wrist and a capital "D" appeared on Mortimer's forehead as he also had done to Wilfred. Mortimer left himself open to the move.

Blood was now running into Mortimer's eyes just as it had with Wilfred. For the first time Redmon spoke quietly, "Mortimer Chatham, I have carved a "D" on your forehead as I did to Wilfred just before I killed him with this blade. You have been branded as you did to me. You will reside in hell for eternity along with your brother with my brand carved on your forehead." A sudden thrust to the heart finished Mortimer Chatham who dropped to the turf of the meadow. His upper torso was covered with his own blood.

Allison wanted to scream out, "Yes!" when she saw the final thrust, but then she changed her attention to Reginald Chatham. He was drawing a pistol and pointing it at Redmon who was standing looking down at Mortimer lying at his feet.

Allison raised her pistol, aimed and fired without any hesitation. Two shots rang out almost simultaneously and Redmon wheeled along with the men who were watching the results of the duel.

They were all so mesmerized by the contest, especially the finish, when Redmon carved a capital D on the forehead of Mortimer Chatham. When Sir Albert realized what the outcome of the contest would be, he began focusing his attention on Reginald Chatham. Just before the final thrust, Reginald pulled a hidden pistol and was pointing it at Redmon Drury. As the fatal thrust took place, Sir Albert shot Reginald Chatham who was squeezing the trigger. Reginald's shot went into the turf halfway to Redmon.

Reginald Chatham stood for only a scant moment and then dropped to the meadow and lay still. Sir Albert could have sworn later that he heard another shot fired an instant before he fired his own pistol.

There was stunned silence as smoke curled away from the muzzle of Sir Albert's pistol. The men realized that if

Sir Albert had not been paying attention that Reginald Chatham would have murdered Redmon. None of the men would ever know that Allison already shot Reginald Chatham from across the meadow a heartbeat before Sir Albert fired his shot. Red Roland, Roddrick, Rodney and Alistair ran for Redmon and surrounded him in case the Chathams had placed another man nearby intending to kill Redmon.

Allison's shot found Reginald Chatham in the heart as did the shot fired by Sir Albert a split second later. When Reginald Chatham was prepared for burial the undertaker would wonder about the size and shape of the bullet hole in Reginald's chest.

The men who witnessed the duel heard horses pounding across the meadow and saw the flowing hair of five women. Allison flew out of the saddle and ran for Redmon. He gathered her into his arms holding his sword behind her back. Roddrick and Alistair did the same with Roselind and Anne. Rodney opened his arms and Jane Chadwick ran into them, "Welcome to the Drury family, Jane. I hope you will still wish to marry me after witnessing all this?"

"I'm wearing your engagement ring. I think being part of the Drury family will always be interesting." Jane said, and then her father was there with Rodney and Jane. "Rodney, your brother is quite a swordsman. I have witnessed many such encounters over the years, but never have seen such complete mastery of the blade. I would very much like to talk to Redmon and hear where he learned such mastery of the blade. Daughter you are marrying into quite a family! I believe my good friend Sir Thomas Dudley and Melissa have finally been properly avenged!"

Madeline flew to her father, "Oh, Father is it finally over? The Chathams can no longer hurt us or anyone else!" Rodney could only utter the words as Jane Chadwick held onto him. "My word! That was quite something," exclaimed Rodney. "My brother was amazing."

The assembled noblemen surrounded the Drurys, and then Sir Albert spoke. "Redmon Drury, you are clearly a true master of the sword. I have never seen a display of the art quite like what I just observed on the field this morning. It would be my suggestion; however, that you and your lovely wife take ship for your western lands as soon as you can manage. The queen may very well issue an order for your arrest. I, along with Sir William, will be safe from the queen's wrath for allowing this contest of honor to occur. The Chathams were not well liked, and after conversing with Mistress Anne, I know they committed the murders of Sir Thomas Dudley and Melissa Dudley. I will inform the queen of this fact. They were, however, considered of the nobility of England."

Redmon addressed the noblemen, "Sir Albert and Sir William, we were planning to go home immediately after returning to Drury Manor. Because our trip to Sheffield to see Rodney and meet Jane is no longer necessary, we will be able to plan our trip home. I hope the queen will not treat you harshly for allowing this contest of honor."

The Drurys, along with Alistair, Anne Chatham, Rodney, Jane Chadwick, and Sir Thomas Chadwick, rode for Darlington Manor. Alistair quietly asked if he and Anne could go to Drury Manor with the Drurys and be married there. The Drury coach drivers had anticipated leaving quickly whether Redmon survived the duel or not, and both coaches were harnessed and waiting to leave in front of the manor house. Lady Joselyn took care of getting the trunks loaded with their belongings, along with having the children ready to leave. Both Clendon and Clarissa kept asking their grandmother that morning as to what was happening. They wanted to know why their father and mother left their rooms so early. Joselyn assured the children that all was well, but they could see the tears in her eyes. Joselyn waited nervously for the outcome of the duel. But, when the Drurys and Chadwicks all rode back into Darlington Manor, there was a scream of frustration and anger from Lydia Chatham.

Sir William Nelson anticipated carrying at least one body away from the meadow so he arranged to have a cart there. He never thought both the bodies of Mortimer and Reginald Chatham would be in the horse-drawn cart. Mortimer and Reginald Chatham's horses were tied to the back of the cart. He, as most others, thought Redmon would be the one carried back to the manor house in the cart. Along with all the other men, Sir Nelson was astounded by the skill displayed by a man of Redmon Drury's size. This would be a story told and retold in manor houses and taverns in middle and northern England for quite some time—how the American cowboy defeated Mortimer Chatham with a sword, and did it easily. All would relate the story of Redmon Drury with a flick of his wrist carving a capital D in Mortimer Chatham's forehead just before killing him. Only Sir Albert Stuart and the Drurys knew the significance of that move.

✦ ✦ ✦

Less than an hour after reaching the manor house, the Drurys, with their horses tied to the back of the coaches, were ready to leave Darlington Manor. Rodney and Jane Chadwick promised to come to Drury Manor as soon as they possibly could. Redmon told Rodney and Jane that he only wished that he and Allison could remain in England long enough to attend their wedding. Rodney hugged Redmon and Allison, wishing them good luck as they traveled home. Rodney quietly told Redmon how very proud of him he was for how he handled Mortimer.

Allison thanked Jane Chadwick for being there to support Redmon as well as Anne Chatham.

After final goodbyes, two coaches traveled back north for Drury lands. Lydia Chatham called them every nasty word imaginable as they were leaving. Anne was the recipient of many of Lydia Chatham's scathing words. Then the cart arrived carrying both her husband and son, and she collapsed in a faint. When she recovered somewhat, the Drurys were gone, including her daughter-in-law, and she vowed vengeance on the Drurys for the deaths of both her sons and husband.

Sir William Nelson attempted to explain to Lydia Chatham that Reginald tried to murder Redmon Drury and was shot by the Marshall on the field, but she would not listen. Sir William made the arrangements to have the bodies of Mortimer and Reginald taken to Chatham Manor for burial. He even instructed the carpenters of Darlington Manor to build caskets before transporting the bodies. Both caskets would be loaded on top of the Chatham coach later that afternoon.

The Drury coaches set a fast pace and reached Drury Manor at dusk. Men carried the trunks to the rooms. Stablemen took care of the horses that were clearly spent. Redmon put coal in the firebox and lit the hot water heater so they could all have hot baths after the coach ride. Anne Chatham was able to retrieve her clothes and personal items from the room she and Mortimer shared at Darlington Manor. Alistair stood guard while Anne quickly packed her small trunk. Most of her clothes were left at Chatham Manor. She told Alistair that she experienced such terrible treatment at the hands of Mortimer and the Chathams, and had such bad memories at Dudley Hall, that she never wanted to see the place again.

Dinner was somewhat subdued because of the hasty exit from Darlington Manor. There was relief that Reginald and Mortimer Chatham were no longer a threat, but they wondered if Lydia Chatham could influence someone in London to come after Redmon and Allison quickly. It was evident that Anne was excited by the prospect of marrying Alistair Worthington. They had planned to marry before Mortimer threatened and blackmailed her and her parents into the marriage. Anne was already more relaxed after getting away from the Chathams. The following morning Redmon and Allison would ride to Gretna Green to find a ship going to America.

Roddrick and Alistair rode to Penrith to arrange to have Rev. Thompkins come to Drury Manor to perform the marriage ceremony. Joselyn, Roselind, and Madeline would prepare a dress for Anne to wear during the ceremony. Joselyn's wedding dress was packed away in a trunk in the attic of Drury House so she offered that for Anne to use.

That night Allison and Roselind made love to their men with a fervor that even surprised Redmon and Roddrick. When they were lying in each other's arms, Allison expressed her feelings. "Redmon, I love you so. I was afraid, but confident at the same time. I was so proud of you. Now I want you to take me home."

Roddrick and Roselind talked about everything that occurred at Darlington Manor. Roselind cried as she talked about the complete ruthlessness of her former family. She told Roddrick how contented she felt to be a Drury. Before falling asleep, they made love to each other. Roselind's slim and supple body still pleased Roddrick even after having their two children.

Anne and Alistair parted for the night with a kiss, with the promise of more to come. Madeline lay in bed and shivered in anticipation for the trip to America. She loved her mother and father, Roddrick, Roselind, and the children but she was ready for new adventures.

That night in their master suite, Red Roland described for Joselyn the duel that Redmon and Mortimer fought. He told Joselyn that their son was the finest swordsman that he had ever seen, and that Mortimer never had a chance. Joselyn told Red Roland how she and Lady Ophelia had comforted each other that morning of the duel. Joselyn sat in a chair at the Darlington house with Clendon and Clarissa close by her. She and Lady Ofelia Nelson held hands and prayed for Redmon. She realized after the fact that all the women followed the men to the dueling field. Ofelia and Joselyn discovered that they shared many of the same beliefs. Joselyn poured out much of the Drury story because she felt that she could trust Lady Nelson. Ofelia, for her part, came to realize that Joselyn could be a special friend because she was honest and she cared for others. Joselyn confided to Lady Ofelia what Allison and Roselind found when they bathed Anne Chatham after the foxhunt.

When Redmon rode back to Darlington Manor with the rest of the family, Joselyn was beside herself with relief. Lady Ofelia actually held her as she cried that relief. Then they heard Lydia screaming her obscenities at Redmon for being alive. There were other noblewomen there who watched Lydia Chatham spew her venom.

Red Roland and Joselyn talked about how the family finally came full circle with Redmon leaving again, along with Madeline. They talked about how hard it would be to lose Madeline, but realized that it was actually for the best.

They were excited about having Jane Chadwick as part of the family. Their conversation ended that night with tender love-making and the knowledge that their children would always be happy and strong as one.

In Gretna Green, Redmon and Allison met Captain Artimus Bream who owned and commanded a sloop named the *Swift*. They procured a good cabin for themselves and one for Madeline. The *Swift* would depart in four days. They just hoped that the queen's men would not come to arrest them before that time.

When they arrived back at Drury Manor, the preacher was there, ready for the wedding. Allison and Redmon changed into better clothes. Allison, Roselind, and Madeline stood with Anne while Roddrick, Redmon, and Clendon stood up with Alistair. Joselyn was very trim and shapely when she married Red Roland. With few alterations the dress fit Anne perfectly. She was thrilled when Joselyn and Roselind dressed her for the ceremony. Red Roland, with Anne on his arm, came forward for the wedding vows. After the ceremony, everyone enjoyed a special dinner. Joselyn and Roselind, with the Drury cook, even baked and decorated a wedding cake while Madeline packed two trunks for the trip with Redmon and Allison.

Neither Alistair nor Anne could believe the luxuries that Drury Manor provided with the wonderful bathroom close to their bedrooms. Alistair decided to do the same thing at Worthington Manor for his parents, brother, sister, and Anne when they went home the following day. The Worthingtons were not at the Darlington festivities as they were away in France. They would be excited to learn that Alistair had brought home a new wife when they came home from France.

Redmon warned Alistair to treat Anne carefully and gently as she had been terribly abused by Mortimer Chatham. Their first night together was a revelation for Anne Worthington. She loved saying her new name. Alistair took careful time with Anne that night and they loved one another slowly and gently. He saw the many bruises on her trim body but knew they would fade away in time. He would protect and love her in a way that would bring back her trust. He was so thankful that Mortimer was dead after what he put Anne through. He would finally have the woman he had always wanted. They were both young and would grow together. Alistair was twenty years old while Anne was now eighteen. In time, people would even forget that she was ever married to Mortimer Chatham. The old adage of time heals all wounds became true for Anne Worthington.

Red Roland sent the coach and a driver to take Alistair and his new wife home, with Alistair's horse trotting behind. Alistair would even manage to take back Anne's parents' Bradbury Manor and lands from the former Dudley estate, and restore them to Sir Edwin and Lady Abigail Bradbury so they could move home from London. Alistair even refurbished the Bradbury Manor house that had fallen into a state of disrepair, and made sure that the manor was supplied with a land manager so the manor did not fall into financial trouble again.

Anne hugged Allison and sobbed as she thanked her many times, and then went to Redmon and he held her. "Oh, Redmon, thank you for freeing me. I will remember what you did to save me for the rest of my life."

The stay at Drury Manor turned out to be a honeymoon of sorts, and the Drurys and Worthingtons would remain friends for life. Roddrick would eventually be knighted and become Sir Roddrick because of his friendship with Alistair and Sir Albert Stuart. Roselind would be Lady Roselind Drury of Eden Hall.

The following morning, keeping a promise, Allison, Roselind, and Madeline, with Roselind and Madeline each wearing a pair of Allison's pants, rode away from Drury Manor on horses wearing men's saddles. The three young women rode for hours, and even enjoyed a picnic lunch along a brook. They laughed and cavorted together and thoroughly reveled in riding free on their horses. When they finally rode back into the stable yard at Drury Manor, Redmon, Roddrick, Joselyn, Red Roland, Clendon, and Clarissa were waiting for them.

The young women were laughing as they saw the concerned looks on their loved ones faces. When they pulled up, Allison and Roselind almost said at the same time, "We were having such fun and lost track of the time. Oh, Rod, that was really such a wonderful time.

Allison is going to send me pairs of these pants when she gets home. I want some of those boots to go with them."

Roddrick looked at Redmon. "Your wife has created a monster. The next thing I know Roselind will be wearing one of those holsters with a pistol on her hip like one of the cowboys you have been telling us about. She will be trying to shoot the feather off some Scotsman's hat." All the Drurys laughed at that.

Clarissa chimed in, "Momma, was it fun riding like that? I want to try, too, and be like you and Aunt Allie." Roddrick threw up his hands and everyone laughed again. The Drurys knew they were a family that could withstand any challenge and survive.

❖ ❖ ❖

Two days later the Drurys saw Redmon, Allison, and Madeline off on the *Swift* in Gretna Green. There were a great number of hugs and tears at the parting. The British Drurys watched the ship sail completely out of sight down Solway Firth, eventually climbing into their coaches and starting home. Little Clarissa had clung to Allison and told her, "Aunt Allie, I love you. I hope maybe one day I can come to see your American ranch."

One of the MacDougals happened to watch the parting and later informed Enis MacDougal that Madeline sailed for America with the sharpshooting couple who had stopped Enis and Angus weeks earlier.

That ended all reason for the MacDougals to continue their pursuit of the Drury's.

Then, a few days after the *Swift* sailed, four of the queen's men came to Drury Manor to arrest both Redmon and Allison Drury for the deaths of Mortimer and Wilfred Chatham. The queen's men, after leaving Drury Manor, learned in Gretna Green, that the people they sought did indeed sail for America. Therefore, the matter was dropped. However, the arrest warrants were still in effect for both Redmon and Allison Drury. They were considered outlaws in England.

Madeline enjoyed every minute of the voyage. But three weeks into the trip, morning sickness came for Allison and she realized that she was finally pregnant. She had missed her last courses and hoped that it was not just the excitement of going home. She was beyond excited by the prospect of having Redmon's child. It became a celebration when she told Redmon and Madeline.

The *Swift* reached its home port of Boston some five weeks after leaving Gretna Green. Allison's morning sickness had now passed and she enjoyed the sights of the city. The Drurys stayed a week in Boston before boarding a train west. While in the city they attended the theater and a concert by John Phillip Sousa and his band. They enjoyed their meals at several of the city's restaurants. Madeline and Allison posted long letters back to Drury Manor that would be carried by a departing ship. Allison announced to her in-laws that she would be having a grandchild for them.

Madeline was as excited as a little girl when she first saw the fresh water of Lake Michigan. As they traveled on west, she was amazed at how many days it took to travel over the Great Plains. The sameness of the landscape was broken up by occasional large herds of buffalo.

Upon arriving in Denver, they spent one night at the Brown Palace. Madeline could hardly wait to see the Rocky Mountains that Redmon and Allison talked about. She was told that they would ride through high mountain passes on the way home. From Denver, Redmon arranged for transportation to Central City and the home of their friends Red and Audrey Brandais.

The reunion with the Brandais' was wonderful. Red and Audrey had had a son soon after Redmon and Allison left Denver. They named the little boy Allen Redmon Brandais. Red told Redmon that he was so proud to have a family and he treated Audrey like a princess. Audrey and Red were excited to learn that Allison was expecting, and they welcomed Madeline as if she were a long-lost relative.

During their stay, Red took fine care of Redmon and Allison's horses until they were fat and ready to travel. Redmon was able to buy a good mare for Madeline to ride, and they started south after a restful several days at Brandais House.

While in Denver, Allison bought pants, shirts, boots, a vest, and a wide-brimmed hat for Madeline, along with a fleece-lined jacket for the cold of the mountains. Madeline couldn't believe how good it felt to ride astride wearing her comfortable clothes. Madeline loved the new mare and decided to name her Lark after she heard a meadowlark singing one morning. Riding through the high mountain passes and seeing the snow-capped peaks was exciting for Madeline.

She took to the camping at night as if she was born to it. Madeline loved it all, and could hardly wait to write home about her adventures. Sitting around the campfire each night, they told stories, looked at the stars, and listened to the breeze through the pine trees. Madeline thought the sound made a kind of soft, soothing music all its own. Redmon and Allison told her that camping out on the plains after the mountains would be different. As they rode for home, they showed her the Rio Grande Gorge and then Taos Pueblo. They followed the Rio Grande River into Santa Fe where they arranged rooms for three nights at the La Fonda Hotel to allow the horses to rest and get corn. After settling in to their rooms, they changed into their dinner clothes, and headed for the dining room where they were seated at a nice table.

The Drurys had just been seated when a tall young man came into the dining room with a beautiful Spanish girl on his arm. Immediately, another young man dressed as a Spanish Don rose from a table and confronted the couple. From his comments, it was apparent that he took exception to the young lady being escorted by the gringo. He called the couple harsh names in the Spanish language for all to hear. Suddenly, the young man Redmon identified as a gringo, put the beautiful Spanish girl behind him and struck the offender, knocking him unconscious with one punch while protecting the girl at the same time.

Redmon interpreted for Madeline because the confrontation was spoken in Spanish. It was a scene not often witnessed in public. Both Allison and Madeline were appalled that the Spanish man would call the girl such names. She was young and beautiful, and looked quite innocent. Redmon explained to Madeline that only a few short years earlier, the Spanish controlled Santa Fe, and that a young senorita from a good family would never dare to be seen on the arm of a gringo, as all Anglos were called by the Spanish.

Redmon chuckled when he heard the young man's speech to the Spanish Dons, where he took and seated the beautiful young Spanish girl. Redmon interpreted for Madeline. It was clear to Redmon that the young anglo man possessed honor.

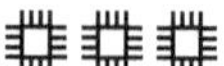

The Drurys stayed one more day in Santa Fe, which allowed Madeline to see the area around the plaza including the wooden staircase in the Loretto Chapel where Redmon and Allison were married. On their walk around the plaza, Redmon bought Madeline a turquoise and silver necklace from an old Pueblo Indian man selling his wares under the porch of the Palace of the Governors. Madeline couldn't believe how beautiful the workmanship was.

Early the next morning as they were saddling their horses and loading their packhorses, the Drurys noticed the Spanish girl from the dining room and the young Anglo man were together at the stable. It appeared that they were going to run away with the help of another young Spaniard. The girl was wearing men's clothes as a disguise which seemed humorous to Redmon. The stableman quietly told Redmon in Spanish that the girl was from a wealthy Spanish family from Las Vegas and that she and the gringo were running away together. The plan would cause much trouble for the young gringo if they were caught.

That night, Redmon, Allison, and Madeline camped on the small creek on the San Cristobal ranch where they had always camped. While around the campfire, Madeline voiced her opinion that she hoped the young couple survived and made a life for themselves. She marveled at the wide sky above them with the myriad of stars. As the fire burned to coals, a three-quarter moon peaked up from the east. The coyotes began their barking and long plaintive song. Madeline laughed and said how wonderful the sound was. Redmon pulled Allison close and whispered in her ear that he felt the same because they were almost home. She snuggled into his arms, felt his need for her, and laughed her tinkling little laugh. The following afternoon Redmon, Allison, and Madeline rode up to the house at the Circle W.

Allison received the shock of her life. She now had a little brother. Grace had presented Franklin with a healthy baby boy three months earlier. They named the baby Jefferson Henry Wilbanks. Just as Red Brandais was with Audrey, Franklin was over the moon proud of Grace. While they were away, Franklin built Grace an artist studio with many windows that looked out toward the plain with views of the mesa and mountains to the south. The house was decorated in art that Grace created. The big house at the R bar A would also soon have some of Grace's art on display.

Franklin held Allison when she climbed off her horse and it felt so good to Allison to be home. Allison embraced Grace, and when she cuddled little Jefferson, she could hardly wait to hold her own baby. Franklin and Grace were excited to learn that Allison would soon have a baby of her own.

Dusk was falling when the Drurys reached their home. Immediately, Henry Sudderth, Jose Ruiz, and Joseph Alvarez came from the bunkhouse and helped unload the packhorses and mules. Redmon had been forced to buy three pack mules to carry Allison's and Madeline's trunks filled with the dresses and accessories he bought for them during their trip. He teased the girls that he could put all his clothes in one little bag while they needed trunks for theirs.

Allison retorted, "Well, mister, you have a whole trunk for your weapons. Madeline and I can put ours in our pocket and still shoot somebody. You men have your priorities in the wrong place. We women need our clothes so you men can strut around with us on your arms." Then she winked at him.

The men carried the trunks into the house. Henry carried Madeline's trunks to her room next to the bathroom, and they laughed about Allison's comments. Henry couldn't seem to take his eyes away from Madeline. Redmon and Allison were amazed when they saw Henry. He looked ten years younger and they decided it was because he was happy on the R bar A. They did not actually know his age, for he never told them. But, it became clear that Henry was not as old as they originally thought him to be. While they were away in England, he shaved off his beard and mustache and that got Redmon to thinking.

That night at the dinner table, Redmon handed Henry a packet, and he and Allison smiled at their cook who looked at the packet in wonder. It was a long letter from Henry's parents, Sir Edward and Lady Edith Sudderth. Henry looked at them in wonder and they explained. "Henry, we went to a foxhunt, dinner, and dancing at Darlington Manor. We also hosted a dinner and dancing at my brother and sister-in-law's home, which was the former Chatham Manor. Sir Albert Stuart, Sir William Nelson, and Lady Ofelia came to the Eden Hall party and then invited us to Darlington Manor for their event. Well, Henry, while at Darlington Manor we met your parents, and brothers and their wives, and told them that you lived on our ranch here in New Mexico. They had not heard a word from you for so long, they thought you might be dead. Henry, the relief on their faces was something to see. Your mother and father asked us to deliver that letter to you when we arrived home." They could all see that Henry's eyes were somewhat misted as he looked at the letter in his hands.

Madeline was excited by the wonderful house that Redmon and Allison had built. Her room would be next to a bathroom. Then, there was Henry Sudderth. She expected an old man by the way Redmon and Allison talked about Henry, but he certainly was not old. And, he was also very handsome.

During the dinner that first night, besides Redmon giving Henry the letter from his parents, Redmon and Allison described their trip. Allison was excited to describe the sea voyage and the whales. She told of the shootout with the highwaymen while riding in the coach to Drury Manor. Then she described actually getting to meet the Queen of England, and finally the confrontation with the Chathams. Henry chuckled when the trouble with Mortimer Chatham was described, along with its eventual outcome. José and Joseph sat forward when Allison and Madeline told of the confrontation with the MacDougals, and finally the sword duel with Mortimer. "Señor Redmon and Señora Allison, you have made such adventures!" Joseph exclaimed after hearing the story.

That night Redmon seemed to spend more time in the bathroom than usual. Allison wanted him to hurry as she wanted to make love to him on their first night back home. When he finally came out, Redmon was in the shadows as he approached the bed. He lifted the covers, slid in, and discovered that Allison was not wearing her nightgown. He pulled her to him and immediately she was shocked when Redmon kissed her. Her hands flew to his face and he laughed. "Redmon, I can hardly wait until morning when I see the man who left England and came to rescue and love me." She rubbed her cheeks against his smooth face and returned his kiss as they fell asleep in each other's embrace, after loving one another.

Two months after Redmon and Allison arrived back at their ranch, a large wedding took place at Chadwick Manor. All the Eden River Drurys were there to see Rodney marry Jane Chadwick. Jane wore a beautiful white gown. She asked Roselind to be one of her maids, along with Anne Worthington. The wedding was a huge event and was attended by all the wealthiest noblemen and their families from northern and central England. Rodney bought an outstanding house in Sheffield. He was one of the most successful barristers in the area. Jane wrote often to Allison and they would continue regular correspondence.

❑❑❑

Redmon and Allison produced two children on the R bar A. A boy they named Trevor Roddrick, and a daughter called Kathleen Joselyn, who quickly became Katie to everyone who knew her. The Drury children grew up strong and proud. Trevor was tall and handsome like his father. He learned to fence from Redmon. Katie was as beautiful as Allison, and humble as well.

Madeline and Henry Sudderth eventually married, moved to the mountains on the Ruidoso River, and settled there. Henry Sudderth was, as it turned out, six years older than Madeline. They grew amongst the mountain community on the Ruidoso River and raised a son and two daughters in the mountains. Regular trips to the R bar A ranch helped them to stay in touch with Redmon and Allison.

⊞ ⊞ ⊞

In England, the family of Sir Thomas and Melissa Dudley petitioned the queen for the return of the Dudley Estate to the family. The petition was granted with the help of Sir Albert Stuart, so Lydia Chatham was ordered off the estate. Soon after, the former Lady Lydia Chatham appeared at the doorstep of Eden Hall and threw herself on the mercy of Roddrick and Roselind Drury. Out of family honor, they set her up in a cottage in Penrith and gave her a small monthly stipend on which to live, but Roselind could never forgive her mother for the terrible things she did and said to her. Lydia Chatham lived out her life in the small cottage, bitter and alone. All that remained for Lydia Chatham through the final years of her life were the memories of once being considered a noble lady who lived in two large manor houses.

She never admitted to herself that any of her words or actions were her fault. She always blamed the Drurys, specifically Redmon and Allison, for ruining her family.

Alistair and Anne Worthington became Sir Alistair and Lady Anne Worthington of Worthington Manor. Alistair joined the House of Lords in Parliament. He was able to have the arrest warrants for Redmon and Allison Drury recalled and deleted from the records.

Rodney Drury and Jane Chadwick were married eight months after the party held at Darlington Manor. All the Eden River Drurys were there for the wedding held at Chadwick Manor. Roddrick was the best man and Roselind was one of the bridesmaids. Red Roland and Joselyn were excited for their son because they wondered if he would ever find the woman he wanted and get married. Rodney and Jane were both thirty years old when they married.

⁂

Red Roland and Joselyn were finally able to sail for America, landing in New York. They rode railroad trains from New York to Santa Fe where Redmon, Allison, and the children met them. They stayed at the ranch for four months. During that time, Red Roland loved riding the ranch and helping to work cattle. They all went to the mountains to visit Madeline, Henry, and their three children. The reunion between Red Roland and Henry Sudderth was fun for the two men. Two years later the newly made Sir Roddrick, with Lady Roselind, Clendon, and Clarissa came to the ranch from Eden Hall.

This time the Drurys met in Denver. They stayed at the Brown Palace, attended the theater, spent time in Central City with the Brandaises, and enjoyed picnics in the mountains. The roads were improved now so the trip to Santa Fe was made quickly. Clarissa at fifteen was beautiful and a hit at every function they attended. She drew attention from young men like flies to honey. When they reached the ranch, the British Drurys were amazed by the amount of land that Redmon and Allison owned. They explored the ranch on horseback, hunted deer and antelope, camped out, and helped Redmon herd and brand the cattle.

Clarissa loved riding astride and doing what the men did. Allison and Redmon bought her everything she needed in Santa Fe. When it was time to go back to England, Clarissa cried. She told Allison privately that she felt so free in America and on the ranch.

Before Redmon and Allison put them on the train in Santa Fe, Clarissa ran to Allison and confided that she didn't want to be an ornament on some young nobleman's arm or in his manor house. "Aunt Allie, I love it here! I don't want to go home." It all came out the night before the train was to leave heading east as the two families sat in the La Fonda dining room. Clarissa wanted to stay in the West. After a great deal of discussion and tears from Roselind, it was decided to allow Clarissa to stay with Redmon and Allison for one year. It was Roddrick who realized Clarissa could be lost to them if they made her go back to England. He loved his daughter enough to let her stay, because he trusted Redmon and Allison to protect her. They knew that Henry and Madeline were planning a trip to see his family, so they could bring Clarissa home if she was ready by then.

The following morning Roddrick, Roselind, and Clendon boarded the train east without Clarissa. They would take three of Grace Wilbanks' fine oil landscapes back with them in crates. Allison took Roselind into her arms and promised that she would protect Clarissa. Clendon even hugged his sister and told her that he loved her. Clendon Drury was always so quiet, but his feelings finally came out when he held his little sister on the train platform.

✶ ✶ ✶

On a trip a few months later to check the mines, Clarissa met the son of a mine owner during a party for mine owners and their families. His name was Lance Calder. Lance was nineteen and Clarissa was now seventeen. A few months after meeting, Lance gave Clarissa a beautiful diamond and sapphire engagement ring. He made regular trips to the ranch to see her at the R bar A.

Redmon wrote to Roddrick and Roselind and told them about Lance Calder, and asked their permission to allow Clarissa to marry. Lance wrote part of the letter and told Roddrick and Roselind about himself and his family. He informed them how much he loved their daughter and also asked Roddrick for permission to marry his daughter. He promised that the wedding would not take place until he and Clarissa received their blessing. A return letter finally arrived granting permission for the young couple to marry. They married in a huge wedding in Denver. The Calder family even hired a photographer to take pictures of the ceremony so the newlyweds would have those to show Roddrick and Roselind.

Allison and Audrey Brandais helped Clarissa with her dress and both acted as if they were the mother of the bride. Allison and Katie were her bridesmaids. Henry and Madeline Sudderth came with their children for the wedding. Redmon walked Clarissa down the aisle of the church. The newlyweds were leaving after the wedding to begin their honeymoon trip to England. The Sudderths would accompany them.

Redmon took Lance aside and talked to him as if he were Clarissa's father. "Lance, Clarissa is special, and I expect her to be treated gently and always with respect in every situation. If you are not gentle with Clarissa, Allison will hunt you down and hurt you!"

Lance Calder had heard stories about many of Redmon Drury's escapades. He took the talk as a warning that he'd better heed especially when they were intimate. Lance would relate the story of Redmon's warning to Roddrick and Roselind when he and Clarissa arrived at Eden Hall. Roddrick and Roselind listened to Lance tell the story of the fearsome look Redmon gave him and laughed. It was clear to them that their new son-in-law treated Clarissa very well, but could see Redmon warning Lance to be gentle with their daughter, and then the warning that Allison would hunt and hurt him. They loved Redmon and Allison all the more for protecting Clarissa.

Roselind hosted a large party for the newlyweds and all their friends came. There were some disappointed young aristocrats when they realized that Clarissa Drury was married to an American. Two in particular had hoped to court the beautiful Clarissa when she came home. Rodney and Jane Drury attended, along with the Chadwicks.

Eventually, Rodney and Jane Drury, with their two children, traveled across the Atlantic on a steamship, and then took trains from New York to Santa Fe. As all the Drurys before them, they were impressed with the large house and ranch that made up the R bar A. Jane Drury was finally able to ride astride with the men and children. She always enjoyed the stories that Roselind told of her, Allison, and Madeline doing such a thing and wanted to try it. They also traveled to Central City and Denver, where they attended the theater and the best restaurants. They were able to see Lance and Clarissa Calder while in Denver and have dinner at their large house. When they arrived back in England, the queen appointed Rodney to the high court as a justice.

As the years passed, visitors to the R bar A saw the volcanic carbine and pistol, along with buckskins, moccasins, Sioux knives, and dueling swords hanging on the wall in the study of the big stone ranch house. There was also a set of longhorns hanging there from the last longhorn bull on the ranch. The R bar A was fenced and raising Hereford cattle brought in from England.

In the large living room, they also saw a large oil painting of Allison Drury when she was twenty-five, wearing her deep burgundy ballgown with the gold and diamond necklace around her neck. Grace Wilbanks had captured the absolute beauty of Allison. There were also paintings of Trevor and Kathleen hanging nearby. Redmon and Allison grew old together and their love was there for all to see.

About the Author:

BILL MACVEIGH LIVES IN CAPITAN, New Mexico, with his wife Dorothy. Having been a teacher of history in Lincoln County, New Mexico schools for twenty-eight years, he is now retired.